THE VANISHING TRICK

First published in Great Britain in 2020 by Simon & Schuster UK Ltd

1 3 5 7 9 10 8 6 4 2

Simon & Schuster UK Ltd
1st Floor, 222 Gray's Inn Road
London WC1X 8HB

www.simonandschuster.co.uk
www.simonandschuster.com.au
www.simonandschuster.co.in

Simon & Schuster Australia, Sydney
Simon & Schuster India, New Delhi

A CIP catalogue record for this book
is available from the British Library.

PB ISBN 978-1-4711-9037-7
eBook ISBN 978-1-4711-9038-4

Typeset in Goudy by M Rules
Printed and bound by CPI Group (UK) Ltd, Croydon, CR0 4YY

MIX
Paper from
responsible sources
FSC
www.fsc.org
FSC® C020471

Jenni Spangler

THE VANISHING TRICK

Illustrated by
Chris Mould

SIMON & SCHUSTER

1
The Fool:
Beginnings,
Fearlessness, Folly

It wasn't a sin to steal if you only took forgotten things.

Leander had been watching the ugly mutton pie in the bakery window for hours. It was lopsided and slightly squashed. All day customers had ignored it in favour of plump loaves, golden apple pies and sugar-sprinkled shortbread. The pie was left alone, unwanted and forgotten.

Leander knew how that felt.

Lurking by the doorway, he breathed in hot, sweet air each time someone went inside and his stomach ached with emptiness. The evening grew dark and people rushed along the cobbles, pulling coats and shawls tight to keep out the chill. Nobody would buy the pie now.

Wastefulness was a sin, too, and Leander was so hungry.

He had tried to find work, but nobody wanted to hire a scruffy orphan with no schooling and no one to vouch for his character. Every now and then, he'd earn a few coppers for a day of labour. Last week he'd spent two days mucking out a pig shed – horrible, cold, smelly work – only for the woman to say his work wasn't up to snuff, and short him half his money. Since then, nothing. People always thought he was up to no good – even when he wasn't. So, if he wanted to eat, he usually had to steal. Honesty and hunger were in constant competition for his soul and today hunger was winning.

Peering through the steam-clouded glass, Leander waited for the wiry baker to turn his back, then darted in. He snatched the pie, shoved it into his pocket and ran.

'Oi!'

The baker was after him. Leander sprinted up the high street, pushing between two men in top hats and dodging an old lady with a cane. He darted across the road, narrowly missing the wheels of a carriage.

'Whoa there!' shouted the driver.

'Thief!' the baker cried, still on Leander's heels.

Leander scrambled over a wall and rounded a corner. If he was caught, he'd get a thrashing or worse – be taken before the law. He dashed into an alley, his panicked footsteps sending rats skittering from their hiding places in the shadows.

Up ahead, warm light spilled from low windows. The inn.

If he was fast and clever, he could lose his pursuer in the crowded alehouse. He shoved the door open, breathless, heart pounding.

'Watch it, son—' He almost collided with a man carrying tankards.

'Sorry!' Leander hopped over the legs of a sleeping drunk and squeezed between tables. Lucky he was so small and skinny for his age. The air was stuffy-warm, heavy with tobacco smoke and the stale scent of old beer. He ducked beneath a man's arm and kicked an overturned chair out of his path.

The baker thundered in. The gaffer was fast.

Leander dropped to the sticky floor and crawled under tables, avoiding booted feet and puddles of drink. This was too close. He raced to the opposite corner and through the narrow black door that led to the adjoining coach house.

Cool night air washed over his flushed cheeks. The coach house was a cavernous room, with wooden beams and an earthy hay smell. The big barn doors were chained and bolted – no escape there. To his right was a row of horse stalls. Could he hide there? No, unsettled horses would give his location away.

Then he saw it. A pristine black carriage, empty and waiting patiently for its owner's return. Perfect. He yanked open the door and jumped inside.

The smell came first, dry and sharp, sour and musty all at once, like last autumn's rotten leaves after the snow melts, and old books, and pine tar, and spoiled meat.

Pots, pans and bundles of herbs hung from the ceiling, brushing against his ears. There was a bench on one side covered with dusty blankets and rugs. The other wall was fitted with dozens of wooden drawers and compartments, some gaping open, leaves and spoons and feathers poking out at all angles. Every other inch was covered with ramshackle shelves crammed with cards and papers and bottles of murky coloured liquids and – Leander leaned in to inspect the biggest jar – was that the skeleton of a rat? Why would anyone want such a thing?

A noise. Someone was here.

Footsteps click-clacked across the flagstones. Not the powerful gait of the baker. These were sure and sharp.

Stupid! He should have checked there was no one around. If he'd been seen climbing into the carriage, he was in bigger trouble than ever.

'Who's there?' a woman's voice called from the far corner. 'Who is in my carriage?'

Leander's heart raced. Whoever owned this collection of strange and eerie things wasn't a person he wanted to meet. He jumped out and darted behind a wooden post.

'What mischief is this?' the woman said.

Click, click, click.

The footsteps came closer, slower now but unhesitating. Blood pounded in Leander's head and he pressed his back against the post. His warm breath made white clouds in the cold air.

'Come out. I know you're there. I can smell you.'

Out of sight, horses shifted in their stalls, hooves scraping over straw and stone.

'Now then, don't be shy.' There was almost a laugh in the woman's voice. She paced round the carriage towards Leander's hiding place.

Beyond the inn door the muffled fury of the baker's voice grew louder. If Leander stayed put, the baker would see him the moment the door opened. But, if he ran for the back door, he'd collide with the carriage owner. He felt like a fox with hounds closing in on both sides.

Thinking quickly, he dived under the carriage, feeling the pie squish in his pocket as he rolled over and tucked himself behind the back wheel.

The inn door was flung open.

'When I get my hands on you—!' the baker roared, stopping abruptly as he noticed the woman. 'Beg pardon, ma'am. Did a boy come this way?'

Leander's chest tightened. Any moment now, he'd be dragged out and . . .

'No,' replied the woman. She stepped in front of the wheel and flicked out her dress, obscuring Leander's hiding place. 'I haven't seen anyone.' Leander could only see her ankles, but from her fancy blue dress and crisp speech he could tell she came from money.

'Been thieving. Yay high,' the man said, panting. 'Long hair, short trousers.'

'I assure you I'm quite alone.'

Leander was confused. Why would this woman lie for him?

'Right you are,' said the baker. 'Sorry to trouble you.'

'Not at all.'

'Sneaky little blighter. I've 'ad a few things go missing lately. First time I've seen who was responsible.'

'Is that so?' the woman said.

'Best keep an eye out, ma'am. He's a wrong'un.'

'Thank you, I shall.'

Leander held his breath as the baker's footsteps retreated. He listened for the *creak-thud* of the inn door closing.

'A thief, is it?' the woman said. 'Out with you, then.'

Not likely. Leander scrabbled away beneath the carriage and out the other side only to find the woman already looming over him. She was tall, with coal-black hair piled high beneath a peacock-green hat. Although she was beautiful, a coldness hung around her, more biting than the November air.

'Why were you in my carriage?' she asked, not unkindly.

'Wasn't.' He sidestepped to get round her, but she blocked his path.

'There's no need to lie, but you must explain yourself.'

The blue satin of the woman's dress brushed against his legs. Any closer and she'd be standing on his feet. He sized her up; something was unsettling. Why would this grand lady have a carriage full of feathers and bones and other oddities? And why would she save him from a beating from the baker … ?

'I wasn't doing anything.' He shrugged. 'Just looking round.'

'And if I should check your pockets?'

'Check them.' He raised his chin defiantly.

'Terrible things happen to liars and thieves, little boy.' Her voice was musical, her lips smiling.

Their eyes met and, for several seconds of hideous silence, Leander didn't dare look away. It seemed the woman could see every dark spot on his soul and every bad thing he had ever done.

'What's around your neck, child?' Her voice was still steady and calm. 'Something of mine?'

'No. Truly I didn't take anything.' The moment she looked away, he'd be out of there. She might have protected him, but he didn't trust this woman with her strange carriage. He desperately wanted to go somewhere safe and eat his pie.

'Come now, I won't hurt you. Show me.'

The woman stared at his throat like a wolf ready to bite. Leander pulled the locket from his grubby linen shirt. 'It was . . .'

'Your mother's,' she finished for him.

A pit opened in Leander's middle. 'How did you know?'

'Ah yes,' she whispered, a dreamy expression crossing her face. 'Now I see. A motherless child – an orphan, yes?'

Leander couldn't form words. What witchcraft was this?

'All alone in the world.' She stroked his cheek with the back of her hand, feather-light. 'Lost.'

He stuck out his chin. 'I can look after myself.'

'May I?' she asked, fingers already curling round the locket. She leaned in, the thick scent of lavender and violets smothering him. 'Interesting.'

He wriggled from her grip. 'I have to go.'

'You are miserable,' she said. 'I know a little about misery. I could help you.'

'Don't need help.' Leander knew she was just pretending to care so she could feel virtuous. He didn't want her pity.

7

Yes, he was alone, but that was fine. No one to let him down. People only cared about themselves.

She laughed. 'I think you do. You can trust me. You must be famished.'

Then again . . . Maybe if he played for sympathy she'd give him some money, or food. He could be nice, for a minute, and run if things went wrong.

'I collect trinkets, as you've seen.' She gestured towards the carriage.

Trinkets? A rat skeleton was hardly a trinket, but Leander bit his tongue.

'I'd be willing to buy your locket, as a kindness. It's clear you need the money.'

'Or you could just *give* me money.' He tried a cheeky smile.

'Impertinent little thing, aren't you?' She laughed. 'No. It must be a fair trade. No nonsense.'

Leander's mind whirred. He'd already pawned his mother's boots and coat, sold her pots and pans and even traded her bed sheets to the ragman. The locket was the last thing he had left. If he sold that, too, there would be nothing of hers to hold. It would be like she never existed. The thought made his eyes sting with tears. No. He couldn't part with it. He *wouldn't*. Then, as if reminding him of the reality of his situation, his stomach growled loudly. What choice did he really have? He had no other way to make money, and the more he stole, the more chance he'd be caught. Today had been a close call with the baker, but what happened when his luck ran out?

'It's not real gold,' said Leander. Should he . . . ?

'Indeed not. But I am a soft-hearted creature, and I've taken a liking to it.'

'I don't ...'

'It would be hard to part with it, I'm sure,' she said. 'But your mother would understand. Do you think she'd rather you went hungry?'

And he was hungry. So hungry. Her words brought the ache back to his belly. The flattened mutton pie wouldn't fill him for long. Three days ago he'd spent his last penny on a pint of pea soup and a hot potato. Yesterday all he'd had were three bruised pears he'd swiped by climbing someone's garden fence. There was never enough food.

'Is the latch still intact? Does it open and close?' she asked.

Leander nodded. To go from being caught stealing to earning some honest money was a good turn of events, but his mother's locket ... Could he?

'I'm sure I can find you a tempting sum. Shall we say ten shillings?'

Ten shillings! He couldn't remember when he last had a full shilling to his name.

Behind the woman, a girl appeared at the open carriage door. Leander blinked in surprise. Where had she come from? There had been no one inside a moment before ... The girl put her finger to her lips, urging him to stay silent. Was she trying to steal something, too? No. She looked too neat and well dressed to be a street child. The woman's daughter perhaps? She looked about eleven, like Leander, and had the same dark hair as the woman.

'Six, seven, eight . . .' The woman counted coins from an embroidered pouch. 'What do you say, boy?'

The girl shook her head frantically and mouthed, 'No,' her expression a picture of panic.

The girl's urgency alarmed Leander back to his senses. He couldn't possibly sell the only thing he had left of his mother!

'No,' he said firmly.

The woman's face fell.

'It's very kind of you, miss, but I couldn't part with the locket.'

She stiffened up and scowled. 'A shame. If you change your mind, I shall be here until morning. Ask for Madame Pinchbeck.'

Was that it? She was letting him leave?

Leander glanced towards the girl. The movement alerted the woman, who spun round.

'How dare you?' She lunged towards the girl, who retreated into the carriage, the door slamming.

Leander took his chance and ran.

2
The Chariot: Opposing Forces, Hasty Decisions

LEANDER

It was past ten o'clock when Leander arrived, cold and muddy, at Litchfield House. The windows were dark, apart from a tiny candle glimmer in the servants' quarters. Even the lowliest scullery maid was in bed at this hour, but he knew the rotten housekeeper, Mrs Smart, might still be waiting for him so he had to be careful. He couldn't risk meeting her empty-handed.

Leander had lived at the grand house for four years. He and his mother moved there shortly after his father died – a fresh start, Mother had said, when she accepted the job as cook. The master allowed them to live in the little gardener's cottage since there were no gardeners any more. There had probably been a hundred servants once, but Lord Litchfield had sent all but six away a year before Leander arrived. Even then, the mansion was beginning to crumble from neglect. Now Leander crept through the overgrown grounds – a long-dead hedge maze, a stagnant fountain, kitchen gardens devoured by insects and weeds.

His mind raced with the events of the evening. He had almost sold his mother's locket to that strange woman. What was he thinking? If not for the girl appearing from nowhere, he would have handed it over – the last thing his mother had given him – and for just ten shillings. He closed his eyes and tried to picture her laughing as she shelled peas, or scolding him for his dirty shoes. It was getting harder to remember what she looked like.

It had been six months since she died and almost at once a new cook had arrived to take her place and with it their cottage. So, not knowing what else to do, Leander had sought shelter and comfort within the dim and dusty library, a sanctuary of quiet which no one ever visited. He had slept there ever since. It wasn't much of a home, but it was all he had. Initially, he had been able to keep his presence a secret, but a few months ago Mrs Smart had stumbled upon him and, since then, had been insisting he pay her money to keep quiet and allow him to stay. Once, when he refused to hand over his last penny, she punished him by taking his pile of blankets and burning them.

Ten shillings would have meant hot dinners all week and money left over to keep Mrs Smart off his back. But, even so, the locket was just too precious.

Leander continued across the lawn, round the side of the house and up to the fourth window along. He pushed open the leaded pane and climbed through, dropping on to the floorboards below. He stopped to listen, holding his breath.

Silence.

He padded across the library floor, keeping to the carpets to muffle his footsteps.

Settling in his favourite corner, he dug out what remained of the mutton pie from his pocket and pulled it apart with grubby fingers. He gobbled chewy chunks of meat, before cramming the pastry into his mouth. It was buttery and salty and gone too fast.

He checked his coat pocket for any leftover crumbs, then turned it inside out and sucked gravy out of the fabric. It tasted musty.

'There you are, little swine.' Mrs Smart appeared at his shoulder. How long had she been lurking in the shadows, waiting for him? 'Thought you could sneak off to bed without giving me what you owe?'

White moonlight shining through the windows made her all hollows and angles so she looked even more menacing to Leander than usual. Her dress was roof-tile grey and her hair was scraped back severely, offering no hint of softness to her face.

'I don't have anything.' He rose to face her. He was too tired for this tonight. Why couldn't she leave him be?

'I don't believe you, toad. Too good to pay board, are you? After I've been so generous to provide a home for you.'

'I couldn't find any work.'

'If you can't pay, you can rot in the workhouse.' She

13

drew herself up to her full height. 'I don't work my back to breaking to provide luxuries for the likes of you. You'll pay me tomorrow, or you can get out and not come back.'

'I'm not scared of you,' he said, sounding braver than he really felt. But she wasn't about to throw him out – she liked his money too much. More than that, she liked having someone to pick on. She had once been the head of a huge household and now she was rotting in an empty house, with only a cook and a few scullery maids to boss around. That suited Leander: it would be impossible to stay hidden in a bustling house full of servants. But he suspected that was why Mrs Smart was so bitter and angry.

Still, he'd heard ghastly things about conditions at the workhouse. As much as he hated the old hag, better here than picking oakum in the spike.

'You should be scared, boy. You will give me my money or I'll haul you before the master. He won't take kindly to a little ratbag thief sneaking round his private estate.' She glided out into the charcoal-dark hallway.

Leander clambered up on to the empty shelf where he slept and rested his head on the grain sack he used as a pillow. The shelf was hard and barely long enough for him to lie down on, but it made him feel sheltered and safe – as safe as anywhere in this horrible world. At first Leander was relieved Mrs Smart hadn't turned him in, but soon another feeling began to gnaw at his insides.

How dare she talk of luxury, and of giving him a home?

Mrs Smart had known Leander's mother and knew he

14

had been left an orphan when she died, but she never troubled herself to check on him. She didn't care about the nights Leander lay shivering and sobbing, no one left to love him. She only cared about the jingle of coins in her apron pocket.

To take his mind off her, Leander reached for his favourite book, the only book in the library he cared about: an illustrated book of fairy tales with gold-edged pages.

As he lifted it, the book fell open to the page he visited most. Although he couldn't read many words, he knew the story by heart. Long before they arrived at Litchfield House, his mother used to tell tales of the Rat King, a man who could turn himself into a rat and creep through cracks in the walls to carry away naughty children. Such stories were never scary by the warm fire with a loving parent. Now, with his mother gone, Leander often lay alone, trying not to dwell on scrabbling noises in the attic and gaps between floorboards, until he could think of nothing else.

On the day he moved into the library, he had found this book fallen from a shelf, open at the picture of the Rat King, and it felt like a message from his mother. He had spent many a lonely night poring over the pictures, wishing she was there to read the rest of the stories to him.

Books ...

The rich lady in the coach house – Madame Pinchbeck had she said? – had a stack of books in her carriage, so she must like them. Perhaps he could sell her some from the library! It was stuffed with books, whole walls covered in

15

shelves, some so high they needed a ladder. Lord Litchfield never read them – what was the harm in taking a few?

Leander knew some books were expensive, but which ones? He could barely pick out his letters. It'd be a shame if he chose worthless ones and carried them all the way to the coach house for just a few coppers. Then again, books weren't the only valuable things in the library.

A thrill of rebellion stirred in him. Madame Pinchbeck had been willing to pay ten whole shillings for his mother's old brass locket. This house was full of many luxurious things, all but forgotten by their owner. Imagine what he could get for those …

He wouldn't take much. Just a little, just the forgotten things from the closed-up rooms. Lord Litchfield would never miss them. Mrs Smart had told him not to come back. Well, she would have her wish and, by the time she noticed anything was gone, he'd be far away.

Leander had never dared take things from the house before; even if his conscience allowed it, he certainly couldn't sell them in the local town where they might be recognized. But Madame Pinchbeck was passing through. He could race back to the coach house now and be waiting for her in the morning. He'd sell the stolen objects and be on his way to the city by noon. Sixty miles to Manchester – he'd surely earn enough for a train fare – then he'd get a bed in a boarding house and find a tradesman who needed an apprentice.

Or he could work in a factory. Manchester was always in

want of strong children for the cotton mills. Whatever the job, he would find somewhere he *was* wanted. Unlike here.

Quickly on his feet, Leander unfolded his sack pillow and tiptoed across the floor.

There was no time to waste. The book of fairy tales went in. If it wasn't worth much money, Leander would keep it himself, for the memories.

He looked around. What else could he take? The mantelpiece held two silver candlesticks, which he slipped into his bag.

In the centre of the room sat a heavy oak writing desk. Two fine pens with gold nibs were nestled in the drawer – he took both.

A glass display case was full of treasures. He chose a sugar bowl with a fancy design.

That should be enough.

He felt a twinge of guilt. But what choice did he have? And once he made his fortune he could send money back to pay for his sins. Maybe he'd visit the master as a wealthy businessman and hear Mrs Smart call him 'sir' as she poured the tea!

Climbing out of the window, Leander hesitated, suddenly remembering the girl from the carriage who had warned him about selling his locket. Had Madame Pinchbeck been trying to cheat him? And how did the woman know the locket belonged to his mother, or that Leander was an orphan? And what to make of her peculiar collection in the carriage?

If he left Litchfield House with these stolen objects, he could never come back. It was risky, but what had caution given him so far? A lonely, hungry life.

Leander made his choice.

The bulging sack bumped his leg with each step. There'd be a bruise tomorrow, but it'd be worth it.

Leander arrived back at the coach house. The carriage was still there – Madame Pinchbeck and the girl were likely asleep in the upstairs rooms. The best thing to do was bed down in the coach house, to be sure he wouldn't miss them in the morning. It was cold, but he could make a nest in the straw and wait.

He slipped through the side door. There, to his surprise, sitting on the steps of the carriage, was the girl. She was dressed in an elegant dark-blue dress and her hair was pinned in two braids to the back of her head. Now he could see she was older than he'd thought at first, older than him certainly. Thirteen or so, almost a lady. She sat in a dainty way, back straight and ankles together, and stared at the flagstones, lost in a daydream.

'Excuse me, miss?'

The girl gasped and leaped up. She dropped her enamel cup and was in the carriage even before it clanged against the stone floor. The door fell closed behind her.

'Beg pardon, miss, didn't mean to scare you,' he called. 'Is your mother there?'

No reply came. This was Leander's chance to ask why she'd

stopped him selling the locket earlier. He hoped she hadn't got into too much trouble.

'You dropped your cup.' He picked it up and opened the carriage door, meaning to hand it back, but he couldn't see her. A small candle burned in a glass jar, but there was no trace of the girl. He climbed inside. 'Where are you?'

Nothing.

'Very clever.' He hated people playing jokes on him. 'Good trick. Show yourself.'

The creak of an opening door. Clicking footsteps. Oh no. He couldn't jump out again – if the woman found him in her carriage a second time, he'd never convince her he wasn't stealing. She'd raise the landlady for sure, and when they saw what was in his sack he'd be done for.

His only choice was to hide. Stay low and not make a sound. He lay on the floor and pulled a blanket over himself. The footsteps were brisk and sharp – it was definitely Madame Pinchbeck. But she might not open the carriage. If he was very lucky and very quiet, he might get the chance to sneak out.

Luck had to be with him. He was so close to a new life.

There was a heavy scraping, the hollow clop of hooves and a soft neigh. The horses! She was tending her horses. Leander closed his eyes and mouthed a thank you in prayer. Hugging his knees to his chest, he breathed as softly as he could, listening for his moment to escape.

Then the carriage began to move.

3

The Empress:
Powerful Woman,
Mother Figure

LEANDER

He was in trouble now. He tried to stand, but the unfamiliar swaying of the carriage made him unsteady and he fell back on to the pile of blankets. Glasses and jars and bottles rattled and shook with the shuddering of the carriage. Hooves clattered against the road and raindrops fell faster and faster, louder and louder, hammering on the thin roof.

He sat up, clutched the edge of a shelf for balance and lifted the corner of the velvet drapes. Black clouds had covered the moon and Leander could see little in the gloom. He pressed his cheek against the cool, rain-streaked glass. Lanterns were lit up front; trees and fence posts emerged into the bubble of weak light as they approached and faded as they passed by, as if pulled by a ghostly tide. Leander had only travelled by coach once, when they first moved to Litchfield House, and it hadn't gone nearly as fast.

It was going too quickly to jump out. He must be alert for the first sign of slowing, but the journey stretched on. There was no way Madame Pinchbeck would trust him after this – he'd be lucky if she didn't call the constabulary. No, once the carriage stopped, he would leap out and leg it. He'd have to find someone else to buy his loot. At least he'd be in a new town, where people might not recognize Lord Litchfield's treasures.

The jars, horses and rain fell into an easy rhythm as the carriage travelled on. It was almost soothing. He'd been awake for such a long time ... But he couldn't, wouldn't, *mustn't* fall asleep ...

Leander jerked upright.

The carriage was moving over different terrain than before. The hoofbeats were softer and less distinct, and the rain had stopped. Another peek through the window showed early-morning sunbeams through bare branches. He *had* slept, then. Leander silently cursed himself. How could he have fallen asleep in such a dangerous situation?

He felt the carriage begin to slow. Leander looked down to see his sack open on the floor, its contents spilled and scattered round the tiny space. He quickly gathered up the candlesticks and shoved them back into the bag. Carriage still in motion, he opened the door, screwed up his eyes and jumped.

Leander hit the ground, rolling through wet leaves until his shoulder slammed against a fallen tree.

The carriage stopped not far from where Leander lay, but the woman climbed down and went straight to the horses without a backward glance.

Phew. She hasn't noticed me, he thought, already planning his next move.

Leander stayed low and crawled in the opposite direction, wary of attracting attention by rustling the straggling bushes. His sack caught on a dead branch. He tugged at it and, with a great crack, the branch snapped. The sack flew free, banging the candlesticks together with an almighty clang that rang through the trees as clear as church bells. He froze.

Fool! He should have left the bag where it was or stayed still so as not to give away his position.

'It's much too far to crawl home, boy,' Madame Pinchbeck called.

Other than the dirt track they were on, there was nothing but woods on all sides. Leander wondered how far away the nearest town was, and in which direction. They might have travelled miles through the night. He was sure he could outrun the woman – long dresses and fancy shoes were hardly made for chasing through the woods – but he had no idea which way to go.

'As you wish.' She moved between her two black horses, adjusting straps and stroking their necks. 'But many a man has come to an unpleasant end in the woods.' She turned her back, travelling cloak swishing round her ankles. 'I shall be here a while if you decide a hot cup of tea would be preferable to perishing in the forest.'

She didn't even sound angry that he'd stowed away. Leander slowly rose to his feet. He could never go back to Litchfield House now; by the time he returned, Mrs Smart would have discovered the theft. She'd kick up a stink and make him pay more for her silence, or worse, tell the master of his stealing. He had no choice but to sell his goods, one way or another.

Madame Pinchbeck was now arranging firewood and paying him no mind. She didn't seem to be a threat. Perhaps he could still convince her to buy his things, or at least let him ride along to the next village. And she was right – he could easily come to harm if he got lost in the wintry woods. It didn't seem he had much choice but to trust her.

'Don't stand idle. Find some dry leaves to get this fire going.' She spoke like a schoolteacher, no doubt in her voice that Leander would obey.

He kicked aside the soggy leaves by his feet to get to the dry, crunchy layer beneath. Then, without letting go of his sack, he gathered up a handful and carried them over to the pile of twigs, dropping them from arm's length.

The woman nodded briskly. 'More, child, more. Don't you know how to build a fire?'

'I wasn't in your carriage.'

Stupid. He shouldn't have started with that. She folded her arms and raised her eyebrows in disbelief.

'I ... I was looking for you. The man at the inn said you

23

went this way, so I followed you. I came to sell some things.'

She put one finger to her lip to shush him. 'Fire first, excuses later. Kindling. Leaves. Twigs.'

'Honest, I came back to the inn,' Leander began, scraping around one-handed for more leaves, his sack clutched tightly to his body. 'But you were gone, so I followed you.'

'My, my. You must have run awfully fast to catch up with me.' A tiny smile almost made it look like she was teasing him.

'I set off right after you.' Leander's words didn't even sound convincing to him. He dropped his next handful of leaves on to the sticks.

'How fortuitous.' She swept back her skirts before crouching by the fire to arrange the kindling. 'And I daresay those boots were a tremendous help as you raced along behind me –' she struck sparks from a piece of flint and coaxed the flames to light – 'for six miles.'

Leander glanced at his shabby shoes, the leather so worn the sole was coming loose. 'I ran quickly so you wouldn't miss out—' he lied.

'Empty vessels make the most sound. See if you can hold your tongue until the kettle sings,' she said, hanging it over the fire, 'and then you can tell me some truths.'

She pulled out two folding stools from the carriage. An age passed as the water came to the boil, Leander's insides churning and bubbling along with it. Had he made a grave mistake? Out in the woods – with no one around – some folks would snatch the sack and abandon him. Madame Pinchbeck looked respectable enough, but you could never tell what was in someone's heart.

But she could have stolen his locket back at the inn, or turned him in as a thief. No one would have believed his word over that of this well-spoken lady.

She handed him a tin cup full of something hot. His cold-numbed fingers throbbed with appreciation at the heat. The last time someone had taken care of him this way was when the church ladies made soup for the needy after Sunday service. But then they started asking questions – wouldn't he be better off in the care of the parish? – so Leander never dared return, for fear of being sent to the workhouse.

'Name?'

'Leander.'

'Manners?'

'Leander, miss.'

'Well then. Let's see what you've brought to sell.'

Leander passed over the dirty sack. He didn't have a clue what the objects were worth, but maybe it didn't matter as long as they made him enough money to get to Manchester. How much did train tickets cost? And he'd need board when he got there. New boots, to look smart.

He puffed up his chest and tried to look confident, like he would know a good price when he heard it.

'Interesting.' She pulled out the silver sugar bowl and turned it over in her hands. 'A handsome little thing. What's this monogram? M. J. L?'

'It's from the big house, Lord Litchfield's place.'

There seemed little point in lying; better to be as honest as he could and try not to raise any more suspicions.

'Oh,' she said, her eyes widening. 'Litchfield House?'

'Yes, miss.' Whatever she offered, he'd tell her to double it. She was obviously wealthy. He wondered why she wasn't travelling with a servant.

'It's a long time since I've heard that name.' She traced the raised letters with her fingertips and smiled. 'Of course, I knew we were in the area . . .'

Did she know Lord Litchfield? It would be a disaster if she was some distant relation, and Leander had presented her with Litchfield's stolen silver. Too late now. He would hold his nerve and hope for the best.

'And how did it come to be in your possession?'

'I live there,' said Leander. It wasn't a lie.

'You can't be Lord Litchfield's son,' she said, watching him from the corner of her eye.

'No, miss.'

She raised her eyebrows. 'A servant?'

'Sort of.' Leander chose his words carefully. 'There aren't many servants any more.'

'No? Why?'

'He went a bit funny, people said, because his daughter went missing.' He slurped the tea. The taste was awful, but the warmth was very welcome. 'He sent most of the servants away.'

'Tell me, does he still grieve for the child?' She leaned towards Leander, her head tipped slightly to one side. There

26

was something unsettling about her expression, as if she hoped the answer was yes. It reminded Leander of a cat that has suddenly spotted something small and furry.

'Suppose so,' said Leander with a shrug. 'I only met him once.'

'And he told you about the girl?' A dark curl fell across her face and she swept it back without breaking eye contact.

'Oh no, miss. People in the town talk about it. We didn't get there until long after the girl was gone.'

'Well, what did he say to you?' She was talking faster now.

'Nothing really. He was telling my mother what her duties were.'

She continued to stare as though she expected more from him.

'I remember he looked very sick, all bundled up under blankets even though it wasn't cold,' Leander added. He leaned away from her. He didn't like the way she was asking her questions. 'Did you know him, miss?'

She smiled and relaxed her shoulders and the tension was broken. 'I met him, a long time ago. Never liked the man. He used to do some interesting work, but I found him to be most untrustworthy. Now what else have we?'

Having been so interested, Madame Pinchbeck now seemed very keen to change the subject. She put the sugar bowl back in the sack and pulled out the candlesticks, turning them upside down, weighing them in her hands.

Leander wondered why Lord Litchfield was untrustworthy,

but it seemed rude to ask. It was probably a good thing that Madame Pinchbeck didn't much like him – she probably wouldn't be too worried about Leander stealing his silver. Leander shook off the strangeness of the conversation and turned his attention back to selling his wares.

'Look lovely in your drawing room, miss,' he said in his most persuasive voice.

She laughed. She was pretty when she laughed. Leander guessed Madame Pinchbeck was about thirty – old enough to be his mother, though not by much. Her eyes were deep brown and lively. She was thin but, unlike Mrs Smart with her hard edges and stern face, it suited her.

She tapped the metal with a fingernail. 'Not the finest I've ever seen . . .'

Leander swallowed a big mouthful of tea to hide his nervousness. It was bitter and burned his throat all the way down. Gritty flecks were left behind on his tongue.

'And I presume you have the master's permission to be selling off his treasures?' Her eyes were piercing, though her expression was gentle.

He looked at his feet. 'They're not needed any more,' he said. Again, it wasn't untrue. 'I want the money for a ticket to the city. I'm going to get myself a position.'

'Is that so?' She smiled.

'An apprentice shoemaker. Or bookbinder. Or I could work in the mills.' He took another gulp of tea. The taste wasn't as bad this time, but the grit was still unpleasant.

'It's a hard life in the mills, child.'

'I can work hard.'

'Ah yes. The plucky orphan. When did your parents die?'

'My father when I was seven. My mother passed this spring.' An unexpected tear stung the corner of Leander's eye. He didn't want to look like a baby and blinked it away, hard.

'You must miss her.'

'Terribly.' He bit his bottom lip so it wouldn't tremble. No one ever asked him about his mother.

She leaned in and lowered her voice. 'I'm a medium, Leander. I help people speak to the dead.'

'You . . . how?'

'It's a gift. To lift the veil that separates our world from the realm of the dead.'

'Heaven?' he said.

'In a manner of speaking. People pay me to help them speak to their loved ones. I could help you, too.'

'You mean . . . I could talk to my mother again?'

'I think we can come to an agreement,' she said. 'But first let us see if you're the sort of boy I'd like to do business with.'

From within the folds of her cloak she withdrew a small metal case, which opened to reveal a deck of cards. Not the hearts and spades the men gambled with in the inn – these cards were red and purple and yellow, with intricate patterns of owls and spiders and bats on the back. She flipped them over and fanned them out – the faces were all different. The top card was a picture of a tower struck by lightning, people falling from the crumbling walls.

She turned them back so the pictures were hidden and shuffled them deftly before fanning them out again, face down.

'Are you going to tell my fortune, miss?' He'd seen a fortune-teller's tent at a fair once, but his mother wouldn't let him go inside. He had always wanted to see how they did it.

'In a sense. Which one?'

'I don't know which to choose, miss.'

'The *cards* know. Take whichever you are drawn to.'

Leander pinched a card between finger and thumb, watching the woman's face for any clue that he had chosen correctly.

'Good. Now show me.'

He handed her the card and she turned it over. The picture showed a boy climbing a mountain, yellow cloak slung about his shoulders and carrying a staff that was bigger than him.

'The Page of Wands,' said the woman.

'What does it mean?' Leander swallowed nervously. What if the card told her he was a thief – could the cards do that?

'It tells me you are loyal, full of energy, capable of learning. It tells me you are about to embark upon a great adventure.'

'One card says all that?' Leander couldn't help smiling. *Loyal and capable.* He sat up a little straighter, pleased that a lady like Madame Pinchbeck saw him as more than just a beggar boy.

She took a small round loaf from a leather pouch and broke it in half, handing Leander the bigger piece. He bit off a huge chunk. Madame Pinchbeck nibbled her piece delicately, so Leander forced himself to chew more slowly, suddenly aware of his bad manners.

'I suppose I can give you a little something for these things, so you can buy your ticket,' she said after a moment. 'Even though it will be very hard to sell them on, with the monogram on them all.' She patted Leander on the knee. 'But I'd like you to find your position.'

He gulped down the dry bread and washed it back with the last of the bitter tea. She was going to buy the silver! He wondered if she'd let him travel to the next town with her. Where was the nearest train station? Or perhaps he should buy himself new boots first, for the journey.

'Although,' she said, 'I wonder ... but no. You wouldn't be interested.' She folded her hands in her lap and sighed.

'Yes, miss?' She looked very sad, and Leander felt strongly that he wanted to help her.

'No, no, you want your money and your job in the mills ... You don't want to hear my worries.'

'If you please, miss, I should like to know.'

'My business keeps me on the road for long stretches. A lady travelling needs a strong pair of hands to help with the horses, fetching and carrying, delivering messages ...'

Did she mean what he thought? Was she offering him a position? He'd never dealt with horses before, but he could learn. *Capable of learning.* That's what the card said.

'I can't offer you much but hot suppers and a dry place to sleep. The occasional penny or two for yourself. Nothing to match the excitement of a town like Manchester.'

Leander nodded his head eagerly. He had missed hot suppers. 'No, miss. I mean, yes, miss. I should like it very much.' He was perching on the very edge of his seat with eagerness.

'But first – how can I be sure you won't rob me in my sleep? We both know these things are stolen. How do I know I can trust you?'

Leander recoiled as though she'd slapped him. So there it was. His job was slipping away. He almost started to beg, but pulled himself back. It was never a good idea to show how desperate you were. It gave other people too much power. He plastered on a cheeky grin and said, 'I'll give you a chance if you give me a chance.' It was said with more confidence than he felt.

She smiled. 'Very well. Let's make an agreement. You give me something of yours as security. I will return it once you've proven your loyalty. How about the locket you're so fond of?'

He hesitated for a moment, then carefully unfastened the clasp of the necklace. After all, he would prove his worth to Madame Pinchbeck and then it would be returned to him. 'And, if I go with you, you'll help me speak to my mother?' he asked hopefully.

Madame Pinchbeck nodded slowly. 'Do we have a deal?' she asked.

Leander lowered the chain into her open hand.

Five of Wands:
Disagreement, Conflict, Strife

LEANDER

The carriage door slammed open and the girl
leaped out.

'Idiot!' she shouted.

The girl from the coach house. Leander had forgotten all
about her! Had she been listening all this time? Why hadn't
Madame Pinchbeck mentioned her?

'Behave, Charlotte,' said Madame Pinchbeck, barely
glancing in the girl's direction. Her slender fingers curled
tightly round Leander's locket and she closed her eyes, a
serene smile on her lips. A strange sensation of tingling
pressure came over Leander, like standing in front of a hot
fire, or a hug that was too tight.

The girl glared at Leander. 'You have no idea what
you've done!'

'Where did you—' Leander tried to shout back at her, but

barely managed a whisper. It was as though all the air had been knocked from his lungs, like the time he fell through the ice into the river. He stood up, knocking the stool over into the dirt as he pulled a long gulp of air into chest and coughed it back out.

The girl was ablaze before him, cheeks flushed red with fury. 'You ran away! Why did you come back?'

Madame Pinchbeck smoothed the fabric of her cloak, watching the girl as if she was of no more consequence than a bluebottle.

She turned her scowl towards Madame Pinchbeck. 'I know what you've done. You traded his locket for a position, instead of money. That was his valuable thing.'

'Yes, dear, how clever of you.' Madame Pinchbeck sounded entirely bored. 'Have you quite finished with your outburst?'

'Never.' She spun round in a blur of silk and crêpe and vanished.

Leander was dizzy with shock, though his breathing was returning to normal. He turned to Madame Pinchbeck for answers.

'I'm sorry, Leander. Charlotte can be quite rude.'

'Who … how …' Leander's brain couldn't settle on the right question.

'Charlotte is my daughter. So to speak.' She pursed her lips. 'My ward. She is an orphan, like you. We've been travelling together for quite some time. Sometimes she forgets her place.'

'I saw her in the coach house,' said Leander. 'But she wasn't in the carriage. I'm sure she wasn't in the carriage.'

Madame Pinchbeck stood up and opened the carriage door like a footman.

Leander craned his neck to see if the girl was there – though she couldn't have passed through the door without opening it. 'But how did she—'

The woman ignored him. '*Exsisto*,' she said.

There was a crackle in the air like the moment before a lightning strike. The hairs on Leander's arms stood on end. From a tiny glass box on a shelf Charlotte began to appear, pouring out like liquid and becoming solid before his eyes. She wore the same scowl as she hopped down from the carriage.

Leander's legs felt as if they had been turned to rubber. It was like falling into a dream and jerking awake – sudden and unsettling. He sank down, forgetting the stool had fallen over until it was too late to right himself, and fell both-buttocks on to the forest floor. He scrambled back to his feet, ashamed to look a fool.

Behind Charlotte was a boy. So now there were two people in the carriage? In the carriage where Leander had sat alone not long ago ...

The boy was younger than Charlotte – Leander guessed about ten years old – with tanned skin and large, serious eyes, dressed in a tweed jacket and bowler hat.

'I am going to find a seamstress in the village, since you can't be trusted with my alterations. I shall be back shortly.'

Madame Pinchbeck hooked a long finger under Charlotte's chin. 'You would be wise not to test my patience further.' She gave Leander's locket to the boy. 'Felix, find a safe place for this, and look after Leander. Teach him our ways.'

She drew her cloak round her body in a sweeping motion, then stalked off up the road without looking back.

'I don't need looking after, miss.' Leander didn't want to stay with these strange children, but he didn't want to annoy his new employer by trailing along where he wasn't wanted. He followed her a few dozen steps along the road, wondering what to do.

Nothing was going the way he expected. Had he made a dreadful mistake by coming here? Leander swallowed the lump at the back of his throat. More than anything, he wanted an explanation. But, whatever the answer, there was no going back now.

Things would be fine. He would be fine.

Probably.

'Disaster,' said Charlotte.

'We'll have to make the best of it,' the boy, Felix, said to her in a measured and calm voice.

'There can't be three of us! This boy—'

'Be kind.'

'Don't tell me to be kind! I didn't cause this mess!'

'Neither did I so don't snap at me.' He folded his arms and frowned.

They spoke as though Leander was invisible.

The surprise of seeing the children appear from nowhere was subsiding in Leander, only to be replaced by a creeping sense of dread. Who were these children who could vanish and return like a witch's familiar?

If Madame Pinchbeck was a medium, as she'd told him, did that mean they were ghosts?

'What are you?' Leander demanded. 'Are you ghosts?'

'I tried to warn him,' Charlotte said to Felix, not even acknowledging that Leander had spoken. 'I thought I'd scared him away.'

'You're not see-through,' Leander continued.

'You did your best, Charlotte,' said Felix.

Leander moved closer and reached out to poke Charlotte's arm. She was solid.

She pulled away with an expression of disgust. 'What are you doing?'

'What's going on?' said Leander.

'You've been stolen, that's what!' Charlotte growled. 'And put us all in danger by doing so.'

'Stop it,' said Felix. 'You'll frighten him.'

'He should be frightened if he has any sense.' She looked Leander up and down. 'Which is unlikely.'

Why did she want to make him afraid? Horrible girl. Leander wouldn't give her the pleasure. 'I'm not scared of you.' He tilted his head back. 'Madame Pinchbeck gave me a job. I have as much right to be here as you.'

'Job?' Charlotte laughed. 'You were *tricked*. Now you're a prisoner. Like us. This—' She snatched Leander's locket from Felix and held it up, hand shaking, although with rage or fear, Leander wasn't sure. 'This is your cage now.'

Cages. Prisoners. *Stolen*. The dread rose again in Leander. 'You're lying. How can we be prisoners? Madame Pinchbeck's not even here. We could just walk away if we wanted.'

Felix put his hand on Leander's shoulder, steering him back to the seats by the already dwindling fire. Definitely solid. Not spirits, then? 'You should sit down.'

Leander shrugged him off. 'I won't. Stop teasing me and explain.'

Felix sat on the carriage step. 'When you gave Pinchbeck your locket, she caught a piece of your soul inside it.'

Leander remembered the tingly feeling, the strange breathlessness when Madame Pinchbeck held the locket. Is that what a broken soul felt like? 'No—'

'Yes,' said Charlotte.

Felix continued. 'When she gives her command, you'll become air and be sucked into it.'

'Sucked into it?' Leander didn't understand.

'Into the locket,' Felix told him.

Impossible. But … 'Like your vanishing trick?' asked Leander.

'It's not a trick. It's her magic. You can do it, too,' said Felix.

'Just cos I don't wear smart clothes and talk fancy doesn't mean I'll believe anything,' said Leander. 'You can't do magic.' Although deep down he wasn't so sure. They were so solemn and their voices so heavy with worry. He didn't like it.

'It's *Pinchbeck's* magic. The only scrap she has, whatever she promised you,' said Charlotte.

38

Leander was suddenly tired and wanted it to stop. He righted the stool and slumped down on to it.

'I know it sounds strange, but you must pay attention,' said Felix. 'If we don't teach you what's expected before she returns, we'll all be in for it.'

'No! I don't want to hear any more. Leave me alone.'

'I wish we could,' said Charlotte through clenched teeth. 'If you weren't so greedy and stupid as to barter with your locket, she wouldn't have caught you.'

'I wasn't greedy!' shouted Leander. 'I was *starving*! Not that you could understand that.' It was obvious from Charlotte's fancy clothes and educated voice that she'd never had to struggle the way Leander had.

'She caught you, too, Charlotte,' said Felix. 'What if I hadn't helped you?'

Charlotte narrowed her eyes and sighed heavily.

'Now, Leander, there are things you need to remember to stay safe. Are you listening?' Felix continued.

Leander nodded. He didn't trust himself to speak – he would surely scream with frustration. How had he found himself here?

'The locket is your Cabinet. You must always leave it open.'

'Cabinet?'

'A magical container,' explained Felix. 'They hold the pieces of our souls which means we can disappear into them.' He unlatched the locket and pulled it open a crack. 'When your Cabinet is open, you can move in and out of it at will. But, if it's closed, Pinchbeck can make you vanish and you'll have to wait for her command to reappear. You don't want to be stuck inside, so never close it.'

'And our Cabinets, too. They can never be shut,' Charlotte said. 'The glass lantern is mine and the violin case is Felix's. You must never close them. Never. Promise!'

'I promise,' answered Leander through gritted teeth. He hated being bossed around, but the look on Charlotte's face made it clear he shouldn't argue.

'Now you should practise vanishing inside your Cabinet,' said Felix. 'Pinchbeck will expect you to be able to do so when she returns.'

It had to be a joke. He would try to disappear and they would both laugh at how gullible he was, before revealing how they did the trick. They probably thought Leander was trying to steal their jobs and replace them, which would explain the frosty reception. But Leander didn't want to replace them. He just wanted to belong.

'We'll help you. You need to learn.' Felix was kinder than the girl. His voice was gentle. He didn't seem the type to play mean games.

Even so, Leander wasn't about to make a fool of himself. 'No.'

'Please yourself,' said Charlotte. 'You'll get a good hiding from Pinchbeck if you won't do as you're told.'

'Why do you have to make this harder?' Felix said to her and Charlotte lowered her gaze.

'I didn't come for magic tricks. I just need a job,' said Leander.

'There is no job,' said Felix.

'You're a slave. A prisoner. Pinchbeck is like . . . the wicked witch in the gingerbread house. The monster who takes children away.' Charlotte's eyes were wet, like she was holding back tears. Like she really meant what she was saying.

'Of course. She's the wicked witch and you must be Hansel and Gretel. Nice to meet you. I'm Robin Hood.' Leander pretended to doff his hat, and Felix gave the tiniest of smiles. Charlotte did not.

'We're not joking,' she said.

Leander thought of the book in his sack, and the story of the Rat King . . . But no. 'Stop treating me like a child. They're just fairy tales.'

'And yet,' said Felix, 'here we are.'

5

Seven of Swords:
Deception, Trickery,
Betrayal

FELIX

Felix loved three things.

The first was music, which flowed through his veins where the blood should be.

The second was his little brother, Isaak, who went to the market one day and never came back. Felix had sworn to find him again if it took him until Judgement Day.

The third was Charlotte.

He hadn't wanted to love her – but she grew on him like lichen on a rock. He'd learned not to become fond of the children Pinchbeck stole. Before Charlotte, there had been four others. Four lost children. Pinchbeck kept them around for a few days or weeks until she decided they weren't useful enough – then they disappeared in the night. Felix didn't like it, but he had promised loyalty to Pinchbeck ... was it eight or nine years ago? Eight, he was fairly sure. It was hard to keep track of time.

Madame Pinchbeck had taken him in when he had no one else and, when it was just the two of them, they rubbed along quite nicely. Felix would play his violin for her, and she seemed to enjoy his company. She had begun performing seances not long before they met, but together they had made her shows into something really special. Other mediums had ghostly knockings, or floating tables, but Felix helped Pinchbeck create an other-worldly performance with music and apparitions and all sorts of unbelievable tricks. And it had been fun. More fun than begging in the streets. Sometimes Felix felt bad about enjoying himself when his brother was still missing, but he comforted himself knowing Pinchbeck would help Felix find him.

Once Pinchbeck stole Charlotte, she mostly stopped taking other children. Pinchbeck never explained why – she wasn't the type to justify her actions – but Felix could tell that Charlotte was different to the other children. Well-spoken, good manners, healthy complexion – she looked like someone from the upper class, which always impressed the wealthy audiences. Not to mention that Charlotte knew how to curl Pinchbeck's hair and embroider her clothes. None of the raggedy stolen orphans had been nearly so useful as a lady's maid. The last child Pinchbeck stole had been three years ago and Felix was relieved.

It wasn't such a bad life. At least Pinchbeck took care of them in her own way, and they were usually fed.

Felix's father had been a drunk, uncaring and useless, so all Felix had was Isaak. Without his brother, what did it matter where he was? At least with Pinchbeck he could travel around and search for him. Felix had Charlotte, and his music, and even an audience during Pinchbeck's performances. He'd accepted his lot a long time ago.

But it was different for Charlotte. She had a home and someone who cared about her. Although they had good days, Charlotte would never be truly happy with Pinchbeck. Felix felt torn between the two of them.

And now there was the new boy, Leander. His arrival threatened to change everything. Charlotte was furious, pacing round the campsite, raging and muttering.

'There can't be three of us,' she said. 'Pinchbeck can't sustain three of us. What does she want him for?'

'Money? He's a thief. She hasn't had much work lately.' Felix busied himself finding more wood for the fire. No use freezing to death while they waited for her.

'And when she has her money, then what? She destroys him? What if it isn't him she chooses to vanish for ever?' She lowered her voice. 'We know that three is too many! Remember Rosa?'

Charlotte's panic was like a mistuned string on a violin, impossible to ignore. But they needed to get through this together.

'Well, we can't just let him flounder. He's here now, so we have to make the best of it. I'm trying to teach him. You could be more helpful.'

'He doesn't believe a word I say. He's useless.'

Despite her harsh words, Felix could tell she was softening.

44

It was Charlotte's way – to lash out in temper before she calmed down enough to think. Felix was used to waiting out her anger the way fishermen waited out a storm.

Charlotte had failed.

CHARLOTTE

From the moment she saw Pinchbeck talking to the boy back at the coach house she knew the woman was trying to steal him. After five years of travelling with this monster, Charlotte understood how her mind worked. She recognized the sweet smiles and encouraging words that covered the truth about Pinchbeck – Charlotte had once fallen for the same act.

Why did the silly boy have to come back? She'd managed to warn him off – much to Pinchbeck's irritation – and had gone into her Cabinet to rest, only to wake too late to stop the boy handing over his locket.

Charlotte was furious. Furious with Leander for falling for Pinchbeck's charms. Furious with her past self for making the same mistake. But, most of all, furious with Pinchbeck, the real villain in all this.

And what did Pinchbeck want with the boy? He was just a street urchin. Charlotte was useful for fixing Pinchbeck's hair and clothes, and Felix for his music. Maybe Felix was right: Leander was a thief and Pinchbeck always wanted more money – perhaps that was the reason. But why now, after all this time?

She tried to take Felix's words to heart and be more helpful. She began dragging out rugs and blankets from the carriage while the boys searched for more dry sticks to burn.

But this was bad news. Pinchbeck couldn't have three captives at once. Charlotte did not fully understand why, but there appeared to be a physical cost to Pinchbeck in keeping the children trapped.

Once, when Charlotte had been with Pinchbeck and Felix for a couple of years the woman took a little girl named Rosa. She was very small – six or seven at the most – and Charlotte had become very fond of her. But Pinchbeck grew drained and tired, as if the Cabinets drew their power from her body. It wasn't long before Rosa and her Cabinet disappeared during the night, and Charlotte and Felix were forbidden from mentioning her name again. She felt sick at the thought of it. Poor Rosa.

The same would surely happen now – one way or another. How could they prevent it?

She shook out a dusty rug and folded it, placing it on the driest spot of dirt she could find. Pinchbeck had told them to teach Leander their ways, and there'd be more immediate trouble if they didn't do as she said.

'Come and sit down,' she called to the boys.

Leander folded his arms. Frustration bubbled up inside Charlotte, but she clenched her teeth together to stop angry words spilling out. She must stay calm, as Felix did.

'Here. I have sweets.' She pulled out a twist of paper from her pocket. Pear drops. She had been making them last as long as possible, and there were still three left. 'Sit down and you can have one.'

That did the trick, and the boys settled down on the blankets.

'If she's really so bad, I'll run away,' Leander said, rolling his pear drop round his tongue.

'You can't. If you go too far from Pinchbeck, you'll become insubstantial,' Charlotte told him.

'What does in-sub—'

'Insubstantial. It means not solid. Like a ghost.'

A frigid wind blew through the trees, whistling round them and whipping up Leander's untidy curls. They pulled the rough blankets round their shoulders.

'You'll turn to vapour. Be too weak to do anything,' Felix added. 'She can't be more than half a mile away now, or we'd feel it.'

'Have you ever tried to run away?'

Charlotte met Felix's eyes for a long moment. 'Yes,' she said at last. Felix had warned her not to. She had run as far as her legs would allow and barely found her way back. Pinchbeck had laughed when she returned. 'It hurts.'

'How long have you been her captives?' said Leander.

Charlotte picked at a loose thread on her skirt. 'She took me five years ago.'

'Eight for me,' said Felix.

'But . . . you must have been just babies?'

Charlotte put her head in her hands. 'That's another thing her magic does. We don't get any older. We're the same age now as when we were stolen, and we always will be. For ever.'

6

The Magician:
Confidence, Power,
Sleight of Hand

The crunch of gravel alerted them to Pinchbeck's
return. She rounded the corner with a large bundle
in her arms and a genial smile.

'Ah, there's my little family!' She handed the parcel to
Felix, ruffling his hair fondly. 'And I smell supper. Such good,
obedient children.'

Leander saw Charlotte roll her eyes, but she said nothing.

'Now then, little Leander,' Pinchbeck said, pointing to the
parcel. 'Come and see what I've brought for you.' She spoke in
a sing-song voice, as if to a small child, and it made Leander
feel funny. He was too old to be 'little Leander', but it had
been a long time since anyone spoke to him so warmly, let
alone brought him gifts.

The sackcloth wrapping fell away to reveal an outfit. Long
trousers! A white linen shirt with lapels. A grey waistcoat

and black frock coat with a single row of buttons. The shirt had been repaired and the outfit was a little mismatched, but they were without doubt the best things Leander had ever owned.

'For me, truly?'

'Truly.' She beamed. Although Leander remained wary, she seemed so kind. It didn't make sense, with Charlotte and Felix acting like she was sent by the devil himself. 'Go and change, then!'

It was difficult to change in the carriage where every space was taken up with some weird object or other. Leander hurriedly put the clothes on to avoid the cold and fearful that someone might open the door and expose him in his threadbare undergarments.

The clothes were a little baggy, but he emerged a different boy. Prisoner or not, this was the first time anyone had cared he was clothed and fed since his mother died. His spirits rose; it was good to be wanted.

Pinchbeck was so kind. A thousand times nicer than anyone he had met since being alone. Could she really be as wicked as the others said? Maybe they were tricking him after all.

'Much better,' said Pinchbeck. 'Though we shall have to do something about that hair. Charlotte?'

Charlotte screwed up her face in disgust. 'He probably has lice.'

'Do not!' Leander said indignantly.

'Just get a comb through it,' Pinchbeck told her.

Charlotte produced a comb and reluctantly dragged it through the straggly mop on Leander's head. He clenched his teeth as she tugged at the knots, determined not to show any pain or weakness.

'Best I can do while he's so filthy,' she said after a while. 'It all needs cutting off.'

Leander hastily dabbed at his eyes so she wouldn't see that they were watering in pain. 'Thank you,' he muttered, cheeks burning.

'Gather close, my cherubs,' said Pinchbeck. 'I have excellent news.' She cleared her throat. 'We have an engagement this evening.'

Felix gave a broad smile. 'A performance, finally.'

Charlotte's lips thinned and her jaw clenched in an expression of irritation. Everything, it seemed to Leander, made this girl annoyed.

'This shall be an excellent initiation for our new little Leander. Charlotte – the red gown, if you please. Felix, ensure the equipment is ready. Chop-chop!' Both children were gone in an instant. Pinchbeck began unpinning her hat, allowing loose dark curls to fall round her face.

'Please, Miss Pinchbeck,' said Leander. She blinked as though she had forgotten he was there. 'What are we doing?'

She laughed again and reached into the deep pocket of her travelling cloak. She produced a gilt-edged visiting card and handed it to Leander who did his best to read it.

'Mmm . . .'

'Madame,' she prompted.

'Madame Aug-us-tin-a Pinchbeck. Clay-voy—' He could feel himself blushing. At least Charlotte wasn't watching. She'd surely have something to say if she knew Leander couldn't read well.

Pinchbeck took back the card and read it aloud. 'Madame Augustina Pinchbeck. Clairvoyant, medium, spiritualist. Miracle worker.' She smiled and curtseyed, as though expecting applause.

Leander had no idea what the words meant, but he wasn't about to admit it. He smiled and nodded and tried to look impressed.

'Oh, Leander, you are so lucky I found you. Most people can hardly dream of such sights as you will see.' She spun round, cloak and skirts swirling about her ankles, then threw her arms up. 'Augustina Pinchbeck, the most gifted medium in all of England. Nay, all of the world. Certainly, any fool can tap on a table and pretend a ghost did it. If you want something more, there's only one person who can help you.'

She made a beckoning motion, encouraging him to speak.

'You, miss?'

'Augustina Pinchbeck, my boy! Only she can summon ghostly apparitions, as real as the flesh! In your very own parlour, she will reach beyond the veil and bring you the answers your heart most desires.' Her voice echoed through the woods, loud and strong, as though she was addressing an audience of hundreds.

Charlatans and tricksters would say anything to part a fool from his money – Leander knew that. But he had heard rumours of rich folks entertaining each other by summoning ghosts – folks far more clever and educated than him.

'Want to be sure dear Grandmama is at peace? Do you seek your fortune?'

Charlotte pushed her way between them, carrying an armful of clothes. Pinchbeck stepped back to let her through without interrupting her patter.

'My spirit guides will advise you on any subject. Are you trying to win the hand of a fair lady?' She leaned in with a conspiratorial wink and a giggle, and added in a whisper, 'It's always about money or love, my dear. Everyone wants to get the better of fate.'

This was a new side to Pinchbeck. There was something magnetic about the way she spoke and moved that made Leander believe she really was magical. Her dark eyes twinkled with mischief. If she was telling the truth, did that mean Charlotte and Felix's talk of magic could be true as well?

Maybe they were all liars. Most people were. He'd stay wary. But, all the same, the talk of spirits made him feel excited. He had never dreamed of witnessing a spirit-summoning.

'Let's work some miracles, shall we?' Pinchbeck ruffled his hair.

This jolly mood made the evening warmer. Charlotte and Felix rushed to and fro, sorting and packing and arranging. Pinchbeck stood statue-still in the centre of the chaos, barking instructions. Leander scrambled to make himself useful. He was handed a crystal ball and a soft cloth to polish it with.

He had only ever seen such things in drawings of fortune-telling gypsies; it was much heavier than he'd expected.

'It doesn't *do* anything. It's a decoration,' said Charlotte, but when she wasn't looking Leander held it close and gazed into the cloudy glass, hoping to catch a glimpse of something other-worldly. There was nothing, just as Charlotte had said, but still Leander was amazed at how little she and Felix were interested in these wonders.

'Shoo!' Charlotte stamped her foot. Leander looked up in time to see a fat black rat scurry away between the wheels of the carriage. He suppressed a shudder.

'Charlotte,' called Pinchbeck. 'Time for the ladies to dress.'

They retired to the carriage. Leander wrapped the crystal ball in its velvet cloth and nestled it gently into a chest. Felix added a half-dozen white tapers.

'Why do we need candles?' Leander asked. 'Won't they have their own?'

'These are trick candles. We break them open and snip the wick an inch from the top. Then we melt the wax a little and stick them back together.'

Leander looked more closely and saw there was a little bulge in the wax, evidence of the repair. 'But why?'

'When the flame reaches the cut part, they go out. With good timing – *pop!* – the room goes dark. Magic.'

What a marvellous trick! Leander thought. Imagine sitting in the gloom, summoning spirits, and witnessing the lights snuffed out by an invisible hand. He shivered.

'I invented that trick,' said Felix, smiling. 'Back in the old

53

days, Pinchbeck and I came up with all sorts of ideas to fool people. We were among the first to hold seances and we had to make things up as we went along.'

To think that Leander had hoped to be apprenticed to a bootmaker, and now he was apprenticed to a magician. He decided that he, too, would invent some new tricks for them to perform. As soon as he had the chance to learn how everything worked, he was sure he could dream up some exciting ideas. That would prove his worth to the others.

Except ... there was that seed of worry again, thoughts of Charlotte and Felix's warning trying to take root in his mind. He shook himself and tried not to think about cages and monsters.

'What other tricks are there?' he asked.

'You'll soon learn.' Felix handed him a thin grey jacket with yellowish smudges around the collar and buttons. 'Put this on. It'll make you look the part.'

'It's dirty,' said Leander. He had only just got his new suit, and wasn't keen to put rags on again.

'It's not dirt,' said Felix. 'Hold it by the firelight. Not too close. See?'

The smudges on the jacket began to glow as they caught the light – an eerie whitish yellow colour Leander had never seen before.

'Phosphorescent powder.' Felix beamed. 'Good, isn't it? Imagine how it looks when you appear out of the darkness and glow in the candlelight.'

Energy crackled through the camp. It seemed even Charlotte

was caught up in it and forgot to be cross when dinner burned and stuck to the bottom of the pan. They ate it anyway – it tasted like charcoal and anticipation. A home-cooked supper, Leander thought, was better than a stolen pie any day.

The sun was almost down when Pinchbeck declared they were ready to depart. Pink-streaked clouds hung low overhead and the last beams of the sunset stretched the dead trees into long, sinister shadows. Pinchbeck was adorned with jewels, the rubies at her neck matching the red of her gown. She pulled out a little black notebook, and checked it against a map. From the undergrowth the black rat emerged, walking right up to the hem of her dress, as bold as anything. Pinchbeck didn't seem bothered. She swished her skirts and the creature departed. Leander moved a little further from the bushes in case it should come back.

'Will she really conjure ghosts?' he whispered to the others as they waited in the cold.

They had shown him some tricks, but surely they weren't enough to make people believe they had seen real spirits? There had to be some truth behind it all … and maybe then he would see his mother again, as Pinchbeck had promised him. It seemed impossible, but if she could make the children disappear, as the others claimed, perhaps it wasn't so far-fetched.

Best not to get my hopes up, he thought. *People always let you down*. But it was hard to resist imagining his mother's voice, the nursery songs she used to sing …

Charlotte gave him her now-familiar look of scorn. 'I told

55

you. It's trickery and games. There's no such thing as ghosts. We're the apparitions.'

He scowled back and turned away from her.

Pinchbeck clapped her hands together. 'Leander, into your Cabinet.'

He froze. 'Umm ... You see, miss, I'm not sure—'

'What? Did the others not teach you how to vanish into your Cabinet?' She cast a meaningful gaze on Charlotte and Felix. 'Have you been sitting idle, children?'

Charlotte twisted her mouth and stared at Leander in an *I-told-you-so* way.

'Then you must learn this instant. Mustn't keep our audience waiting.'

Everyone looked at Leander. His neck and ears felt hot.

'Just try to imagine yourself as smoke,' said Felix. 'Picture the inside of the locket.'

'Think of emptiness,' instructed Charlotte, arms folded.

'I can't,' Leander protested, feeling foolish.

'Time is short,' said Pinchbeck, returning her black book to a pocket in her dress. 'The horses are hitched and the carriage packed.'

Her tone was much sharper now. She frowned at Leander and he felt ashamed at disappointing her so soon. He should have tried to practise the vanishing trick, as the others had told him. Still not quite believing it possible, despite everything he had seen, he resolved to try his best.

He took a deep breath and closed his eyes. *Picture the inside of the locket* and *think of smoke ... emptiness ...*

Something happened. A lightness in his feet. The ground beneath him was softer – no, it wasn't there at all.

'I don't like it!' He clenched his hands into fists and the earth became solid again. Charlotte tutted.

'Nearly,' Felix said encouragingly.

Pinchbeck looked up at the darkening sky and held her hand out to check for rain. '*Abeo*,' she said in a bored tone.

Lightness, again, but this time Leander wasn't doing it. He resisted, pushing back with his limbs, feeling frantically for something to anchor him to the world.

'Don't fight,' Felix's voice floated from beyond, but Leander couldn't help it.

His skin burned and froze; grinding pressure gnawed at his bones as though they would be crushed to powder. Air was squeezed from his ribcage and his stomach turned over violently like he was vomiting, but nothing came out of him because there was no him. He had no control at all as the world darkened and his flesh became smoke.

Then he was in the locket – or so he assumed. He felt like air and space and nothing more.

The sensation was peculiar. Or rather there was no sensation at all. He had taken for granted the weight of fabric against his skin, the pressure of the ground beneath his feet, the rush of air in and out of his lungs. Now he could hear, but see nothing. It was strange, but not so bad as the vanishing.

So this was the magic he would do for his new mistress? It was terrible. What had he got himself into?

'Come out, Leander,' came Pinchbeck's voice from far away. 'Your Cabinet is open – you can emerge by yourself.'

Would appearing hurt as much as vanishing? But he didn't want to stay inside. He tried to hold his breath, braced for pain, but there was no breath to hold.

'Just imagine yourself free,' Pinchbeck pressed. He could hear irritation creeping into her voice again.

He thought *out* and out he came, hair and bones and skin real again. It didn't hurt this time, only a strange rushing sensation and a shock of cold, like jumping into the river. The earth felt good beneath him. Smell was the last sense to return, the dry soil and decaying leaves and the exotic spices of Pinchbeck's perfume.

'*Thank you*, Leander,' Charlotte said haughtily as she appeared beside him, smoothing out her dress. She climbed into the carriage and let the door slam behind her.

'The "*abeo*" command works on all of us at once,' offered Felix by way of explanation. 'When Madame Pinchbeck pushed you into your Cabinet, she pushed us into ours, too.'

'It hurts,' said Leander.

'Only if you resist,' said Pinchbeck casually. 'Practise a few times.'

Leander swallowed hard. He didn't want to go inside the locket again, but the memory of the pain of being forced to vanish made it hard to refuse. Felix watched, quietly urging him on, and Leander didn't want to look cowardly.

Deep breath. In. Feel for the locket, think of air . . .

His insides tingled, his head became light and the world around him became dark.

Not painful. Not anything.

And out . . .

Leander tried a few more times, finding he could do it more quickly with each attempt. Now he wasn't so afraid, he could reach for the locket with his mind and slip inside without any resistance. The pain was gone, but vanishing was still unnerving and unpleasant, like he was breaking the rules of reality, and the air itself disapproved.

When Pinchbeck gave the order to leave, the three children climbed into the carriage. He placed his locket into the chest alongside Charlotte's lantern and the violin case.

'You did well, Leander,' said Felix.

'And now I can vanish and come back whenever I like?' asked Leander.

'Only as long as your Cabinet is open. Remember what we told you? Once the latch is closed, only Pinchbeck's command will allow it. Always be careful. You might need to hide there, or shelter if we have nowhere to sleep. You don't want to be stuck outside.'

'Or inside,' muttered Charlotte darkly.

7
Seven of Cups:
Fantasy, Imagination, Illusion

LEANDER

L eander sat squeezed between the other two inside the carriage. It wasn't a comfortable fit, and over every bump in the road he was poked by an elbow or a pan handle, or hit in the face by a bundle of herbs. The carriage would have been big enough for four or five passengers if it wasn't for all of Pinchbeck's jars and drawers.

'It's all about getting people to believe in Pinchbeck – that she's able to reach across the void to the realm of the dead,' Felix told Leander, explaining how the seances worked.

Leander shivered. 'That's creepy.'

'It's not real,' sighed Charlotte, lifting a corner of the velvet drapes to look out of the window.

'People pay her to come into their homes and pass them messages from those they've lost. They all sit round a table with just a few candles for light. She goes into a trance—'

Charlotte snorted.

'Well, that's the idea anyway,' continued Felix. 'And then I appear and play my music. She tells them that I'm her guide.'

'Why do people pay money to be scared?' asked Leander.

'Not just scared,' said Felix. 'Amazed. Delighted. Surprised. People *like* to be scared sometimes. A safe kind of scared. Have you never felt that?'

Leander nodded. He supposed that was how he had felt when his mother told him the story of the Rat King as they basked in the warm firelight. But, since she'd gone, there had only been bad-scared. Scared of Mrs Smart, or of being caught stealing, or starving to death. He thought how lucky these people were to live such lives that they needed to invite horror and fear into their houses to amuse themselves.

'So, should I try to frighten them?' Leander asked.

'When Pinchbeck summons you out of your Cabinet, all you need to do is stand on the table. You don't say anything; you don't move. They'll think you're a ghost.'

'But I'm not see-through,' protested Leander, pulling a stray sage leaf from his hair. 'They'll know I'm just a boy.'

'A glowing boy, who appears from thin air in the middle of their dining table,' said Charlotte. 'They'll believe it, trust me.'

The carriage was riding over cobbles now. It rattled their teeth and the bottles and jars.

'Don't let them touch you, though,' said Felix. 'It spoils the effect.'

'What if I do it wrong?' said Leander.

'There's nothing to get wrong,' Felix reassured him. 'Charlotte and Pinchbeck and I will do all the tricks this time. All you have to do is appear and disappear.'

'How does she talk to the real ghosts?' asked Leander.

'She doesn't,' said Charlotte. 'How many times? It's like putting on a play. There's no such thing as ghosts.'

But Leander refused to let his hope die. Maybe these seances for the rich were nothing more than clever tricks and children in costumes, but that didn't mean Pinchbeck couldn't talk to the dead at all. She clearly had magic at her disposal: the vanishing trick alone was proof of that. And she knew things that surely proved some special skills beyond normal understanding – the fact that Leander was an orphan, that the locket was his mother's – so Leander held on to the flicker of hope that Pinchbeck would keep her promise that he could talk to his mother again.

A short distance from their destination Pinchbeck told them all to go inside their Cabinets. It was important that her customers didn't see the children before they appeared as spirits. Nervous and excited, Leander could barely wait. He listened to the oddly distant sounds of the world beyond. A knock on the door. The scrape of furniture being arranged. Voices greeting Pinchbeck and each other as people took their seats.

'... something quite remarkable, I hear ...'

'... never seen anything like it ...'

'... of course, I don't normally believe ...'

At last something was happening. A hush fell. Pinchbeck

began speaking in a low, melodic voice, but Leander couldn't understand the words.

'*Exsisto*.' Like a carp on the fisherman's line, he was pulled from the cool depths at Pinchbeck's command. A queasy sensation, but he didn't dare fight it. He stepped out on to the table, relishing the weight of his own body. The air smelled of vinegar and spent matches.

Leander gasped along with the spectators; the ritual was eerier than he'd imagined. He was standing on a round wooden table, surrounded by three men and four women, including Pinchbeck. A ring of candles threw enough light to see their pale faces cast with harsh shadows.

Pinchbeck was chanting, almost singing, in a dark voice, head thrown back as if in a trance. The cards she had used earlier with Leander were spread out before her, overlapping in a complicated star-shaped pattern, gold leaf twinkling in the candlelight.

He remembered Felix's instructions. All he had to do was stand there, say nothing and keep still until he was told to return to the locket.

A long, ghostly wail rose in the darkness, trembling like the clasped hands of the people at the table. Leander couldn't tell where it was coming from. The elegant room beyond the candle beams was so dark he could almost believe they had fallen off the edge of the world into nothingness. The wailing climbed and dipped and Leander realized it was a violin. Felix was playing in some hidden corner, his melody dark and unsettling.

Faster and faster the violin laughed and cried its unearthly song. The man in front of Leander was stony-faced, but his eyes were wide and shiny, and Leander detected a twitch of nervousness at the corners of his mouth. A woman in a red dress whimpered and closed her eyes, hiding against the man's shoulder. The man's eyes moved, but his body remained rigid as though he was afraid the slightest movement might break the spell.

A deep, hollow knocking sound came from the table beneath Leander's feet. It was answered with a series of lighter taps, like fingernails on glass, from the other side of the room. *Knock*, *tap*, *tap*, back and forth like a conversation. Leander turned round in a circle; the sitters were all holding hands on the tabletop, Pinchbeck included. *Who is knocking, then?* Leander wondered. It couldn't be Felix since his music was still playing. Which left Charlotte. But the noises came from opposite ends of the room – how could she be in two places at once?

There are no ghosts here. Charlotte said it's all pretend, Leander reassured himself, but the sitters obviously believed it. The knocking became a scraping.

'The veil is thin tonight,' said Pinchbeck softly. 'The spirits are strong.'

There are no ghosts. There are no ghosts. Leander wasn't scared. He wouldn't let himself feel scared. His mouth was dry. The room was so dark.

'If there is someone here who would like to make contact, please give us a sign,' Pinchbeck called.

A candle went out. Then another, at the other side of the table. A collective gasp rose, the trick candles doing their job of convincing the party. Four more candles went out, one by one, until only three remained. The growing gloom made the room feel smaller.

There was a softening in the violin music and then a moment of stillness. Goosebumps formed on Leander's arms and he clasped his hands together to stop them from trembling. An image came into his mind, unbidden, of a real spirit, ancient and awful, lingering in the thick darkness, waiting its turn to reveal itself.

There are no ghosts, he told himself again.

Something brushed his ankle. He yanked his foot back with a yell and nearly lost his balance.

The woman beside Pinchbeck had touched him. She was smiling, open-mouthed, and the knuckles of her other hand were white from clutching her neighbour so tightly.

'He's real!'

There was a ripple of excitement and Leander felt like a fox surrounded by dogs as they leered at him. What should he do? Would he be in trouble if he returned to his locket before Madame Pinchbeck gave the command? Or would she be even more angry if her tricks were discovered?

Charlotte appeared behind the sitters, at the edge of the circle of light, unnoticed by the men in front of her. She lifted both hands, then brought them down on to their shoulders, hard. Both started, one standing up from his chair so rapidly that Charlotte had to hop back. The woman in red fainted.

'*Abeo!*' came the shouted command. The pressure on Leander's bones and the stinging pain began to rise. *Don't fight.* He relaxed, let his body go limp and the pain ebbed away. With no small sense of relief, Leander's flesh became mist and he returned to his locket. The violin came to a harsh, screeching halt. Outside he could hear great confusion. Heavy, hurried footsteps, the scraping of furniture and agitated voices. Muffled speech was punctuated with little bursts of nervous laughter. What queer things the upper classes did for entertainment.

Later that night, when Leander felt himself pulled from his Cabinet at Pinchbeck's command, he didn't fight it. He let himself pour out of the locket and breathe the November air into his still-forming body.

'Home sweet home,' Pinchbeck said. She took Leander's hands and spun round in a circle as though they were dancing. 'Wasn't it marvellous? They adored me.'

'Home', it seemed, was a large brick farmhouse, with a sturdy oak door and many darkened windows staring down at them like empty, glassy eyes. The carriage stood on the paving stones, hidden from the road by overgrown hedges.

'Whose house is this?' said Charlotte.

Pinchbeck wasn't listening or didn't care. She released Leander and strode over to the front door, lantern in hand, and ushered them inside.

It was as though the house had been lost in time. Curtains still hung at the windows, though here and there they were rotted to rags by years of neglect. The kitchen had plates and bowls on the table, pokers by the stove, a single teacup left in the sink. Sturdy work boots waited by the back door. The parlour was the same – candlesticks sat on the mantelpiece, a blanket hung over the back of a chair and a thick layer of dust covered everything. It was as though the owners had gone for a walk twenty years ago and never returned.

'What is this place?' Charlotte asked again.

Leander picked up a ceramic milkmaid ornament from the sideboard and the arm came off in his hand. He hastily put it down.

'A secluded little spot for us to rehearse,' said Pinchbeck. 'It'll be a very pleasant stay once you get the place cleaned up.'

The house smelled of mould, and the cold had settled deep into the stone, but it wasn't so bad. If they could get a fire going in the hearth, it might even be cosy. Leander had slept in worse places.

'Who lives here?' he asked.

'We do.' Pinchbeck ruffled his hair.

'And if the owners come back?' said Charlotte.

'Nobody comes here since the family left. People think the house is cursed.' Pinchbeck winked at Leander.

'Cursed? Why?'

'Some children went missing.' The ghost of a wicked smile crossed Pinchbeck's face. 'Hop to it, then! Boys, you can find some wood and build me a fire in the parlour. Charlotte, you can make up my bed in there, and air out a bedroom in the morning.'

Charlotte sighed heavily and folded her arms. 'Fine.'

'Pardon?'

'Yes, Madame.' She forced a smile and a sarcastic curtsey, but Pinchbeck was already busy unpinning her hat.

The boys changed out of their seance clothes first, quickly using the carriage before letting Charlotte do the same. There was no time for Leander to feel worried about his shabby underclothes now: it was clear that Pinchbeck would stand for no shirking or delay in getting things ready. Leander was happy to swap his glowing jacket for the frock coat Pinchbeck had given him. It was deliciously warm compared to his old one, and it had all the buttons, too. He smiled to himself as he smoothed out the fabric.

'Hurry up, Leander!' Felix already had an armful of wood. 'There's still a few logs in the woodshed. Watch out for the damp ones.'

'It's just like Pinchbeck to know a place like this,' muttered Charlotte as she climbed out of the carriage now wearing her plain dress and pinafore. There was a blanket flung over her shoulder and she carried a pillow under each arm. 'Somewhere she can play house with somebody else's belongings.'

Leander wanted to ask what she meant, but she had already disappeared inside. He scuttled off round the back of the house and loaded up his arms with chunks of firewood. There wasn't much left, but it should get them through the night.

The parlour contained a small settee – a little cobwebby

but still strong – which Charlotte turned into a bed for Pinchbeck. The boys cleaned out the hearth and lit the kindling, then fed the flames with larger pieces of wood until they had a roaring fire. Pinchbeck promptly chased them out of the warmth and closed the door behind them.

They gathered the few remaining rugs from the carriage and set them out in front of the kitchen stove. They scraped together enough wood and sticks to light a fire of their own, albeit much smaller. The three of them sat as close to the stove as possible in the draughty room so that their fronts roasted and their backs stayed frozen.

'I hope there's no rats,' said Leander, peering nervously into the dark corners of the room. He couldn't shake the image of the rat he had seen by the roadside. Strange for it to be so unafraid of humans. Nothing to stop a creature like that running over their legs as they tried to sleep. 'Not that I'm scared of rats. I'm not.'

'I'm sure there'll be no rats here,' said Charlotte. 'When the people left, so did the food. The rats will be long gone.'

CHARLOTTE

Felix sat at the table, lovingly polishing his violin, wiping away the rosin dust and bringing the old wood to a gentle shine, then crept away outside. Leander began to softly snore. Charlotte lay awake, listening to the scrabbling of rats in the walls. She had lied to Leander. There were always rats everywhere they went. She had been as squeamish as Leander once, having grown up in luxurious surroundings where vermin were thankfully rare. But, since she'd met Pinchbeck, she saw and heard them every day. If not for Leander mentioning them, she probably wouldn't have noticed their scratching.

No point scaring the boy. He'd be used to the rats soon enough.

Charlotte couldn't stop thinking about what would happen next. It wasn't possible for Pinchbeck to keep all of them. Three magical Cabinets took too much strength. She was buoyant tonight after her great performance, but soon she'd grow weak and weary with the effort, and dispose of Leander.

Well, dispose of someone.

No, it would be Leander. Charlotte was certain. She and Felix were too valuable. Pinchbeck wouldn't have kept them around for so long if she didn't need them. She had often threatened Charlotte and Felix that she'd force them into their Cabinets and then smash them if they stepped too far out of line. And Charlotte knew Pinchbeck was more than capable of that. She still thought about little Rosa, and how Pinchbeck had made her disappear for ever. As much as Charlotte wanted rid of that annoying street urchin, she wouldn't let Leander be harmed. Charlotte couldn't see that happen to another child.

He was so frustrating, though. Even after all her warnings, it was clear he still believed that Pinchbeck would follow through on her hollow promises, and was so happy when the woman showed him the tiniest bit of affection. The poor boy must have had an awful life to be so desperate for kindness. It seemed that he'd been alone for a while and of course Charlotte felt sorry for him. But she was also annoyed at his presence because it threatened the life that she and Felix had. As awful as it was to be trapped, the alternative was unthinkable.

Outside, Felix began to play. Each night since she'd met him, Felix played songs of his own creation, sweet and mournful, beautiful and mysterious. Felix didn't talk about his feelings, but Charlotte knew what he was thinking by the colours that flowed from his strings. Tonight the melody was first fretful, then sad, and Charlotte felt he was playing just for her.

FELIX

Felix woke before dawn and was away before the others were even stirring. He and Pinchbeck had an agreement: when they arrived at a new place, Felix was allowed to search for his lost brother. He slung his violin case over his shoulder and walked through the crisp air.

Of course, he couldn't go too far from her without becoming weak. Still, he knew he could wander into the centre of the village without any problem.

The village was filled with the music of a market day – the click of clogs on cobbles, carts dragged on creaking wheels, the sing-song cries of the costermongers.

'Excuse me, sir,' he began, but the first seller grunted

and waved him off. He tried again. 'Excuse me, ma'am, I'm looking for someone.'

The woman was friendly, but had never heard of Felix's brother. There was little chance of anyone knowing the little boy here, far from where he had gone missing, but Felix never wasted an opportunity. He dreamed his brother had somewhere grown to be a young man.

'His name is Isaak Reisbeck – or he may go by Peasmarsh, our mother's name.'

'No one by those names around here.' The jam maker couldn't help. One after another, the stallholders shook their heads.

'He'd be about fourteen, dark hair.'

'Sorry, lad.'

'He may have passed this way as a child – you might remember him; the tip of his third finger is missing.'

A stone road marker provided a convenient platform to stand on and get a good view of the folks milling about. Felix drew out his holey stone – a smooth pebble with a hole worn right through the centre by the tide – and peered through it, hoping for some shimmer of a clue. Pinchbeck had given it to him when they first met, to help him with his search. After his violin, it was his most treasured possession. No luck.

In the churchyard, he checked each grave for any sign of his brother, but there was nothing. Even finding Isaak's name on a burial plot would be something. The vicar was nowhere to be found. Felix looked through the holey stone again, but everything appeared normal; it always did. Pinchbeck said it would reveal hidden things, lost things, magical things, and that he would know it when he saw it. He carried it with him always, but had never seen anything through it.

Of course, he hadn't expected to find anything today. They had been through this village before, four or five times, and with every passing year the chances grew slimmer that someone would remember Isaak. Besides, Felix and Isaak came from Kent – that was where Isaak went missing – and now they were in the Midlands, about two hundred miles to the north. It felt to Felix as if there were now few corners of the country that he had not searched.

He sat on the wall and took out his violin. He always played in the hope Isaak would hear the music and be guided back to him. Felix had played his violin in a hundred villages or more since his little brother disappeared. The music summoned memories from his mind like spirits from Cabinets.

Their mother had died when Isaak was an infant, and their father was no provider – he cared only for the drink until he perished from it. So it was their grandfather who saw that they were fed, and taught Felix how to play the violin. Before Grandfather passed away, he made Felix promise to keep Isaak safe, no matter what. Felix would play music in the marketplace for enough pennies to buy food for them both, even though he was only ten years old. Isaak was five, or was it six?

That's what they were doing when they first met Pinchbeck. She had a husband, then, and the two of them travelled from town to town, selling potions, lifting curses, finding things that were lost. Pinchbeck had watched Felix play and given him a whole sixpence for the song.

'That's a beautiful violin,' she'd said. Felix remembered she was dressed in fashionable clothes, not like her husband who wore odd garments decorated with feathers and twigs and crosses.

'Thank you, miss.'

'I wonder if you could be persuaded to part with it.'

'I couldn't, miss. It's how I make my living.'

'I would pay you very handsomely. Think of all the wonderful things you could buy. Cakes and pastries, new boots . . . Name your price.'

They were standing outside a cheesemonger's shop with empty, hollow tummies. Isaak crept closer, eager for a treat. The lady saw that he was listening and added, 'Toy soldiers, for your little brother?'

Felix shook his head. He could never part with his grandfather's violin for all the cake and boots and toy soldiers in the world. Apart from Isaak, music was all that mattered to him.

'Sell it!' Isaak begged as the lady walked away. 'The money!'

'We can't! When the money's all spent, then what? I need the violin to make more.'

Isaak pouted and kicked the wall. 'You should've sold it.'

But of course, Felix now knew, if he had sold the violin that day, he would have been under Pinchbeck's spell immediately. Although perhaps Pinchbeck might have allowed Isaak to travel with them, and the boys would at least have been together.

Felix shook the thoughts away. There was no use dwelling on what-ifs. He couldn't go back and change things now, no matter how much he wanted to. He had to make the best of reality. He set the violin back carefully in its case, loosened the strings of the bow and settled it securely in its spot, then headed back towards the house.

8
Page of Wands:
Discovery, New Information,
Unexpected News

LEANDER

O ver their morning tea, Pinchbeck laid out instructions to Leander for the next performance. 'Leander, it'll fall to you to make sure I am compensated fairly for my skills, if you see what I mean.'

He didn't but he didn't want to look stupid. Charlotte watched, scowling, as if waiting for him to show his ignorance.

'Payment for services provided,' Pinchbeck prompted.

What was he supposed to say? 'Sending the bills, Madame?'

'Robbery,' snapped Charlotte. 'You'll be stealing their valuables while we keep them busy. I imagine you'll be good at that.' She was in a foul mood again. He was already sick of her and her changeable temper.

'At least I'm good at something,' he jabbed back. 'What do you do except look pretty and be rude?'

A wry smile crossed Pinchbeck's lips. 'Children, children.

We're all family here. Get to your work, Charlotte, or shall I fetch the horsewhip?' Pinchbeck stood.

'I'm not scared of your whip,' said Charlotte, glowering at her.

'I know what you *are* scared of.'

That did the trick. Charlotte left the table and Pinchbeck sat back down.

'She'll come around,' she said to Leander. 'You'll be jolly friends in no time.'

He shrugged. 'Don't care. Don't want to make friends anyway.'

Pinchbeck tilted her head and said gently, 'No man is an island, Leander. You've been alone for a long time, but you'll be happy here, with us.'

Jolly friends! Leander was doubtful Charlotte knew how to be jolly. No one liked thieves, of course not, and if the world hadn't been so unkind he never would have taken anything that wasn't his. But he'd had to steal to survive, and he'd do it again if need be. Charlotte could look down at him all she wanted. He wouldn't make a show of shame for her benefit. In fact, he'd do such a good job of stealing for Madame Pinchbeck that they would have no choice but to thank him for it. He was sure even Charlotte couldn't be nasty to him if he put food on the table.

With the others out of earshot, Leander took his chance. 'Madame Pinchbeck, I wanted to ask you, please ... about my mother.'

From a small satchel Pinchbeck produced a bundle of papers. 'Fold these for me, my lamb. I need to have them delivered.'

Leander took the stack and started work. 'You said you could help me. I wondered ... may I talk to her?' he pressed.

Even asking the question made him shiver. Charlotte said Pinchbeck couldn't talk to the dead, and last night he'd seen for himself the tricks used to fool her patrons, but if there was even a tiny chance—

'Ah, little Leander. Of course I will help you. Soon. Very soon. But these things can't be rushed.' She reached for an ink bottle and began scratching out a letter, copying the address from her black notebook that she quickly tucked back into her pocket.

'You can do it, then? Really talk to the dead?'

A laugh. 'Of course.'

'Charlotte said it's impossible.'

'Charlotte doesn't have the imagination for magic, Leander. Not like you.'

'But ... if you can talk to ghosts, why do you need us to pretend?' He almost whispered the words, half afraid that he would anger her. But he had to know.

She paused, the nib of her pen hovering over the ink. 'How can I explain? It's showmanship, my sweet. Putting on a spectacle for our customers. Of course, I could simply pass on messages from the dead, but where's the performance in that? They wouldn't be half as entertained.'

'Oh,' said Leander. That made sense. If people were paying money to see a seance, of course they wanted something exciting and showy. 'I see.'

'And besides –' she lowered her voice and leaned closer,

until her breath tickled his ear – 'it's tiring work. I save my real power for people who truly need it. People who truly deserve it.' She tapped him on the nose and then sat back in her chair and returned to her writing. 'But now tell me about your old home. Litchfield House. How many people live there?'

'Only the master. He hasn't got any family since the girl disappeared.'

Pinchbeck took out her small black book and flipped carefully through the pages. It was packed densely with writing and drawings. She found a page with a little empty space and scribbled something Leander couldn't make out. 'Servants?'

'A cook, couple of maids and a groom, I think. And a horrible, wicked housekeeper. Why do you ask, miss?' He leaned over to get a better look at the book, but she moved it away and covered it with her arm.

'Never you mind,' she said. 'You want to earn the chance to speak to your mother, don't you? Here's your chance to begin. Impress me by answering my questions.'

Leander straightened up and nodded. Besides, it was nice to have someone interested in what he had to say. No one had ever asked about his life before.

'Only five servants? Are you sure? So few, in such a grand house?'

'It used to be grand, but now it's in a right state. The garden's all overgrown. There's this huge fountain with statues of all these ladies with scrolls, fancy-like, but it doesn't work any more.'

Charlotte stopped what she was doing and began watching him from across the room, brow furrowed. When Pinchbeck glanced in her direction, she hurried away.

Pinchbeck continued to question Leander for a long time, asking strange things like how many staircases were in the big house, and how many chairs were in the parlour. Once she was satisfied with his answers, she tucked the little book away and began to shuffle through a stack of newspaper cuttings. Now and then she read out headlines such as 'Spirit Phenomena' and 'Psychic Demonstration'.

'Always good to know what our competition is up to. My seances must always be the best in the business.'

Leander picked up a piece of paper. It showed a photograph of a lady posing next to a ghost – Leander supposed it was meant to be a ghost anyway. It looked more like a person wrapped in a tablecloth, creased white fabric covering the face and shoulders.

'Yes, that's an interesting one, isn't it? Spotted that in the *Illustrated London News* back in September,' Pinchbeck muttered. 'Fred Hudson, the old fraud.'

'Who's Fred Hudson?' asked Leander.

'A medium. Calling himself a "spirit photographer" these days. Somewhat famous. Not a patch on me, of course. It should be *my* name in all the papers. And it will be. Soon.' She stood up. 'Speaking of which, time to get our newest member properly trained. The performance tonight must be perfect!'

The newspaper cuttings fluttered down to the table.

Charlotte swooped in to tidy them away, peering at Hudson's 'ghost photograph' as Pinchbeck showed Leander some of the wondrous contraptions and devices she had dreamed up.

A wooden block on wheels made the sound of ghostly footsteps when pushed down the stairs. Pigeon feathers rained from the sky when blown out of miniature bellows. An oily substance painted on Leander's palms left damp, shimmery handprints that faded to nothing.

Then she called Felix in from tending the horses and made him play his violin, while Charlotte and Leander rehearsed appearing at the perfect moment in time with the music. Pinchbeck shouted questions and the children would respond with a series of knocks and taps on the walls and furniture. They practised creeping silently about the room, beneath the table, up the stairs, so that they could move unnoticed while the audience was distracted. Leander learned the hand and whistle signals that Charlotte and Felix used to indicate what the other should do. And, when he revealed that he had taken a handkerchief from Charlotte's apron pocket without her knowledge, Pinchbeck laughed with delight.

'Wonderful! I knew you'd be a natural.'

After hours of rehearsal, Pinchbeck grew weary and sent the children out to buy food, entrusting Felix with several coins.

'We shall have a feast!' she declared. 'To celebrate new beginnings and excitements to come!'

Once they were clear of the house, Felix said, 'Pinchbeck

must have a very wealthy client in mind. It's been a long time since she's had us working so hard.'

'Never mind that,' said Charlotte, stopping so suddenly Leander walked into her. 'Leander, I overheard you talking to her about your home. Why was she so interested?' She gripped his forearm.

'I don't know.' Leander shrugged.

'Where did you come from?' Her fingers were digging into his flesh. He shook her off.

'Near where I met you. The big estate, Litchfield House.'

A strangled noise came from Charlotte's throat. She was trying to suppress a sob.

'Oh,' said Felix. 'I see.'

Leander didn't.

'When you said about the fountain and the library ...' Charlotte's voice trailed off.

'Were you a servant?' Felix asked Leander.

'No, there's hardly any servants. I lived there in secret, in the library. It was cold. My mother was the cook at the house before ... before she died. I didn't have anywhere else to go.'

Charlotte shuddered. 'What happened to all the servants?'

'I don't know. Lord Litchfield had sent most of them away and shut the house up before we arrived. They said there were lots of servants, but when the lord's daughter went missing the old man went mad. Locked himself away.'

'Is he ... is he still alive?' said Charlotte, as pale as cambric.

'Yes, but I only saw him once, in all the time I was there.

He never came out of his rooms. He went peculiar from pining for his daughter.'

'Not his daughter.' Charlotte's arm dropped to her side. 'His niece. His niece went missing.'

'How do you know that?'

'It's me. I'm Charlotte Litchfield.'

It couldn't be. The girl from the big house went missing five years ago at least and Leander's mother had said the girl was thirteen when she disappeared, so she'd be an adult by now. But Charlotte said she would never grow older, and she was captured five years ago . . .

'How did Pinchbeck get you?' he asked, but Charlotte was no longer listening. The mask of anger fell away and tears filled her eyes. Ashen, she sank on to a low wall.

Cheery whistling made Leander look behind him. A bearded man pushing a handcart sauntered merrily past in the direction of the farmhouse, strangely out of place after this terrible revelation. Leander blinked hard. He had forgotten for a moment that the world around them carried on as normal, even as his own world had changed for ever.

'Morning!' the man called to the children. Then, noticing Charlotte's pained expression, he added, 'Cheer up, love! It might never happen!'

Leander watched the man head off into the distance, then turned back to Charlotte whose shoulders were beginning to shake with barely contained sobs.

Felix nudged Leander away. 'Come, let's buy something to eat.'

'Charlotte?' said Leander, but she didn't respond.

'Leave her be. She needs solitude.'

Leander tried to ask Felix more as they walked on, but the other boy shook his head and couldn't be pushed. It was Charlotte's story to tell, he said.

A feast, Pinchbeck had demanded, and a feast they bought. A round of cheese and a big, heavy meat pie, straight from the oven, stinking of sage and grease. Two loaves of the whitest bread money could buy. A half-dozen eggs to be cooked over the fire and, best of all to Leander's eyes, a pennyworth of dark, sticky parkin. Lastly they purchased a paper cone of roasted chestnuts and ate them as they walked, burning their fingers in their haste to get to the warm, sweet nuts. They laughed together and for a little while they were simply two boys who belonged, instead of two stolen children. Leander could almost imagine being friends with Felix. It was a long time since he'd had a friend.

When they reached the edge of the woods, Felix dropped a chestnut and a corner of bread on to a flat stone.

'For the fey,' he said.

'There's no such thing as fairies,' said Leander, then, doubting himself, added, 'is there?' His world had been turned inside out. Anything could be real now.

'I've never witnessed a jot of magic other than Pinchbeck's wicked tricks. But there's no hurt in being sure. The squirrels will eat it if not.'

What a world Leander had stepped into. He raked over

the morning's events and then said, 'Do you think Madame Pinchbeck *is* wicked?'

He knew there couldn't be many worse sins than stealing children, but Leander was fed and warm and not lonely for the first time in for ever. Felix seemed content, too. Maybe that meant Pinchbeck wasn't that bad after all? But what about Charlotte, who once had a life of comfort and an uncle who loved her? Surely taking her from a loving home showed Pinchbeck's cruelty.

Felix picked out another chestnut and peeled away the brittle, charred shell. 'I'm not sure people are all good or all bad, but a little of each.'

'Even you?' Leander had done many wrong things, but it was hard to imagine sensible, serious Felix ever being bad.

Felix broke the last chestnut in half to share. 'Last night we fooled those people,' he said. 'Made them think we were the children they lost in infancy – wasn't that wicked? Yet I enjoyed it, and the food it bought.'

Leander considered that. Those people around the table had lost their children? Which meant it wasn't just about entertainment, as Pinchbeck had said to him. They were turning to her for proof that their loved ones still existed somewhere. They wanted the same thing Leander wanted. And Pinchbeck had tricked them. It *was* wicked. Leander slowly chewed his chestnut to make the flavour last as long as possible. 'Why do you stay with her, then? Why not run away?'

'Do you still not understand? We don't have a choice.

We're butterflies in a jar. We told you, Charlotte tried to run away in the beginning. She tested how far she could get before she became insubstantial. Then she realized that we couldn't vanish into our Cabinets if there were walls in the way.' He moved his hands to demonstrate. 'So Charlotte locked her lantern inside an outhouse to stop Pinchbeck ordering her inside. But it didn't work – turns out *we* might not be able to vanish through walls, but Pinchbeck's command *is* strong enough, even through them. Pinchbeck left her locked inside the outhouse for two days as punishment. If it was possible to run away or bypass her magic, Charlotte would have done it. Besides –' he paused – 'I agreed to go with Pinchbeck. I promised and I can't go back on my word.'

'Why did you agree to go?'

'She promised to help me find something I'd lost.' They were almost back at the farmhouse and when Leander opened his mouth to ask more Felix shook his head. 'I don't wish to talk about it.'

Leander kicked at a stone and thought of the bargain he had made with Pinchbeck. Had he made a terrible mistake?

FELIX

Pretending that he wanted to see to the horses, Felix left Leander to take their purchases indoors and wandered to the back of the farmhouse. Thinking about what had happened, the reason he was with Pinchbeck, was something he tried to avoid. But now his mind was whirring with memories of that day.

Isaak had disappeared while Felix was asleep. After that first meeting with Pinchbeck, they had argued all day. Isaak was convinced they should sell the violin. He wanted to buy food and toys and comforts, and couldn't understand how quickly the money would run out, and how hard it would be to make more. They'd only earned enough for cabbage and potatoes that week, and the violin would fetch a lot of money even if it was old.

'What can we sell, then?' he had asked as they huddled down beneath blankets that night, his untidy brown hair falling across his face.

'Nothing,' said Felix. 'Everything we have, we need.' It was true. Their clothes were little more than rags as it was – they had nothing to spare.

'I'm hungry.'

'Do you think I'm not?' Felix snapped.

'My tummy hurts.'

'Close your eyes. You won't feel it when you're asleep.'

'But I can't sleep without something to eat,' Isaak whined. 'You should've sold your violin.'

'Stop!' Felix shouted. 'You don't know what you're talking about. You make everything so much harder!'

'Why don't you just go off on your own, then?' said Isaak. 'I don't need you anyway.'

'Maybe I will!'

Isaak scowled and turned his back to Felix.

'I'm sorry, Isaak,' said Felix after a few minutes of stony silence between the brothers. 'I didn't mean it.'

Isaak didn't reply. His eyes were closed tight.

'I'll get you something to eat in the morning,' said Felix.

'Don't bother,' said Isaak, still not opening his eyes.

'I'll look after you, I promise. Do you hear me? I promise.'

But, when Felix awoke at dawn, Isaak wasn't beside him. Felix wasn't worried at first, thinking his brother had gone down to the stream to watch the frogs, or climb trees in the meadow, but when he wasn't back by midday Felix was concerned. He checked all of Isaak's usual haunts and wandered the woods, calling his name, but found no sign. When dusk fell and Isaak still wasn't home, a panicky, queasy feeling settled in Felix's stomach. What if Isaak was hurt or in danger? Felix had promised to take care of his brother, and he had let him down.

For two days, Felix searched for his brother in every corner of the village and all the surrounding land. It was as though he had disappeared completely, whisked off by wood-folk into fairyland like in the songs his ma used to sing to them.

That's why he went back to Pinchbeck and her husband, Pellar, to their funny little cart with signs advertising their magical services.

She listened seriously as he told her about his fear for his brother and then drew a deck of cards from a shelf. She shuffled them, laying them out in the shape of a cross, before examining them closely, nodding and whispering as though they were speaking to her. He watched silently as her fingers danced over angels and demons, kings and warriors, seeking truth from somewhere far beyond the tiny room. After several minutes, she shook herself, and blinked hard, as though she had forgotten Felix was there.

'I have a strong feeling,' she said, eyes shining in the lamplight, 'that your brother has left this village.'

'Left? Where is he?' The argument. Isaak had run away because of Felix, left the village and got lost or hurt . . . Felix was sure he wouldn't stay away this long through choice.

'Far away . . . I'm not sure.'

'Is he –' Felix swallowed hard, his mouth suddenly dry – 'is he alive?'

Pinchbeck nodded, and placed her hand over Felix's in a reassuring gesture.

'I foresee a long journey to find him. But I think I can help.'

She told Felix that she and her husband travelled the length of the country, sharing her magical gift – for a price. If Felix promised to help with her work and serve faithfully, he could travel with them, and at every stop along the way look for his brother. It was an easy choice to make. Felix had promised to look after Isaak. He had to find him. She gave him the holey stone, to help in his search, and he handed over his violin as proof of his loyalty to her – on the condition she would never sell it and he might be allowed to play it every day. With Isaak gone, it was easy to leave the village behind – Felix had nothing to stay for – and so his new life with Madame Pinchbeck had begun.

And, all this time, she had kept her promises. He had

been clothed, fed and sheltered. And he was always allowed to search for Isaak as they travelled. Perhaps he wasn't free, but what was freedom worth if you were alone and cold and starving? He had his violin, Charlotte and hope.

'*Why not run away?*' Leander had asked. But it wasn't that simple.

He couldn't break his promise to Pinchbeck. Promises must never be broken.

And, even if he did want to go back on his word, stopping Pinchbeck was impossible. The source and methods of her magic were inscrutable. If there was a way to free their souls from the Cabinets, Felix would have helped Charlotte escape years ago when she first tried to run.

But there wasn't.

Was there?

CHARLOTTE

It took some time for Charlotte to regain her composure after the discovery that Leander had lived at Litchfield House. Fragments of understanding were coming to her and she couldn't show Pinchbeck that she was beginning to guess what she was up to.

Despite the clear skies, it was a cold day with a sharp, biting wind that whipped at her dress and blew loose strands of hair into her eyes. What were the odds of Leander finding them – a boy who had met her uncle and lived in her house? It seemed like more than a coincidence. And Pinchbeck was asking him so many questions – she wasn't a woman who took an interest in other people unless it benefited her.

It might be safest to play at being good, for a while, until she could figure out what Pinchbeck was plotting.

The man with the handcart returned, interrupting her thoughts. 'Shame to see a pretty girl like you without a smile,' he said. Charlotte scowled in reply.

Drying her eyes, she headed back to the house. Pinchbeck was hunched over the table with her black commonplace book, feeding silver wire into a clockwork lamp. The lamp rested on a square wooden box, half draped in cloth, with a brass tube protruding from the top like the eyepiece of a telescope. Something new. On the sideboard was a basket filled with an assortment of large green bottles. Sackcloth and brown paper lay crumpled on the table around it, as though a package had been opened in a great hurry. The man with the handcart must have delivered the box to Pinchbeck. Charlotte wondered what it could be.

As soon as she saw Charlotte, Pinchbeck hastily stashed the notebook in her pocket, and moved the wooden box and lamp to a corner. She set them down with great care, wincing as she stooped over, limbs stiff.

Felix and Leander returned together and Charlotte nudged Felix, nodding towards Pinchbeck, making sure he noticed. Pinchbeck was clearly beginning to feel the strain of another captive.

Despite her apparent discomfort, Pinchbeck was merry. She laughed her tinkliest laugh when she saw what food the boys had brought and arranged it on the table like afternoon tea. Charlotte and the boys rinsed the dust from plates left behind by the previous owner. Pinchbeck found the best cutlery and laid it out – never one to use brass when silver was available. They often stole things from strangers, but this felt worse somehow, more personal. The family who ought to be there was gone, and they had taken their place, like real ghosts haunting the wrong house.

They unwrapped the paper bundles of food and took their seats round the table.

'Isn't this cosy?' Pinchbeck raised her cup. 'To new friends.'

Even though Charlotte's stomach was tight with anxiety, the sight was too enticing to resist. It was days since they'd had a filling meal and much, much longer since anything so appetizing was spread before them. A successful seance was always rewarded. At times like this, they almost looked like a real family.

All eyes were on the pie as Pinchbeck deftly cut thick slices for each of them. It was warm and salty and they all devoured it to the last crumb. Mild, soft cheese crumbled in Charlotte's fingers as she squashed it on to chunks of cloud-soft bread. Back at Litchfield House, even the nursery supper would have been far grander, but hunger was a sweet sauce.

It wasn't until they were cleaning up that Charlotte realized what the wooden box was. It was lying on its side, so at first glance she didn't realize that the brass tube was a lens. It was a camera.

'Beautiful, isn't it?' Pinchbeck purred.

'What's it for?'

'A new hobby. Taking pictures of my family.' She stroked the top of it like a cat. 'Why not?'

A camera was an extravagant purchase and Pinchbeck didn't have hobbies, unless acquiring money and deceiving people counted. This explained why she had been even more penny-pinching than usual lately. Despite Pinchbeck's casual tone, Charlotte knew this wasn't something she had bought on a whim. She must have ordered it weeks ago, and planned ahead to have it delivered to this address. Pinchbeck wouldn't go to such trouble without some sort of scheme in mind.

'Did you ever have your portrait taken?' Pinchbeck asked her.

'Once,' Charlotte said. 'I didn't care for sitting still for so long.'

'It's much quicker now. Done in seconds if the light is bright enough. People can make copies of the picture to sell.' She gazed off into the middle distance, head tilted, lost in thought. 'Even print photographs in the papers.'

The newspaper. Of course! The clipping Pinchbeck had been looking at earlier that day was about a medium who claimed to have photographed a ghost, and now Pinchbeck wanted to do the same. Even from her quick glance, Charlotte could easily tell that Hudson's photograph was a fake, so Pinchbeck had an advantage. Her spirits would be exactly like real children. She'd have to work to make them look ghostly, since her vanishing trick wouldn't be captured in a photograph. But Charlotte knew Pinchbeck would come up

93

with a solution for that problem. She might be evil, but she was also very clever.

In an instant, things became clear to Charlotte: if the photographs were printed in the papers, Pinchbeck would be famous. Every wealthy person in England would want to hire her. She'd be rich. Pinchbeck loved luxury, and she loved being admired. More than that, photographs of spirits could be sold as souvenirs to the sitters, to be traded and displayed as curiosities. How fancy to have a photograph of your own personal ghost.

But she'd require a lot more children. Showing the same ones again and again would never do – people would realize it was a trick. She'd need a steady stream of freshly captured children to keep up with demand, and when she'd finished with each of them ...

Leander was only the first.

9

Ace of Wands: A New Business Venture, Profit

I mmediately after dinner, Pinchbeck packed them up for another seance. Leander was even allowed to ride up at the front of the carriage with Pinchbeck for a little way, which made him feel very important indeed.

'I'll leave your Cabinet open in a dark corner,' said Pinchbeck as they clattered down the narrow street. 'Come out when you hear the music, but try not to show yourself.'

She had instructed him to keep his black coat on this time, instead of changing into the glowing jacket. She didn't need him to be a ghost for the performance that evening – it seemed her only concern was testing the camera. Charlotte would do the knocking and whispering, while Felix would take centre stage with his violin.

'See if you can find anything worth taking, but don't steal

too much. It's a small house and they will notice. We must avoid suspicion.'

'Yes, Madame,' said Leander.

When the first notes came from Felix's violin, Leander thought *out* and felt his body take shape. His head pressed against something hard and he crouched down quickly before he was solid enough for it to hurt. It took a moment to get his bearings. He was under a small table in the corner of a dark parlour.

A group of people sat in a horseshoe shape with their backs to him. Felix stood in front of them with his violin, swaying in time to the music. His eyes were half closed and he seemed so peaceful and happy, even in this spooky setting.

'My spirit guide comes forth from the haunted violin,' said Pinchbeck. 'His ghostly music calls the spirits through the void.' She stood behind the watchers with the camera set up on three tapered wooden legs and pointed towards Felix. She lifted the clockwork lamp and touched a taper to the silver wick.

A lightning-white light filled the room. Leander shaded his eyes with his hands. Felix's fingers slipped on the strings, the flat note like a stain in the air. The light lasted six or seven seconds and then it was gone, and the room seemed much darker than before.

The watchers murmured with approval, impressed by the camera as much as the ghost.

Leander took his chance to move before their eyes adjusted

back to the darkness. Felix had quickly found his rhythm again and now his music became louder and faster. Keeping low to the ground, Leander slipped his hand into the pocket of the nearest man and drew out a watch. No. It'd be too quickly missed. He put it back.

The lady beside him had a small beaded purse hanging from the chair back. He opened it silently and took out two coins – a sixpence and a shilling, he guessed by the feel – and left the other three behind.

Just then a knocking sound came from the opposite corner of the room: Charlotte was tapping on the windowpane. The watchers turned in their seats, looking for the source of the noise. Leander flattened himself to the ground, relying on the shadows to keep him hidden.

Pinchbeck chanted and sang her way through the rest of the seance. It felt to Leander as though she was rushing to finish, now that she'd taken her photograph. He helped himself to two teaspoons from the sideboard drawer, swiftly and silently. It was almost too easy. He felt a little thrill of pleasure at his own skill, followed by the familiar pang of guilt.

There wasn't much else for him to steal in the room and he couldn't reach the door without being spotted, so he stuffed his ill-gotten gains into his pockets and vanished back into his Cabinet. A few moments later, he heard the violin stop with a great tuneless screech. The seance was over.

*

Back at the farmhouse, Pinchbeck went straight into the small larder. She draped the tiny window with the thickest rug and stuffed rags into every crack and cranny.

'We'll show Fred Hudson how it's done, children!' She rushed about, carrying sheets, transforming the little room into a cave of fabric. 'To bed then, and don't disturb me on any account! I must have complete darkness when working on photographs.' She slammed the door.

With the blankets all taken by Pinchbeck, it was bitterly cold. The children did their best to build up a fire, though most of the remaining wood was too damp to burn.

'We should try to get some rest,' said Felix.

'Not yet,' said Charlotte. 'We can use this time, while she's occupied.'

'I'm too tired.' Leander rubbed his eyes.

'I need to explain—'

'I don't want to listen.'

'For goodness' sake, Leander, this is important,' said Charlotte. 'You're in danger. I'm trying to help you.'

'Stop lecturing me! I know. We're prisoners. I understand!' His eyes stung with the threat of tears and he angrily blinked them away. 'I don't care. I like it here. I wasn't rich like you. I didn't have a fancy home with servants. I was alone and I don't want to go back.'

Charlotte pressed her lips together into a thin line and took a deep breath. Leander could tell she was fighting the urge to shout at him again.

'And I'm doing my bit. Look.' Leander took the spoons and

money out of his pockets and dropped them on to the kitchen table. The sixpence landed on its edge and spun round and round before falling flat.

'It's not about doing your bit,' said Charlotte. 'It's about your safety. You've had new clothes and a couple of meals and a bit of fun at the seances, and you think everything is wonderful. You're wrong.'

A look was exchanged between Charlotte and Felix.

'We've told you about the magic Pinchbeck uses to keep us trapped like this,' Felix began. 'Well, we don't know how it works, but we *do* know she can't keep more than two Cabinets at a time.'

'Good,' said Leander. 'Then she'll let one of us go. Hopefully *you*.' He pointed at Charlotte.

'You're a fool—' Charlotte began.

Felix put his hand on her shoulder in a calming gesture. 'Pinchbeck doesn't let people go,' he said. 'I don't think she can.'

'There have been other children. Children she stole, then . . .' Charlotte wiped her eye with her sleeve. Was she crying? 'Come and see.'

She walked to the door and Felix followed with a candle. Leander stayed put, arms folded. He wasn't in the mood to be ordered about by Charlotte.

'Come on!' she said.

He sighed and got up. They unlatched the front door and walked to the carriage, clambering in one by one. Leander sat on the bench with Felix beside him.

'Look,' said Charlotte, stooping beneath the low ceiling.

'Here, and here.' She pointed out glass jars of various sizes. 'And here.'

'What?' said Leander. He picked up the nearest one. It contained shards of pottery. Another had pieces of broken glass.

'They're Cabinets,' said Charlotte.

'They were all children she captured,' said Felix. 'Destroying the Cabinet is the only way to get rid of them.'

Leander furrowed his brow, trying to make sense of what they were saying. 'So ... if we destroy our Cabinets, we'll be free?' But even before he finished his sentence he knew that wasn't what they meant. Their faces were grave in the candlelight.

'No,' said Charlotte. 'If the Cabinets are destroyed, we're ...'

'Dead,' said Felix. The word hung in the air like dust.

'Pinchbeck can't keep three Cabinets for long. It hurts her. It drains her power. She'll have to get rid of one of us soon.'

'Or what?' said Leander.

There had to be another option. They couldn't really be saying that Pinchbeck would just kill one of them. Whatever the others said, the woman had been so kind to him. And, when he and Felix had spoken in town, there had been almost a fondness in Felix's voice. Leander hadn't even got used to the idea that he was a prisoner, not really, and now they were saying she was a ... murderer?

'Or nothing,' said Charlotte. 'She gets older, and weaker, and ...'

'Would she die?' said Leander. He rolled the jar in his

100

hand, watching the fragments of blue-and-white pottery fall against each other.

'No,' said Charlotte. 'I mean, we don't know if she could die that way, but it doesn't matter because she'd never let that happen. Pinchbeck will preserve herself at any cost. She'll destroy a Cabinet and go back to being healthy and young.'

'She wouldn't,' said Leander. His throat felt tight and his shoulders were tense. 'You're trying to frighten me. Why would she take me in just to hurt me?'

'To use you. We're objects to her, like all this stuff,' said Charlotte. 'When we stop being useful, she'll throw us out.'

Maybe Charlotte was trying to upset him. She didn't want him here in the first place. Leander looked at Felix for confirmation.

'It's true,' Felix said with a sigh.

'You think you know who she is, but she's a stranger to you,' said Charlotte. 'She's trying to win you over so you don't question her.'

'But . . .' Leander put the jar back on the shelf. He didn't want to touch it for a moment longer. 'She's going to help me speak to my mother again. She said she kept her real power for people who deserved it. People like me.'

Charlotte scrunched her eyes up and exhaled hard. Leander waited for her next set of mean words, but instead she kneeled down by his feet and took his hand.

'I'm sorry,' she said, 'but that's not going to happen. Pinchbeck can't speak to the dead. She lied to you.'

They went back to the kitchen and huddled round the

dying embers in the stove. Charlotte tried to explain to Leander and Felix about the camera – her suspicions that Pinchbeck was going to snatch more children in order to produce spirit photographs in large numbers – but Leander couldn't take it in. He felt numb. He wanted to speak to his mother more than ever before.

Eventually, the others fell asleep, Felix propped up between two chairs and Charlotte with her head down on the table. But Leander couldn't rest.

Early the next morning, Pinchbeck summoned them to stand shivering in the hallway and admire the photograph of Felix playing his violin. She held it up to the light so they could see. It was smudgy and Felix's arm was blurry because he was moving the bow. Pinchbeck said this was a good thing. If the photograph was too crisp, people would see he was just a boy.

If Leander didn't know better, he would have believed Felix was a ghost. The harsh shadows from the clockwork lamp made Felix's eyes look huge and dark, and the polished wood of the violin caught the light and gleamed. Where Felix was blurry, the people watching with their backs to the camera were completely sharp and still, making it seem like Felix wasn't made of the same substance as the watchers.

The photo itself was imperfect, a blotch covering one corner. 'A little light got in when I was fixing the image,' said Pinchbeck. 'Next time I shall be more careful to have absolute darkness.'

'Yes, miss,' said Leander, although he didn't really understand anything she had said. Pinchbeck didn't seem to care, and continued lecturing the children on how she printed a copy of the photograph with paper soaked in egg white.

'A little work to refine my technique,' she said, 'and people will be fighting to hire me. We'll be rich. We'll sleep in the finest hotels. Have a different outfit for every day of the week!'

Leander wanted to be excited, but Charlotte's words were still echoing in his mind.

Pinchbeck scribbled a letter and folded it with the picture of Felix, then put on her hat to take the letter into the village.

'Madame,' said Leander as he helped her on with her cloak. 'Perhaps today we could speak to my mother?'

'Another time. When I'm not so busy,' she said, brushing him easily off.

The next few days were miserable. Each morning Pinchbeck walked into town to check for messages, and returned in a meaner mood when there were none. She told them she expected an invitation from a very important person, and nothing else would please her. Leander politely asked about his mother once or twice, his heart sinking each time Pinchbeck shooed him away.

The others were right after all. Pinchbeck couldn't speak to the dead. Of all the lies, this one hurt the most. He knew he should never trust her again.

Pinchbeck spent most of her time in the darkroom, experimenting with chemicals and light, trying to create the perfect photograph. She wrote endless notes in her little black book, which she always kept close to her chest. From time to time she shouted for one of them to pose for her, and woe betide them if they weren't quick to answer.

'When I call you, you come right away,' she snarled at Leander, twisting his shirt as she pushed his back against the wall. He noticed thin strands of white were beginning to appear in Pinchbeck's jet-dark hair. She growled at him and he swore that he caught a glimpse of long, sharp teeth behind her thin, sneering lips. He stared. A strange expression flickered over her face for a moment and she let him go, flashing him a pleasant smile with her usual normal-sized teeth.

They weren't safe with her. He understood it now. Not just understood but felt it in his bones.

Once Pinchbeck shut herself back in the darkroom, Leander went looking for Charlotte and Felix. Leander always felt a pang of jealousy whenever he saw them together, as close as brother and sister. He wanted a friendship like that.

He found them inside the carriage. Charlotte was poring over one of Pinchbeck's magical books.

'I believe you,' said Leander.

'What?' said Charlotte, moving her legs so he could climb in. She shuffled along the bench seat to make room for him.

'I understand now, about Pinchbeck. You were right when you tried to warn me. She's evil. We need to escape. I want to help.'

Felix, sitting on the floor in the narrow gap between

the shelves and bench, leaned to one side so Leander could get past.

'Finally,' said Charlotte. 'Working together, all three of us, is our best chance of defeating her.'

'Did you find anything in the books?' Leander asked.

'It's useless,' said Charlotte. 'We've read every book a hundred times. If the answer was here, I'd have found it years ago.'

At her feet, Felix was dealing out Pinchbeck's cards on to the floor. He shook his head, gathered them up and shuffled them back together. 'The cards aren't making any sense tonight.'

'How is it done?' Leander asked.

'It's hard to explain.' Felix handed the cards to Leander and beckoned to him to sit down. Leander squeezed into the gap between the bench and drawers to sit facing Felix. With his back against the carriage door, there was just about room to lay the cards out between them.

'Spread them out like this,' said Felix, pointing to different spots on the floor as Leander dealt each card in turn.

'How do I know which cards to put down?' asked Leander.

'You don't. The cards decide what they want to tell you. Now put one in the middle. That means today.'

The middle card was a king draped in fur robes and holding a huge silver sword.

Charlotte sighed. 'This is just superstition,' she muttered.

'I don't know what it means,' said Leander.

'It's less about knowing,' said Felix. He squinted and rubbed his ear. 'More about feeling. Quiet your mind and listen.'

Leander didn't hear anything.

'I can't make any sense of them,' said Felix. 'Perhaps they're not ready to give us their message today.'

They certainly looked magical, but Leander felt as if he was missing some secret. He looked at each one in turn, trying to take in every detail of the drawings in the hope that he would spot ... what exactly?

The snap of a book made him look up.

'Here.' Charlotte dropped it into his lap. 'You look. I've read it over and over. If the answer is here, I'm not seeing it.'

'Same here,' said Felix, beginning to tidy up the cards again.

Leander felt his cheeks flush with shame. 'I can't read,' he admitted. 'Not properly.'

As if Charlotte needed any more reasons to think he was an idiot.

'Of course not.' She rolled her eyes, then paused as if catching herself and spoke more gently. 'It doesn't matter. The answer isn't here anyway. We're wasting time.'

Felix picked up the last card – the fur-cloaked King of Swords. The golden edge glinted and sparked something in Leander's mind. Golden edges. A king ...

'There's another book,' said Leander. 'I brought one with me. A book you haven't checked yet.'

It was a silly idea. The book he'd brought from Litchfield House wasn't a book about magic, like all of these. It was only fairy tales. But he had nothing to lose by showing them, and a tiny voice in his head told him it might be important.

He reached past Felix, who squashed himself against the

106

shelves to make room. Stuffed in a corner under the bench was the sack of stolen items from Litchfield, forgotten by Pinchbeck the moment she'd captured Leander. The book of fairy tales was still inside. He handed it to Charlotte and her eyes grew wide.

'I remember this! It was mine as a child.' She clutched it to her chest and then, to his great surprise, she hugged Leander. It was an awkward, lopsided hug because of the cramped space, and Leander sat stiffly, not sure how to react. 'It's lovely to see this, Leander. But they're just stories. It can't help us.'

It was Charlotte's book. All those nights in the library he had been holding a book belonging to the missing girl, the very girl who was now sitting right beside him. The book that contained the same story his mother used to tell him, with golden edges that matched the fortune-telling cards . . . There were too many coincidences. They had to mean something. He felt a spark of hope in his heart. Maybe a book of fairy tales couldn't contain the answer to their problems, but it felt like a message of encouragement nevertheless. From the cards, from his mother, from fate!

'Look at this,' said Leander. He took the book and flipped through the pages until he came to the drawing that had given him so many nightmares. 'The Rat King.'

The drawing showed a child asleep, one foot poking out from the bedcovers. Standing in the doorway in half-shadow was the Rat King, beady-eyed, wizened and hunched, his fingers reaching towards the child, ready to grab—

'The child-snatcher,' said Charlotte. The three of them

leaned in as she traced her fingers over the words. 'This was a strange tale. He sold his soul for the power to transform into an animal, until he used up all his magic and was stuck as a rat for ever.'

Leander shivered, his gaze drawn to the rat skeleton in the jar.

'Charlotte! Felix! Leander!' came Pinchbeck's cry. Charlotte snapped the book shut and hid it behind the others. They all tumbled out of the carriage and raced indoors.

Pinchbeck was waiting in the hallway, hands on hips. 'About time! Idle beasts. I don't know why I feed you.'

10
Three of Pentacles:
Co-operation, Teamwork,
Friendship

CHARLOTTE

Charlotte ached with hunger. There had been nothing to eat since the feast before the last seance. Was it three days? Or four? They wouldn't starve – they never got sick, either. Just as they didn't get any older, Pinchbeck's magic seemed to protect them from other types of harm. To the best of Charlotte's knowledge, there were only two ways she and the other stolen children could actually die: if their Cabinets were destroyed, or if Pinchbeck herself was killed while they were captive.

But they still felt hunger and pain and cold, and days without food made Charlotte's stomach feel both empty and heavy, like an earthenware pot in her middle. Soon she'd have no choice but to start spending more and more time inside her Cabinet where she had no bodily feelings at all, as gloomy as that prospect was.

She pinned Pinchbeck's curls, trying to disguise her revulsion. This had been her task for years and she had done it without thinking, but Leander's arrival was a fresh reminder that this woman was a monster, and Charlotte could hardly bear to touch her.

'Will you walk to town today?' said Charlotte.

'I will. My invitation will arrive at any moment. You and the boys must be ready to travel.'

'Yes, Madame.'

'I am teetering on the brink of greatness, Charlotte. Queen Victoria herself attends seances. These photographs are my ticket to the palace. Finally, I shall be mixing with people of quality, in my rightful place.'

Pinchbeck had laid out her favourite images across the table to admire her work. The children looking back were dirty, exhausted and unhappy, adding to the unsettling effect. In two or three, she had even managed to make them appear transparent, with details of the brickwork and furniture visible through their clothing.

'This next performance is the big one. The world is about to hear about Augustina Pinchbeck.'

'We haven't eaten for a long time.' Charlotte eased a pearl hairpin into place. 'You'll be too weak to perform if we don't get some food.'

'True. One doesn't want to look too thin – it's unbecoming.'

'Will you bring us something back from town?'

'I shall be much too busy. You'll have to get the food yourself. And have something ready for me when I get home.'

'May I have some money, please?'

'There is none. You will have to use other methods.'

Charlotte woke the boys. 'There's no money but we need food. We'll have to lift something.'

'Stealing?' said Leander. 'I thought you didn't like thieves.'

'I don't,' she said. 'But we're desperate.'

Leander looked at her hard. 'I was always desperate. Every time I stole, I only did it because I had to.'

Guilt rattled through Charlotte. 'You're right. I'm sorry.' She hated stealing. It left her feeling ashamed, and angry at Pinchbeck for putting them in that situation. Leander had been an unpleasant reminder of those feelings, but it wasn't his fault.

'What if someone recognizes us from the seance?' said Leander.

'They won't. We look different in our day clothes. Poor children are always invisible,' said Felix.

'Wear your deepest pockets, Felix. We'll split up and go to different stalls.'

'No,' said Leander. 'The best thing is to steal some money, and then buy the food. If we only steal once, there's less chance of being caught.'

Charlotte exchanged a look with Felix. As much as she hated to admit it out loud, it did sound like a good plan.

'And,' continued Leander with a smile, 'I have another idea, too.'

*

In town, Felix laid his violin case on the cobbles and began to play his sweetest melodies, weaving in phrases from favourite hymns and familiar songs that gave people a warm sensation and the desire to part with their money. Charlotte watched from a distance. The first penny was thrown into his case within a minute or two – if they stayed there all day, they might scrape together enough for a meal. But there wasn't time.

Leander had come up with a plan to use Charlotte as a distraction while he picked somebody's pocket. Felix would change his melody to warn them if somebody was watching. As directed, Charlotte sat on a bench, a nervous tickle forming at the back of her throat. Several feet away, Leander gave a nod.

She let her head fall forward and shook her shoulders, pretending to cry. Sometimes she would pretend to weep during a seance so she knew how to make it convincing. She held her eyes wide open, shielded by her hands, until they started to water, then quickly blinked six times. She repeated the pattern until tears began to roll down her cheeks.

Had anyone noticed yet? She took a long breath and released it in a heavy sob.

It worked.

A shift of the boards as someone sat beside her. 'Miss? Is something wrong? Are you hurt?'

His voice was so kind it caught her off guard and her act threatened to become real tears for her own sorrows. 'No, sir.' She added a sniff for good measure.

He offered her a handkerchief and she dabbed her eyes.

'What's troubling you?'

'Forgive me, sir ...'

His eyes were warm and brown and sincere. A shiver of madness came over her – *Tell him the truth*. She bit her lip to hold it back. The tears became hotter.

'Yes?'

'I'm fearful, sir, for my sister.' It was hard to think of anything to say when her mind was so full of worry. 'She ... she has fits.'

They were here to get bread, and that was all. She would not think of her poor uncle, mad with grief. She would not think about Pinchbeck's camera and her plan to— *Oh*.

'... grow out of them, you know ...' The man was still talking, but she barely heard him over the thunder inside her head.

The camera. Pinchbeck questioning Leander about Litchfield House. Asking Charlotte if she'd ever had a photograph taken ...

Of course.

Anyone who understood photography could probably make a ghostly looking picture. That would never be enough for Pinchbeck. She would want her pictures to be so much more.

It all began to make sense. How did she not see it before? Pinchbeck would take Charlotte's photograph and it would be a perfect match for the portrait of her at Litchfield House. Charlotte hadn't aged a day since she last saw her uncle – of course she would look exactly the same. Like a ghost.

It would be a sensation. A miracle. Perfect proof of Pinchbeck's skills as a medium. It would be in all the papers.

But, once everyone knew Charlotte's face, Pinchbeck wouldn't risk anyone recognizing her in the street ...

I'm the one she's going to kill, Charlotte thought. And the tears that fell after that were all too real.

LEANDER

Leander had certainly proven himself now.

His plan worked perfectly. Charlotte's performance kept the smartly dressed man busy while Leander effortlessly lifted his wallet. Felix, who'd been keeping watch to warn Leander with his music should anyone spot him, wound his last melody to a close and packed his violin. They took their time before meeting up by the bakery, waiting until the kind man was well out of sight.

The money was quickly counted and divided. Charlotte took a few pennies to buy soap, a luxury they had gone without for too long. The boys were left to choose the food. A penny left over, Leander spotted a bright display of ribbons in a shop window, and had an idea to cheer Charlotte up – not that he cared if she was cheerful, of course ... He didn't need her to like him. All the same, he bought a length of yellow silk for her hair.

'Thank you,' she said when he gave it to her. She squeezed his hand and smiled weakly before tying the ribbon into her dark hair.

'Good work, Robin Hood,' said Felix.

Leander flushed with pleasure. See? Not as useless as everyone thought.

Charlotte had been silent for most of the walk back, but once the carriage came into sight she blurted out, 'Felix, it's me.'

'What?'

'Pinchbeck isn't going to kill Leander. She's going to get rid of *me*.'

It couldn't be. Not his Charlotte. Why would Pinchbeck keep her for this long and then throw her away?

'Explain.'

'The camera, and this big invitation she's waiting for, the one that's going to change her fortune? I think it's my uncle.' Her voice shook. She paused and bit her lip and started again. 'I thought the camera was the new plan, that she'd photograph Leander, then get a new child to replace him and so on. But then I remembered: Pinchbeck asked if I'd ever posed for a photograph.'

Felix's mouth went dry. Tendrils of dreadful understanding were beginning to uncurl, but he stayed quiet and waited for her to finish. Leander looked nervous and confused.

'Don't you see?' she said. 'Pinchbeck's plan is as perfect as it's cruel. My uncle already has a photograph of me. So, if she gets him to hold a seance and then takes a photograph of me appearing, no one can deny that it's really me.'

'Do you think that's why she was so interested in what I knew about the house? Why she asked me so many questions about where everything's kept, what state the master is in?' asked Leander.

Charlotte nodded sadly.

'When you went missing, it was such a famous mystery . . .' Felix began to think aloud. 'Everyone will hear about it if she summons you. She'll be in great demand. The first person to prove she can call on the dead.' Dread rumbled through him like an ominous bass note.

'Ironic, really,' said Charlotte. 'My uncle despised mediums. That's what a lot of his work was about – trying to prove they were fakes. I don't think Pinchbeck would even have met me if not for that. And now he's hiring her to help him find me.'

Felix looked away. Charlotte had no idea of the real reason Pinchbeck snatched her away, but he did . . .

It was true that Lord Litchfield had been an outspoken sceptic. Often, Pinchbeck would read out pieces he had written for the London papers, denouncing the spiritualists, exposing them as frauds and liars. That's why she had volunteered to perform for him five years ago.

'*He shan't catch me out*,' Pinchbeck had said to Felix, so confident that Lord Litchfield wouldn't be able to see through her tricks and would sing her praises as the only true medium he had ever met. Charlotte hadn't been at the seance, but Pinchbeck had been introduced to her that same evening, in the lord's parlour – Felix remembered hearing their voices from inside his Cabinet.

And later he remembered Pinchbeck's rage as she read her own name in Lord Litchfield's scornful articles.

'That scoundrel!' she had said, waving the paper in the air like she was swatting a fly. *'That crook! How dare he tarnish my reputation? He cheated me!'* She had raved about it for weeks.

Biding her time, it was months later that Pinchbeck sought her revenge. She had loitered around the woodlands surrounding Litchfield House, waiting to engineer a chance encounter when Charlotte was out walking, then used their brief introduction on the evening of the seance as an excuse to strike up a conversation. Charlotte, intelligent but sheltered, had no reason to distrust the woman.

Charlotte had often said to Felix that she was sure Pinchbeck wanted to steal a rich girl as a sort of lady's maid, someone whom Pinchbeck believed to be of the right rank to tend to her needs, and it was Charlotte's ill fortune that she had found her. But, though Pinchbeck had never told him her plans, Felix was sure the woman had wanted Charlotte in particular. Lord Litchfield hadn't given her the praise Pinchbeck felt she deserved, and he had paid the price with the loss of his niece.

And now it seemed that simply leaving the lord bereft wasn't enough for Pinchbeck. No, the cunning woman had been waiting all these years, planning to return to Litchfield House when the old man was beyond hope. It was exactly her idea of justice. The man who criticized her would become the man to make her name.

Leander reached out to touch Charlotte's shoulder, but she edged away.

'She'll have my photograph in the papers within days,' she said. 'The whole country will know my face. She'll never risk me being seen outside the seances. So I'm the one she'll throw out.'

'Maybe she'll still need you,' said Leander. 'Folks might want to see the famous ghost conjured for them, too?'

'Maybe,' said Charlotte with the tiniest of sniffles. She did not seem comforted.

'We'll do something. We'll find a way to free you,' Felix said. He could not lose her as well.

'There is no way. I've been with her five years and never found one. You've been here longer still. If there was a way to get free, you'd have gone years ago.'

Would I? He didn't meet her gaze.

In truth, though he truly wished to break Pinchbeck's spell for Charlotte and Leander's sake, he still wasn't completely sure he wanted to leave. He had been with Pinchbeck for almost half his life. He'd had more years with her than he ever got with Isaak, or his mother, or Charlotte. Performing for Pinchbeck was better than begging, and at least it felt like he was searching for his brother when they travelled round the country. If Felix was freed somehow, how would he continue his search?

He had been wondering, secretly, if there was some way he could release Leander and Charlotte but not himself. Pinchbeck would be angry, of course, but Felix was special to her. Important. She would surely come around and they could carry on together. He owed her some loyalty. He had promised to stay with her, and he did not believe in breaking promises.

Now, with this new development, things were becoming more complicated. Pinchbeck was showing her wicked side more and more, and Felix felt pulled apart by conflicting loyalties. He couldn't let anything happen to Charlotte. They had to think of something, and fast.

'We can alert your uncle. He'll help us,' he suggested.

'Pinchbeck won't risk letting us speak to him. If she sees us talking to my uncle . . .'

'Then we shall find another way. We're all in this together. We won't let her hurt you, will we, Leander?'

11
Five of Swords:
Cowardice, Failure, Defeat

CHARLOTTE

Pinchbeck's moods had been so unpredictable, and disaster was so close at hand, that the children thought it best to keep her happy. They had brushed the horses, polished the carriage and cleaned and aired their best clothes as well as they could without a proper washpot. Keeping the rats away from their dwindling food supplies had been a constant struggle. Dinner was being cooked – potatoes boiled then fried with chopped sausages. Mushrooms had been found growing behind the farmhouse.

'Which are the poisonous kind?' said Charlotte. 'If she was too sick to travel . . .'

'Too dangerous,' said Felix. 'If she eats too many, it might kill her.'

'Good,' said Leander. 'Then we're free, right?'

Charlotte looked at him in surprise at his ruthless tone.

'No,' said Felix. 'If she dies, we all die.'

'*If anything happens to me, you're dust*,' said Charlotte. 'That's what Pinchbeck always says to us.'

'But we don't know that for sure,' said Leander. 'It's just her word. Wouldn't it be worth the risk?'

Charlotte shivered. The idea had occurred to her, too, once. Many years ago, soon after Charlotte was stolen, they had visited an apothecary. An old woman, skin like crumpled paper, was buying a tonic for a terrible hacking cough that seemed to cause her great pain.

Pinchbeck whispered in Charlotte's ear. 'That will never happen to you. You'll never grow old, and you'll never get sick. The suffering I've saved you.' She held on to Charlotte's hand too tightly, bones crunching together. Perhaps she'd noticed Charlotte's gaze lingering on the rat poison. 'So long as I'm safe, you're safe. I hope we understand each other.'

Even so, Charlotte had been tempted. After five years with Pinchbeck, death sometimes seemed better than eternal captivity. What stopped her, even after all this time, was the faint and distant hope that she might one day see her uncle again, and care for him in his old age.

'Besides,' said Felix, rousing her from her thoughts, 'she'd notice we weren't eating the mushrooms and get suspicious. Better we behave and not end up locked in our Cabinets.'

While they prepared dinner, they spoke of magic and charms, but came no closer to working out the secret to breaking Pinchbeck's hold over them. The magic in her books was nothing more than herbal medicines and fortune-telling. But something kept bringing Charlotte's mind back to her book of fairy tales that Leander had brought with him – the idea of the Rat King using up all his magic to steal children. It was just like Pinchbeck and the obvious strain she felt holding three Cabinets.

Time was running out. Either Pinchbeck would use up her magic and then who knew what would happen, or she would run out of patience and get rid of one of them for good.

After hours of deliberation, their only idea was to write a letter and leave it behind when they performed at Litchfield House; Charlotte had written it on a stolen piece of paper and held it close to her chest.

Uncle,

I know this will be hard to understand, but Augustina Pinchbeck has been holding me captive since my disappearance. She has imprisoned me and two other children.

Please do not believe her lies. I am not dead, just being held against my will.

You must apprehend her, and see that none of her possessions are destroyed or we will be lost for ever.

Your loving niece,
Charlotte

Next to her name she drew a honeybee – his nickname for her when she was small. She didn't seek to explain the weird magic binding them to Pinchbeck – it was too implausible, and might confuse matters. Charlotte wasn't even sure he would believe the note, but they had to try. It was better than doing nothing, but still a wild and desperate plan.

'It's here!' Pinchbeck burst through the door, smiling and waving a sheet of folded paper. 'My invitation has finally arrived! My big moment is fast approaching. We won't be stuck in this old place much longer!' She sat down in the best chair, reading the letter.

A small grey rat poked its head out of a crack in the wall to see what the commotion was about. Charlotte stamped her foot to scare it away. Then she scraped the food on to their mismatched crockery and the four of them once again sat down to eat, a mockery of a family.

'We'll pack the darkroom tonight, ready to leave in the morning.' Pinchbeck was gleeful. She scribbled a note into her commonplace book and tucked it safely into her pocket. 'I will develop the photograph immediately after the seance so the sitter can watch and see there's no swindle.'

This made Charlotte all the more certain the next performance was going to be for her uncle. He wasn't the type to accept Pinchbeck's word, for all her showmanship. He'd want to inspect the equipment and be present for every step.

'Where are we going?' said Leander through a mouthful of bread. 'Is it back to my old house?'

Tactless idiot! Charlotte glared at him. She would have asked questions gently, searching for subtle hints and clues, teasing out Pinchbeck's plan without making her wary. Charlotte braced herself for an outburst, but none came.

'That's right, dear boy. I suppose Charlotte has already told you who she is.' Pinchbeck smiled, but it was not a pleasant smile. 'It is time to tell Lord Litchfield of the tragedy that befell his poor little niece. I'm going to tell him she drowned in the lake, at just thirteen.' She drew out the vowels in the word 'drowned', savouring it.

The heat drained from Charlotte's body. 'You can't. You'll break his heart.'

'No. It's a kindness. More kindness than he deserves, the rogue. Better than always wondering what happened to you. Maybe you will finally have a funeral. Imagine that.'

'My uncle's no rogue,' said Charlotte, unable to resist arguing back. How dare Pinchbeck the child-snatcher call Charlotte's beloved uncle a rogue? 'He's a gentleman.'

'Your memory is playing tricks on you. Remember, dear Uncle had no time for a little girl, what with his very important work.' Pinchbeck patted Charlotte's arm in a condescending way. 'I'm sure you were fond of the old man, but you were keen to get away from him. He deserves to wonder what became of you. It's extremely kind of me to end his misery.'

It took all of Charlotte's will not to lunge for Pinchbeck's throat. But she had to stay in control. If Pinchbeck suspected that Charlotte would rebel during the seance, she'd have them sealed in their Cabinets in an instant. And then any hope of getting the note to her uncle would be lost. Worse still, Charlotte would become useless to Pinchbeck at once, and then what would stop her from destroying her Cabinet? So she swallowed down her rage and did her best to lie. 'Yes. Perhaps it is a kindness.'

When Charlotte first met Pinchbeck, her relationship with her uncle had been strained. He was always a hard worker, writing articles and giving lectures, but in the past year or two he had become obsessed with his work. He spent every hour in the study, scribbling away, or meeting with other gentlemen and holding heated conversations into the early hours. Though they had been very close when she was small, she had begun to feel like he didn't know her any more. On the rare occasion they ate dinner together, he would ask silly questions about her dolls or her drawings as though she was still a little girl. He had barely noticed that she was almost grown.

On the night before she was taken, they had argued fiercely about just that. Charlotte remembered feeling furious with him for treating her like a child. Perhaps that's why she had fallen for Pinchbeck's trap. The woman had talked with her as an equal when they'd met, suggesting that Charlotte might like to travel with her as her female companion, promising to show her more of the world, and Charlotte had believed her. Then, once she was captured by her magic, Pinchbeck had tried to convince Charlotte that her uncle didn't want her anyway. She would tell her that the old man would be much happier without her now he could focus on his work without distraction. She even claimed that her wealthy clients said Lord Litchfield had gone travelling to research his latest article and was relieved to be free of his burden.

At first Charlotte nodded along with whatever Pinchbeck said, mostly because it eased her guilt to think of him happy without her, instead of grieving her loss. But, deep down, Charlotte knew that her uncle loved her. And, as the years had passed, she had cursed her foolishness for ever trusting Pinchbeck.

Then Leander's appearance with tales of her uncle's misery proved Pinchbeck had lied from the very start. She had hurt Lord Litchfield by stealing Charlotte, and now she was going back to twist the knife.

As if she knew what Charlotte was thinking, Pinchbeck set down her teacup and glared.

'I will not tolerate anything that prevents me from doing this.' Her tone was darker, sharper. The shadows around her eyes seemed to darken, too, and her lips, for the barest second, looked almost black. 'If anyone should be uncooperative, I will be most displeased.'

The children watched her the way one dare not turn away from a venomous snake. A thick yellow silence filled the room like smoke.

Pinchbeck laughed, a hollow, brittle sound. 'Now then! Such serious faces. I daresay there will be a few extra pennies left over for well-behaved children.' The creases on her cheeks were more prominent than a day ago. She was transforming from a young woman into a crone, hour by hour.

126

LEANDER

As soon as Pinchbeck was asleep in the enormous wooden bed, camera within arm's reach, the children crowded into the carriage to discuss their plans once more.

'What's in that book she always carries around?' Leander asked.

'All sorts,' said Felix. 'Notes on the seances. Addresses. Charms.'

'Notes on photography now probably,' added Charlotte.

'I think we need to get hold of it,' said Leander.

'She's never apart from it,' said Charlotte.

'That's what I mean!' Leander swept his hair back, fingers catching in the tangles that had already returned. 'She wouldn't keep it so close if it didn't have something important inside. Maybe the way to break her magic . . .'

'We'll never get it away from her,' said Felix.

'I can,' said Leander. 'I'm a thief, remember?'

'No,' said Charlotte. 'It's too dangerous.'

'I wouldn't get caught.' Leander was insistent.

'You have too much courage and not enough brain.' Charlotte fixed her face in her favourite frown.

Leander smiled to himself. Even though she called him stupid, she also said he was brave. He was winning her over.

'We know you're good at lifting things,' said Felix, 'but, even so, don't do anything foolish, Leander. We don't know how Pinchbeck would react if she caught you.'

'But—'

'No,' Charlotte interrupted. 'Felix is right. You mustn't try and take the book. We'll have to hope the letter works. Do you promise?'

'I promise,' muttered Leander.

He lied. Of course he was going to steal it. The book had to hold the secret that could help them break the magic. He would be the one to take it, and prove to Charlotte and Felix that he was worth something after all.

Charlotte and Felix feel asleep, as close as kittens. They were anxious, but days of fear and secrecy had taken their toll.

Leander was about to be a traitor and a hero all at once. Pinchbeck had fed and clothed him. Well, sometimes she'd fed him. Either way, she'd given him more in the last week than any other adult since his mother had passed away. He understood now that she wasn't to be trusted, but it still felt like a betrayal to turn against her.

Silently, he tiptoed into the house and towards Pinchbeck's room. He paused behind the door.

Can I really do this? The others were so sure it would end in disaster, but Leander was good at picking pockets. He'd had lots of practice. Doubt pecked at his insides, and that old feeling of guilt began to gnaw. He seemed to be making a habit of being a thief, even though he didn't choose that path. His soul was heavy with sin.

Stealing from a monster doesn't count.

He felt useful and important and worthy for once. He'd show

128

Charlotte. She wouldn't be rude to him when he saved her life. It was worth the cold panic seeping upward from his toes.

He listened for stirring. The night was full of sounds. Dry leaves skittered over the flagstones with every puff of wind. Night-time birds cooed and, in the corners of his vision, bright-eyed rats scuttled between shadows. But inside the room was silent.

Fingers on the door, edging it open as lightly as an autumn breeze. One, two, three, four steps brought Leander over to the side of the bed. The bed curtains were missing, but the canopy above was still intact, thick with a decade of dust and cobwebs. Pinchbeck lay on her back, one arm beneath her head and the other across her chest. Leander stood over her.

The sheets and blankets, like those from the carriage, had been repurposed to make the darkroom where she developed her photographs. The house was cold, so she was sleeping fully dressed with her cloak wrapped round her for warmth. Her breathing made a steady rhythm, the folds of her cloak moving in time with her ribs. The pocket that held the book was on her right hip. If Leander was quick and careful, he could reach in at exactly the right moment.

If she catches me, I'll be dead.

But they were all in danger anyway. He must be strong.

Trembling fingers reached out. He was close enough to feel Pinchbeck's hot breath. In. Out. In. Out. *Do it!* Why couldn't he do it? It was as though she was surrounded by a fog of fear; it coiled round his throat like the hangman's noose and threatened to choke him.

He slipped his fingers under the cloak, reaching for the pocket. *The book!* He touched the corner of it, but withdrew his hand. The angle was wrong – the slightest catch on the fabric could be his undoing. *Would she only punish me? Or would she think we were all in it together?*

Now.

On the in-breath, he reached in and gripped the corner of the book between thumb and forefinger. He started to pull gently, gently—

Pinchbeck stirred.

No, no, no.

The woman gave a single great snore and Leander snatched his hand away. He stayed frozen. If he moved, Pinchbeck would surely wake but, if he stayed where he was, she might wake anyway, and he would have no explanation for his presence.

Pinchbeck mumbled in her sleep and moved her arm. Her sleeve brushed Leander's jacket.

Ten seconds later, Leander finally dared to breathe again. This shift of position had worked against him: the edge of Pinchbeck's cloak now covered the pocket and her arm was blocking the way. He tried to swallow, but his throat was as dry as sawdust.

Try again. Again, Leander!

But his hands wouldn't co-operate. Tears filled his eyes. He crouched by the sleeping woman for what felt like for ever, willing himself to reach for the book, but his courage was gone.

130

He slunk out of the room, hating himself. He had failed and now they'd never be free.

He was as useless as Charlotte said he was and she and Felix would never accept him now.

He returned to the kitchen where the others were sleeping. Felix opened one eye.

'Leander? What's wrong?' he whispered.

'Nothing,' Leander lied.

12
The Hermit:
Solitude, Caution, Vigilance

Less than a full day later, they were back at Litchfield House.

The air around him sighed with relief as the locket opened. Leander heard his name and stepped out into the brightly lit parlour, marvelling at how easily he could appear now. The room was beautiful. Two enormous candelabra sat atop a vast table, a fire blazed beneath an ornate mantelpiece and huge portraits frowned from brass frames on every wall. Pinchbeck's camera stood to attention on the stand before the hearth.

'Move, boy!' Pinchbeck hissed at him and pointed to a door in the far corner. Leander obeyed, slipping through the door and closing it as softly as he could. His eyes took a little while to adjust to the gloom in the hallway. Behind him he could hear people coming into the room. Polite greetings were exchanged and chairs scraped the floor. A man with a deep, oaky voice commented on the camera.

While the seance was taking place, Leander had been instructed by Pinchbeck to sneak through the house and fill his pockets. The untended rooms in the wings would be full of treasures that wouldn't immediately be missed.

'Not too much,' Pinchbeck had warned. 'Nothing too obvious. Just a little to tide us over until word spreads about my talents, then we shall have more money than we know what to do with.'

But Pinchbeck was unaware that Leander had another mission, too. He, Charlotte and Felix had come up with a plan. Leander had volunteered to go right into the heart of the old house and leave a note in the master's chambers. Charlotte had taught him the way by tracing maps into the dirt and Leander had recited the directions until he knew them perfectly. He'd never ventured into this part of the house before; as a servant's child and then a stowaway, he knew better than to be seen near the lord's rooms. But he was the only one who had permission to go out of Pinchbeck's sight, and his days of thieving had taught him how to sneak around. It was all down to him.

While Leander was creeping about, Charlotte and Felix would play their part and perform the seance, just as Pinchbeck wished. That way she wouldn't suspect anything. If Pinchbeck thought they were up to no good, she could seal them in their Cabinets, or worse, destroy them completely, so they had to make her believe they were obedient.

Leander might have been an unschooled orphan, but even he knew the plan was weak. What if Lord Litchfield didn't believe the letter? It sounded like such nonsense written down. No sensible man would believe magic. And then – what if he *wasn't* sensible? Rumours had been rife among the remaining servants at Litchfield House that the old man had gone strange in the head after Charlotte went missing. He had seemed ordinary enough the one time Leander met him, but that meeting had been brief. So much of their hope rested on the lord being open-minded enough to believe in Pinchbeck's twisted magic, but not too frail and muddled to help them escape. Leander knew it might be a hopeless mission.

For the seventh time, Leander checked his pocket to make sure the letter was still there and recited the directions in his head: *Left down the corridor. Staircase on the right.* A step creaked and Leander froze, expecting someone to burst out of the parlour and catch him. No one came. He continued up the stairs on the balls of his feet: he wouldn't be chicken again. On the landing, he headed towards the master's bedroom, counting the doors as he passed. *Two, three, four . . .*

A door opened. Leander was sure it was the door to the very room he was looking for . . . But Charlotte had said this room was out of bounds because her uncle feared the servants would disturb his work. Why was someone there? Panic gripped him. Charlotte had been gone for years; things could be different now. Maybe Lord Litchfield didn't use this room any more. Leander flattened himself against the nearest door, relying on the deep indentation in the panelled wall to hide his small frame.

A woman crossed the hallway to the servants' staircase, barely an arm's length from where Leander was hidden.

Mrs Smart! What was she doing in the master's private room?

She disappeared from view and Leander stole across the carpet and opened the study door ...

A creak came from the servants' stairs – Mrs Smart was coming back!

Leander darted into the room and crouched behind the nearest chair. The woman entered a moment later and crossed to the tall cupboard on the other side of the room.

She hasn't seen me, Leander thought. *Breathe quietly. Don't move.*

Mrs Smart rummaged through a drawer. Moving over to the shelves, she stroked the spines of the books with a bony finger. She opened a small wooden box and peered inside, pulled out a coin and dropped it into her apron pocket.

She was stealing!

She had waited until the master was distracted with visitors so she could use the opportunity to rifle through his things.

Mrs Smart was very close to Leander now, and it was only because she was engrossed in her task that she hadn't noticed him, inches from her skirt hem. As she leaned over to examine something on the writing desk, the fabric of her dress brushed Leander's knee. He shuffled backwards. If he could edge round to the other side of the chair, he'd have a chance of sneaking out unnoticed. Mrs Smart found something and held it up to examine it in the light, stepping back as she did so.

Leander hopped aside, but overbalanced and fell. The housekeeper whipped round towards him. Her shock faded to wicked joy when she recognized him.

'Here's the sneak thief.' She stuffed her trophy into her pocket with one hand and grabbed Leander's wrist with the other. 'I thought you'd gone to the sewers with the rest of the vermin.'

'Let go of me!'

'Oh no,' she replied as she yanked him to his feet. 'Sneaking around His Lordship's chambers! No doubt you're up to your usual pilfering ways.'

'You're the thief! I saw you put money in your pocket.' He wrenched his hand from her claw, but she caught him by his coat before he could get away.

'This half-sovereign that I stopped you from taking when I caught you red-handed?' she asked, producing the coin. 'Oh, the master will be most pleased with me, catching a ne'er-do-well in his chambers. I daresay I shall be rewarded handsomely, once you've been handed over to the constable.'

'I'll turn *you* in!' he protested. 'Let go!'

'I'd like to see you try. To the master with you.' She dropped the coin back into her pocket and gripped his shoulder, wrestling him through the doorway.

The letter! He had to leave it otherwise all would be lost. Quickly, Leander pulled it out of his coat and twisted round to flick it into the room. It landed on the corner of the rug, almost invisible against the pattern. The door closed behind them.

Please let him find it, he pleaded to himself.

'Stop squirming!' Mrs Smart shook him and gave his arm a hard pinch.

'The master's got visitors,' said Leander. 'He'll be angry if you interrupt.'

'And what would you know of that?' She shoved him through the door to the servants' staircase. It was darker in here, and her long, pinched face looked skeletal in the shadows. She smelled of camphor and damp.

'Wait!' Leander cried.

She did not.

'The master is finding out what happened to Charlotte.'

That stopped her.

'What did you say?'

'His visitors. One of them's a medium come to show him the spirit of his lost niece. You'll be for it if you disturb him.'

She stared at him for a long time. 'How do you know about Lady Charlotte?'

He couldn't resist a smirk – it was fun to see her wrong-footed. 'Just do.'

'How does a ruffian like you know these things?'

'I know a lot of things,' Leander said. He avoided her gaze until she squeezed his cheek and twisted his head towards her.

He had to get out of here.

His Cabinet! He closed his eyes and willed himself to disappear, imagining his bones turning to air ... Nothing

137

happened. Perhaps he was too far away, or there were too many walls between him and his locket. He took a deep breath and tried again. He imagined steam, smoke, breeze.

But Mrs Smart was off again, dragging Leander down the stairs too fast for his short legs. Pinchbeck would be irate if this woman interrupted her seance. And if she didn't reveal Charlotte then Lord Litchfield might not believe the note – if he found it at all. To make things worse, Leander hadn't stolen anything for Pinchbeck. *She'll be furious if I disobey!*

He could hear Felix's violin and all manner of knocking and banging. The sound was comforting to Leander, but Mrs Smart was clearly uneasy. As they neared the bottom of the staircase, her pace slowed and her breathing quickened. No real ghosts, but she didn't know that. As they got closer to the parlour door, her march became more of a shuffle.

'You're scared,' said Leander.

'No. But it seems the master is busy, and I shan't disturb him. Mark my words, though, we're going to stay right here until he's finished, if it takes all night.'

Again he tried to become vapour and return to the safety of his Cabinet. The sensation was like pushing against stretched canvas; the air around him wanted to yield to his will, but he wasn't quite strong enough to break through. If he could reach the parlour door ...

He had to get away. He couldn't let anything ruin their plans. The others were counting on him.

He stamped on Mrs Smart's foot, hard.

Mrs Smart yelped and hopped on one foot, cursing him.

He yanked himself free of her grasp, shoving past her and sprinting down the hall.

'Get back here—' She tripped over the hem of her dress and fell, sprawling face down on the floor. The coin flew from her apron pocket, rolling along the carpet towards Leander.

'Serves you right!' Leander said, snatching it up. He pushed on the parlour door, opening it just a little, and willed himself to vanish.

This time the air accepted his plea and his spirit flowed through the gap into his locket, retaining his vision long enough to see Mrs Smart slack-jawed with astonishment.

CHARLOTTE

Charlotte stepped out into the parlour of her childhood home. It looked strangely cold, all harsh shadows in the dazzling light from the clockwork lamp, but the smell was unmistakably home. Her chest was filled with an ache of longing so strong it threatened to burst out of her. She belonged here.

Most of the sitters were men. She dimly recognized one man as an old friend of her uncle, far greyer and plumper than she had known him. Another man, balding and flushed, she remembered being some sort of important figure from the next town, but his name was missing from her mind.

And then she saw him ...

Uncle!

Had he always been small and frail? No, he had been such

a vibrant man. But now his hair was completely white and his eyes were sunk deeply into his skull. His posture was hunched as if the weight of his sorrows pushed his shoulders towards the ground. Was it because of her he was like this? No ... not *her*. Pinchbeck!

Charlotte stepped forward, eyes fixed on her uncle. *Recognize me! Please recognize me.*

'Charlotte ...' The old man barely whispered, but she heard it over the howl of Felix's violin and the gasps of the other men. She leaned over the table, over the arms of the nearest men, and reached her hand out towards her uncle. She wanted to call his name, but she was too overcome with emotion to speak and didn't want to do anything to draw Pinchbeck's negative attention.

The spluttering lantern behind her uncle blinked and burned out. Only the watery candlelight remained. As her eyes adjusted to the gloom, Charlotte could see Pinchbeck's smile as the woman draped a dark cloth over the camera lens. She had taken the photograph. The reward would be hers for certain. But, even without the photograph, Charlotte could see her uncle was in awe of Pinchbeck. *Oh, devious witch! This is too, too cruel.*

'*Abeo!*' Pinchbeck's voice commanded Charlotte into her lantern. She tried to scream no, no, not yet, a few moments longer. To shout at her uncle that this was the woman who had taken her, and she wasn't dead, and he must find a way to save her.

She pushed and fought, desperate to keep her form, but

the magic pulled her in, tugging at her flesh like a million fish hooks, burning, smothering. But it was nothing next to the pain at being parted from her uncle again.

The lantern door snapped shut as Pinchbeck ensured she couldn't come back out.

FELIX

'The craftsmanship is unremarkable,' the voice said. 'No real value.'

How dare they? Felix hated it when people touched his violin. Even in his Cabinet he knew; he could picture them turning it over in their hands, running their fingers over the worn patches on the finish, noticing the tiny crack in the tuning peg. Insulting its quality.

'The music, though,' said another man. 'I've never heard anything like it before.'

'Well, it was played by a ghost, my dear,' said a woman with a titter. 'One can't expect the spirits to be capable of Bach.' They laughed.

Felix was furious. *Of course I can play Bach! Then you'd complain it wasn't mystical enough!*

He should pop out of the violin case and give them a fright. But he wouldn't, of course. Especially not tonight.

Pinchbeck knew how Felix felt about his violin, and yet she had left it out here for them to toy with. After her performance, Pinchbeck had requested to be shown to a dark place where she could develop the long-awaited photograph, and had deliberately left behind the remainder of her belongings. She knew Lord Litchfield would want to check for any sign she was creating illusions, and none would be found. Pinchbeck was too canny to bring her showy tricks in here. The seance had been performed with nothing but music and heartbreak to set the mood.

'James, are you unwell?'

'Yes,' said a man – Charlotte's uncle? – in a soft voice. 'Shaken. It was . . . I could never have believed it . . .'

'Dreadful news. We're so sorry,' said the woman.

'I hope you find some comfort in . . .' The man trailed off.

'Knowing she's at peace,' the woman finished.

'Yes,' said the uncle. 'Of course, yes. I always knew she couldn't be alive . . . after all these years. I always knew.' The last words were little more than a whisper. Felix could taste the old man's pain and he thought of Charlotte, locked away in matching agony. He felt guilty for fretting over his violin.

'. . . quite startling. Such a clear manifestation.' The woman spoke as if she had seen many ghosts. These gatherings were quite fashionable among certain circles.

'Exactly as I remember her,' said Lord Litchfield.

'I'm certain no one in London could compare to this medium. She truly has a gift.'

'That's why I invited her.' Charlotte's uncle cleared his throat. 'I saw many frauds and illusionists back in the old days. I'm sure you remember, Alfred.'

'Of course.'

'This was the only one who didn't . . . I couldn't find any

evidence against her. You'll think me a foolish old man, I suppose. I miss Charlotte so dearly.'

There was a moment of deep, empty silence.

The old man continued. 'Thank you for coming tonight. I have rather neglected my old friends, it seems. Without you, I might not have trusted my own eyes.'

The woman began to say something, but the door burst open and Pinchbeck's crowing voice called, 'I have done it!'

The people all spoke at once, their voices mixing and fading as they moved away from Felix's Cabinet. Pinchbeck's plan, it seemed, was working perfectly.

13
Strength:
Courage, Determination,
Cleverness

CHARLOTTE

The carriage was already far from Litchfield House when Pinchbeck finally opened their Cabinets and allowed them to come out. They had stopped by the side of a dark and winding country lane, and almost immediately Pinchbeck gathered the children round the lantern, eager to show off the photograph.

'One for us, and one for your uncle to show off to all his rich friends. Come, see what clever Mama has done!'

The boys looked at the image, curious, but Charlotte hung back. She might as well be looking at her own burial gown.

'You should be grateful,' Pinchbeck said to her sharply. 'You saw your uncle and brought him comfort. And this picture will bring comfort to many more. They'll believe this is proof their loved ones go on after death!'

It was a striking photograph. Though Charlotte had been

reaching for her uncle, Pinchbeck had angled the camera perfectly, making it appear that Charlotte was staring right at the viewer, arm outstretched, eyes black in the harsh light. She even looked transparent: the furniture was visible through her dress.

'Double exposure,' explained Pinchbeck with a wink. 'Two pictures over the top of each other on the same plate. One of the empty room, and one with you in it. The walls and furniture look solid because they're in both pictures, but you are not.' She was obviously pleased with her own cleverness.

Charlotte pushed down her anger. As soon as Pinchbeck had gone to sleep, there would be a chance to find out if Leander had succeeded in planting the letter. Until then, Charlotte needed to stay calm and not arouse suspicion.

'Glorious day, children! Mark this day! Remember this day!' Pinchbeck said with glee. It was obvious now that she wasn't just buoyant from the seance, she was drunk, too. No doubt she had been offered sherry and wine at the house, to thank her for the success of the session. Charlotte was revolted at the thought that her uncle was rewarding the woman who was the source of all his pain. Giggling, Pinchbeck took down a large wicker basket from the driving seat and handed it to Felix.

'A gift from your grateful uncle, Charlotte dear. Help yourselves.'

'I got this,' said Leander, producing a gold coin from his pocket.

'A half-sovereign!' Pinchbeck clasped her hands over

145

Leander's. 'Well done, my little Leander! You'll have pocket money when we reach the city. Good lad.'

Leander managed a half-smile in response.

'Oh,' said Pinchbeck, pulling Leander's locket out of her pocket. 'Put this away safely.'

Leander put the chain round his neck.

'Will we camp here or go back to the farmhouse?' asked Felix.

Pinchbeck shook her head and made big sweeping gestures. 'Neither. Onward, children. Onward to better things!'

'I'll ride up front with you,' said Charlotte. She'd charm Pinchbeck while she was vague with drink and try to learn more about her plans. *If she's going to smash my lantern and kill me, why not do it now? Why the urgency to travel through the night?* She put on her sweetest smile. 'I can hold the reins while you eat. Keep you company.'

The boys were already rummaging through the hamper. She crouched beside them so their heads were very close. 'She might give something away while she's drunk. You hunt through her books for ideas. If she falls asleep –' she glanced at Pinchbeck, wobbling precariously as she heaved herself up to her seat – 'I'll pull off the road and tell you what I've found out.'

Charlotte took out a small pigeon pie and a wimberry tart, which should keep Pinchbeck awake for a few miles, at least. Felix nudged Leander to get into the carriage and handed him the hamper. A rat scampered from the hedgerow and stood boldly watching them from behind the carriage wheel, as if waiting for its share of the spoils. Charlotte stamped her foot and it retreated. Vile creatures.

'Blankets.' Felix passed Charlotte an armful of rugs. 'Good luck.'

It was impossible to climb gracefully while wearing a crinoline, but she didn't waste time changing. Pinchbeck's gown was thankfully more modern, not sticking out as far, or there wouldn't have been room for the two of them to sit together. Charlotte arranged the blankets over their laps to protect their clothes from dirt and their skin from the cold.

'Everyone in?' Pinchbeck shouted and didn't wait for an answer. Felix hopped into the carriage as it started moving and slammed the door.

The white in Pinchbeck's hair was gradually taking over and her hands were bony, though she drove the horses like a demon until Charlotte persuaded her to hand over the reins.

'Where are we heading?' said Charlotte, gripping tightly to keep her hands from shaking with fear.

'To Stafford, for some well-earned rest and luxury. Your uncle is a generous man, Charlotte. My work was richly rewarded and he'll no doubt be sharing news of my talent far and wide soon, too.'

She opened her mouth as wide as a snake to take a huge bite of the fruit pie, the purple-red syrup staining her lips blood red.

'I'll need some new gowns in the most fashionable styles before mixing with high society in London. And I shall need to hire a driver. It won't do for a woman to travel alone among

147

the upper class. Another limitation of this wretched female form. I should have been a man, Charlotte. I could have chosen a—' She stopped herself abruptly. 'Oh well. Too late now. At least I'm beautiful. All eyes will be on me very soon.'

As well as talking nonsense, Charlotte noticed that Madame Pinchbeck's balance had been affected by the drink; every bump in the road made her sway dangerously. It'd be so easy to push her off the seat. Charlotte imagined the sound of her head hitting the ground, legs pulled beneath the carriage wheels, the cry of pain—

No! What kind of monster had she become? Was she capable of such a thing? Besides, hurting Pinchbeck wouldn't grant their freedom. But if it would . . . could she do it?

'Keep on this road until the village of Coven.'

'What's in Coven?'

'No concern of yours. Your work is done.'

Your work is done. So Charlotte had been right to worry. She was no longer useful to Pinchbeck. The cold, biting wind stung her face and matched the lump of ice in her gut. The carriage passed along the narrow, winding road, the world around them shades of navy and black. It was spooky, but what need was there to fear the dark when the monster was already beside you?

Perhaps flattery would get her talking. Pinchbeck was a prideful creature, and might let something slip if Charlotte encouraged bragging. 'I was wondering . . .' *Ease into it. Don't rush.* 'Using us as spirits in a seance . . . it's such a clever idea. How did you ever think of it?'

Pinchbeck laughed. 'I'm a clever person, Charlotte. Don't you forget it. I simply had to use my gifts to my advantage.'

'And before you were a medium?' Charlotte's mouth was as dry as parchment, and it was a struggle to keep her voice light.

Pinchbeck stared at her for a long time. 'A lady must have a few secrets, Charlotte.' She leaned back and closed her eyes.

'How did you learn to perform so well?'

'I won't be tempted into talking, girl. My secrets have been buried for eight years, and it'll take more than a prying child to uncover them.'

FELIX

Felix scoured the books yet again, searching for any tiny clue they might have overlooked – anything to stop Pinchbeck harming Charlotte. Leander's reading wasn't good enough to be of any use, so he mostly sat guard over the well-stuffed food hamper. He'd already devoured his chunk of fruitcake and pocketed handfuls of biscuits and sugarplums when he thought Felix wasn't looking, but Felix pretended not to notice. He knew it wasn't greed. Leander had spent months never knowing when his next meal would come. The longer Felix knew him, the more Leander reminded him of Isaak; though he was much older, Leander had the same stubbornness, the same false bravery and puppy-dog hopefulness. Felix was growing fond of the boy, and that was the last thing he wanted to do. *Never get attached.*

The carriage swayed to a stop and the door opened to reveal Charlotte.

'She's asleep. I've covered her with blankets, but we don't have long. The air's biting.'

Felix shifted the pile of papers so she could squeeze in.

'Did she say anything?' he asked.

'Mostly bragging about her own genius and complaining about the hardships of being a woman, as if I didn't know.'

Leander held a piece of cake out, but she shook her head. Felix saw him pretend to put it back in the basket, but instead slip it into his pocket.

'The letter,' said Charlotte. 'Did you leave it in my uncle's study?'

'Yes,' said Leander. 'Well, sort of. I got caught by the housekeeper and had to drop it on to the carpet. I hope he sees it.'

Charlotte nodded. 'At least we tried.' She rubbed her hands together, then stuck them under her arms for warmth.

'I suppose we just have to wait and hope,' said Leander.

'We're on our way to Stafford, through Coven. What's in Stafford?' asked Charlotte.

'Coven?' said Felix, a memory stirring but still foggy. 'Did she mention anything else?'

'She said her secrets have been buried for eight years, whatever that means. I think she was suspicious. I might have been too nice.' Charlotte was shivering. Felix didn't know if it was because of the cold or the horror of the night's events.

'No luck here, either,' said Leander. 'We—'

'Wait.' Felix cut him off. Charlotte's words had loosened something in a dusty corner of his mind. An idea was waiting just beyond his grasp. *Buried for eight years.* He dropped to the floor, combing through papers they'd already checked. 'Leander, quick. *The Grimoire of Marsh and Blight,* where did we put it?'

'Which one is it?' Leander joined him on the floor.

'The blue one with the golden edges.' Charlotte pulled her feet up on to the bench to give them space.

'Got it.'

Felix clambered on to the seat beside Charlotte. Leander began tidying away the papers.

'Where is it, where is it?' Felix turned the book upside down and shook it, causing a shower of dried petals and paper scraps to fall into his lap. He discarded the book to sort through them. 'I saw a note. I had a nagging feeling it might mean something.'

He pushed a scrap of paper into Charlotte's hand and she unfolded it, revealing a verse written in a scratchy, slanted hand.

> *Be gone from this house,*
> *Be gone down the hill,*
> *Go back to your king,*
> *You have eaten your fill.*

'Poetry?' Charlotte suggested.

'Not poetry,' said Felix. 'It's a letter to the rats, asking them to leave a house.'

Leander shuddered and tucked his legs in, as though the mention of rats might summon them. 'Ask them to leave? Why not just kill them?'

Felix shook his head. 'You should never kill a rat. There are whole kingdoms of them. Kill one and dozens will come for revenge. If you ask nicely . . .'

'But what's the use in writing a note? Rats can't read, can they?' Leander said.

'Of course they can't read!' Charlotte's tone was scornful.

'What would you know?' said Felix. 'You've never understood the old ways.'

'Just because something is old doesn't mean it's right.'

'Just because someone had a tutor once doesn't mean they know everything,' snapped Felix. Now was not the time for Charlotte's opinions. He was on to something, he knew it . . .

'I don't need a tutor to tell me rats can't read!'

'You have to be right all the time!' Felix slammed his hand down on the book. The thud brought him to his senses and they all fell silent, listening for any sign that Pinchbeck had heard them.

Felix took a deep breath and closed his eyes for a moment. 'It's not important whether rats can read or not. Let me think.'

He ran his fingers over the looping scrawl on the fragile yellowing paper. This wasn't Pinchbeck's handwriting. It belonged to her husband, Edmund Pellar.

Pinchbeck had introduced Felix proudly to Pellar on that first day. *'He'll draw in custom for us. Listen to how well he can play,'* she'd said, and Felix had delighted in their praise as he performed for them. He remembered the tune he'd played for Pellar, and wished he could play it again to summon the memory.

Pellar had been gruff but kind, setting up a bed for Felix and making sure the boy had enough to eat. He was a tall man, older than Pinchbeck, with a strong, commanding presence.

That same evening, Pinchbeck was serving Pellar dinner at the tiny table in the wagon. 'Remember I mentioned the spirit rappings, and how much money they make? When we do it, Felix here could play music to set the mood.'

'Hmm.' Pellar had been stony-faced, giving nothing away.

'And just imagine if the boy had a disappearing trick, to make it seem like the violin was haunted!' Pinchbeck spoke like someone telling a child that spinach was delicious – high and false and overly cheerful. She fussed and fluttered round her husband, almost giddy.

'No.' Pellar's voice was a bass drum.

'But darling, consider—'

He grabbed Pinchbeck by the arm. Felix pressed back into the corner, fearful things would get violent. 'No. That's my final word, Augustina. Don't test me.'

He walked out and Pinchbeck stomped and sulked her way through the evening. That night Felix woke to the sound of hushed arguing.

'You've already done it, haven't you?' came Pellar's voice, demanding and low.

'No.'

'You promised you would stop, but he's like them, isn't he?'

Though it was pitch-dark, Felix could picture the disgust on Pellar's face. 'You betrayed my trust!'

'*Shh!* The boy will hear,' said Pinchbeck.

Felix pulled his blanket over his head and screwed up his eyes, wishing he was back at home, wishing for Isaak.

There came the scrape of chair legs on the wooden floor, the click of a latch, then the door swung shut, shaking the flimsy walls. Their voices faded away. Felix stayed put under his blanket, listening for their return, but the next morning he was alone. He stayed by the cart, sweeping and dusting and collecting firewood, but Pellar and Pinchbeck were still gone when he settled himself back down to sleep that evening.

When she finally returned, a full day later, Pinchbeck wore a black veil. 'Edmund took ill in the night. I didn't want to frighten you. We went for the doctor, but it was too late to save him,' she said. She was gentle, reassuring, holding Felix's hand tightly like she was afraid to lose him, too. 'It was the fever.'

There was no further explanation. It struck Felix as a little strange because the man hadn't seemed unwell, but what did he know of doctors and fevers? His tentative questions were met with tears and he quickly learned it was not his place to wonder. He tagged along to the church, the stonemason, the coffin-maker, as Pinchbeck made arrangements. Back at the wagon, she filled a crate with the tools of Pellar's trade – bundles of herbs, cloth poppets, salt crystals. 'We'll bury them with him. It's what he would have wanted.'

That was it. Felix shook his head and blinked hard to dismiss thoughts of the past.

'Coven,' he said. 'That's where Pinchbeck's husband is buried. I was there … it was eight years ago.'

'Secrets buried for eight years,' said Charlotte.

The candle spluttered and flickered. Leander scrambled to light another before it burned out.

'She buried him with his own charms and trinkets—' said Felix, and Charlotte was quick to follow his thought.

'You think she buried something important with her husband?' she asked. 'Something we could use?'

'There was a whole boxful of things to go in the coffin. Mostly rubbish, I thought, but maybe … After all, Coven isn't the quickest way to get to Stafford. There must be a reason to go there.'

His thoughts were in tangles. He hadn't thought about Pellar in a long time. But, now that he did, Felix remembered he had travelled through Coven with Pinchbeck many times, even though it was a tiny, unimportant village, without even a proper inn. It had been years since their last visit, soon after she stole Charlotte. Or was it after she stole the last little girl, Rosa? Pinchbeck must have a reason for heading back that way now.

'We need to look in the coffin,' Felix said.

'Disturbing a grave – that's hideous,' Leander said.

'It's all we've got.' Felix felt like he was shivering on the inside, but managed to keep his voice steady. Pinchbeck trusted him. And she had taken him all round the country so he could look for Isaak. If he did this, it would be a betrayal he could never recover from. But he couldn't lose Charlotte. And now there was Leander to consider, too. Felix felt as if his soul was being pulled in two directions, in danger of tearing at the seams.

'What if she buried another grimoire, one that tells us how to break her spell? Or, or what if one of the amulets she buried is the source of her magic somehow?'

It made sense that she would hide any object that could undo her magic somewhere the children could never reach it.

'If that's where she gets her magic from –' Leander jumped up, excited, and banged his head against a pan hanging from the ceiling – 'maybe she'll get more, and keep all of us.'

'I don't—' Felix began, but Leander interrupted.

'I know we want to escape. But if she could keep all of us that'd be the next best thing, yes? At least we'd be together and safe.'

'No!' Charlotte grabbed his wrist. 'You didn't hear her. She's finished with me. She doesn't want me any more.'

'And, even if she could keep all three of us, it will never be enough,' said Felix. 'She'll want fresh children for her ghostly photographs. She'll have to steal more.'

'And it won't be any old children,' said Charlotte. 'Now that she's seen what someone like my uncle will pay to see a child he loved again, don't you think Pinchbeck will want more of the same?'

Leander's eyes widened. 'You mean . . . she'll take children from families? Happy children? Safe children?' He stared at the others as the realization sank in. Felix had never seen him looking so pale. 'It'll be a whole new business. Stealing children just so she can summon their "ghosts" for profit.'

The wind whipped round the carriage and blew in through the cracks, bitter and cruel.

'We're the only ones who can stop her,' whispered Leander.

'It's only a few miles to Coven. She'll wake before then,' said Felix.

Charlotte produced a green glass bottle, no bigger than her thumb, from one of the drawers. 'Laudanum. Let's get the carriage as close to Coven as we can. Then we'll help her down into the carriage to warm up, and I'll put a few drops in her drink.'

14

The Hanged Man:
An Involuntary Pause,
Reversal of Fortune, Change

LEANDER

The night was as cold and clear and still as glass. The three children left Pinchbeck slumbering beneath her blankets in the carriage and set out under the moonlight. Foxes were fighting in the distance, making an awful sound like a baby wailing in the darkness. The trees reached out with gnarled branches, and half-dead brambles scratched and snagged at their clothes.

Exactly the right kind of night for grave robbing.

It was wrong to be excited, but Leander was giddy, like his blood was full of bubbles, and red-hot fear pulsed through his chest with each breath. The world had never seemed so vivid and alive. It was very late, and they'd had no rest, but they moved tirelessly on. Leander carried a shovel, Felix the lamp from the front of the carriage.

'Where's the grave, Felix?' whispered Charlotte. 'Do you remember what the headstone looked like?'

'In a corner, near the walls. I've never seen the stone; we moved on before the soil settled.'

'What if there isn't one?' said Leander. If the grave wasn't marked, they were lost. They'd drugged Pinchbeck for nothing.

'There is. I remember us visiting the mason,' said Felix.

They split up to find the stone. Charlotte had printed the name on a scrap of paper so Leander could match it to the inscriptions, but the stones were worn and mossy. The others worked faster, checking three or four stones to Leander's one. He was shamefully slow.

John Walker Cartwright, aged sixty-six.
In Loving Memory of Catherine George.
Benjamin Shotton, at peace.
Sacred to the memory of Edmund Pellar.

Pellar!

Leander's heart thumped against his ribs. He'd found it! He whistled and the others were with him in a trice.

The headstone was surprisingly grand, though very overgrown and set crookedly in the ground. No one had tended this grave in years. Apart from the name, the only thing engraved on the stone was a strange symbol made up of triangles and a single curving line, which, if Leander squinted his eyes, could almost be the outline of a rat.

'Quickly,' said Charlotte, 'before I change my mind.'

But digging up a grave was not quick. The clay-rich soil was almost frozen, hard and heavy. They had only one shovel between them – the one Pinchbeck kept on hand in case a carriage wheel got stuck in the mud. A trowel was lying discarded by the wall and they grabbed it, two digging while the other stood stamping their feet and tucking their hands under their arms for warmth. Progress was painfully slow, bodies burning with the effort, fingers numb with the cold. The longer it took, the more chance of them being discovered, or of Pinchbeck waking to find them gone. Leander's imagination twisted the trees into Pinchbeck's shape and transformed every sound into the swish of her skirts or the click of her heels.

'Not much further,' said Felix after an age. The edge of the hole was already at his shoulders. 'I can feel something.' They scrabbled and scraped at the dirt, revealing the long, thin shape of a coffin.

This was it, then. They were going to commit a terrible sin. Now they were actually here, the plan seemed foolish – and gruesome. In Leander's old life, he would've scoffed at fairy tales about curses and hidden spellbooks. But here they were, three enchanted children in an open grave. Would Edmund Pellar's resting place hold magic that could save their lives, or nothing but a mouldering pile of bones and rags?

The coffin lid shifted beneath them. All three shuffled back as close to the muddy edges as possible lest it crack completely.

'We've made a terrible mistake.' Charlotte's voice shook.

160

'If Pinchbeck comes here, she'll see the earth disturbed and know what we've done.'

'If we find the answer here, it won't matter,' said Felix.

'And, if we don't, she'll kill us all.'

'Too late now.'

The wind dropped and the world was silent apart from their ragged, terrified breath.

'I'll do it.' Leander surprised even himself. As frightened as he was, this was his chance to be the hero, and make up for his earlier cowardice. 'I'll prise it open.'

The other two climbed out to give him room, and stood like mourners above him, caked in grave dirt. Charlotte's hair was half loose from her braids and they all glistened with sweat despite the chilly air.

Leander lined up the shovel with the edge of the coffin lid and planted his foot on top of it. He would be brave. There was no other choice. He made the sign of the cross, then forced the shovel into the coffin and leaned on the handle with all his weight.

The lid budged a little, then stopped. He shoved against the handle again and this time there was a hard crack, like the snap of a whip. The old wood splintered and gave way, leaving a hole in the lid the size of a dinner plate.

'I can't bear to look. Is it awful?' said Charlotte, covering her eyes.

'I can't see anything,' said Felix, peering into the gap.

Determined, Leander shifted the shovel and repeated the action nearer to the tapered top. Nails began to pull

161

away from wood. After a third time, he crouched in the narrow space and forced his fingers under the lid. In his imagination, he saw ghostly fingers touching his; he pushed the vision away.

Closing his eyes as tight as he could, he flung back the lid. It hit the other side of the pit with a wet thud.

Breathing shallow and shaky, he straightened up and pushed his shoulders back against the edge of the hole. He didn't care about the others seeing how scared he was now. He wanted to be far away from the corpse before he opened his eyes.

Would it still have skin?

Would it look like a person?

He clutched the shovel to his chest for protection and opened his eyes.

The coffin was empty.

Well, at least there was no body. Instead, the wooden box was filled with broken rocks and twigs and long-dead leaves.

'How can it be?' said Felix.

'Where is he?' said Leander, flooded with relief.

Charlotte dared to peep. 'Bodysnatchers? Or has it rotted away?'

'Wood rots faster than bones,' said Felix. 'And graverobbers wouldn't trouble themselves to leave bricks in his place.'

'How did Edmund Pellar die?' Charlotte asked him.

'I don't know. Pinchbeck said something about a fever.'

'Did you see him?' Leander asked. 'Did you see the body laid out before the funeral?'

Felix slowly shook his head. 'Do you think he was never in the coffin at all?'

Leander crouched down and rummaged through the debris, hoping they were missing something in the dark. There were a few scraps of fabric – perhaps the remains of the poppets Felix described – and bundles of skeletal leaves that were probably once herbs. He passed them up to the others as he found them. A rusted spoon. A few feathers. A knotted piece of string. No mysterious objects or books or anything that looked remotely magical.

'Why bury an empty coffin?' said Leander. If Pellar was dead, what had Pinchbeck done with the body? If Pellar wasn't dead, why go to the expense of a funeral? Pinchbeck loved money – why waste so much if it wasn't needed?

The disappointment in the air was palpable. Their plan had come to nothing. As if in sympathy, the first cloud of the night passed over the moon and the churchyard grew as dark as pitch.

'What now?' said Charlotte, defeated.

The moon reappeared from its shroud and in the new light Leander noticed something he had missed at the bottom of the coffin. It was a tiny hinged box of dark, cracked leather.

'What's this?' He passed it up to Charlotte before scrabbling out of the grave, toes slipping and fingers struggling to find purchase on the loose soil.

'A jewellery box?' she said. 'Maybe for a wedding ring?'

'Come on. We need to fill in the earth and go,' said Felix. 'We've taken too long already.'

'Here, you can have it,' Charlotte said and tossed the small box to Leander. He opened it, then turned it upside down and shook it. Nothing.

Then a smell of earth after a great storm made the hairs on every part of his body stand on end. There was a sensation in his chest as if he had breathed out too deeply and his lungs were empty. It was just like the odd sensation he felt when Pinchbeck first captured him.

Suddenly a figure coughed into life before them. A full-grown man had emerged and was bent over, leaning heavily on the headstone as though he hadn't the strength to stand. He was coughing the deep, coarse rattle of the nearly dead. The children all stepped back. Charlotte's cold hand found its way into Leander's and he took it gratefully.

'Where is she?' said the man, though his voice was as dry as pine cones and old paper, and the children could barely hear him. None of them answered, too struck with fear to speak.

Then ...

'Pellar,' whispered Felix.

Leander and Charlotte turned to look at Felix. This was Edmund Pellar? Not *dead* but *captive* all these years. Leander's heart thudded with anticipation and understanding. The jewellery box was a Cabinet!

Pellar was a very tall man, despite his stoop. His hair was white and wild, standing up several inches around his head

164

in all directions in a fiendish imitation of a halo. His clothes were equally strange. Beneath his wrinkled greatcoat was a smart waistcoat in emerald green, decorated with all manner of peculiar charms – feathers and sticks and buttons and animal teeth.

Leander felt himself shaking with fear. The man in front of them would have been frightening even without the eerie setting.

'Where is Augustina?' he said in a gruff voice.

FELIX

Felix took a tentative half-step towards the man. Pellar was another prisoner, like them – no need to be scared. 'Mister Pellar, I'm—'

'You're the little brat she stole last.' Pellar glared like a hawk, ready to swoop on an injured rabbit. 'And you –' he jabbed a finger towards Charlotte and Leander – 'more cursed wretches, no doubt.' Raising his voice started his cough again.

'Pinchbeck captured you, too?' But Felix knew the answer. Had Pellar already been a prisoner when Felix met them? Or did Pinchbeck trap him the night Felix heard the argument? Pellar's Cabinet was a jewellery box – perhaps Charlotte had been right and it was a ring box … maybe that once contained a wedding ring.

Pellar came towards the children, moving with care as though taking the first cautious steps on to a frozen lake.

'Sent you back to get me, has she? Well, I won't go down

without a fight.' He whipped a jackknife from his pocket and waved it at them, wheezing with the effort. The sight was in equal parts terrifying and pathetic.

'Sir, we need help.' Felix put himself between the others and the blade. He had known Pellar once. Maybe he could reason with him.

The man made a snarling noise and began to shuffle away towards the churchyard gates. Felix followed, Leander and Charlotte a few steps behind. It was easy to outpace the broken old man.

Leander hopped in front of him. 'Can you tell us how to break Pinchbeck's spell?' But the man walked on as though the children were nothing more than flies buzzing round him.

Then Pellar halted. 'She promised me she'd never take another child. I said we'd be damned for such a sin. And then she dared to trap me, too!'

'We—' Charlotte tried to interject. Pellar noticed the ring box and snatched it from her grasp.

'Mine!' He stuffed it into his pocket. 'Tell your witch-mistress I shan't help her again!'

'No! Pinchbeck didn't send us.' Charlotte's desperation hurt Felix's heart. 'We need help! We dosed her. She doesn't even know we're here.'

Pellar stopped, as still as a statue except for his eyes, which darted from side to side. 'That so? Drugged her, eh?'

'We want to stop her. That's why we need your help,' said Leander.

'I'll stop her all right,' Pellar snarled. He folded in half from

166

the strength of his next cough, gesturing through splutters towards the bench by the churchyard wall.

Hesitantly, Felix offered the man his arm to lean on, and helped him over to the seat. There was a good man underneath this madness if only Felix could reach him.

'Where is she, then?' Pellar lowered himself on to the bench.

'But a quarter-mile away, sir, slumbering in her carriage,' said Felix.

Pellar sniffed the air. 'I've a fearsome hunger. Did you bring vittles?'

'No, we—'

'Here.' Leander dug into his coat pocket and produced a fistful of sweets and broken biscuits, which he dropped into Pellar's outstretched hands.

Pellar plucked a piece of fluff from the corner of a biscuit. 'Beggars en't choosers, eh?' He tipped the sugarplums into his mouth all at once and crunched through them with a force which surely must have hurt his teeth.

'Can you help us?' said Charlotte as the broken biscuits disappeared into his mouth.

'Why should I trust you? I was tricked before by Augustina.'

'We're the same as you,' pleaded Charlotte.

'There's three of us. We don't think she has enough magic to keep us all,' added Leander. 'We need to find a way to break her spell and we thought you could help.'

'We'll *die* if you don't,' said Felix.

'Die? You'd be lucky,' the man said. The words were a trickle

167

of cold water down Felix's spine. 'Augustina collects spirits. Yer not the first, you won't be the last. But she's not a killer—'

'She is!' Leander cried. 'She's got jars of broken Cabinets and—'

'Let a man speak!' bellowed Pellar, which started another round of great hacking coughs. They echoed off stone walls, loud enough to wake the dead.

The children crowded close together in the near darkness. The man obviously wouldn't be rushed, and Felix tried to remain patient, but was starting to worry about how much longer the laudanum would keep Pinchbeck asleep.

At last Pellar spoke again. 'Augustina en't a killer so much as she's a miser. A hoarder. First lot of children she took – first I knew of, at least – she said they were dyin'. Said stealin' them was the only way to save them. Like a fool I believed her. Didn't like it, mind, but she promised we'd find a way to set it right.'

'You helped her steal children?' said Leander. 'So you're as wicked as she is!'

Pellar turned to Leander with a stare that could melt lead. 'Nay! I told you, she made me believe it was for good reasons. And so I helped her hide them away once she had them, so she wouldn't be weakened. Just until we found out how to set them free without them dyin', or so she told me. Then *you* came –' he poked Felix square in the chest – 'and when she took you I realized she'd never really stopped. She was still collectin' spirits, just in secret. She couldn't help herself.'

Felix's head was swimming. There was truth in the old

man's tale, he could tell. That's why they'd argued on the night Pinchbeck had taken him, and why she'd decided to take Pellar captive, too. She didn't want him getting in the way of her plans.

'No. She can't collect spirits!' said Charlotte. 'Pinchbeck can only hold two captives at once. That's why it's been just me and Felix for so long. She's already weak from the three of us. If there were more—'

'There are ways of containin' magic, child, of keepin' it under wraps so it don't spill out and contaminate you,' Pellar interrupted. 'Kept me contained at the same time as you three, didn't she?'

The leaves in the coffin: now Felix understood what they meant. Pinchbeck had used Pellar's own charms and talismans and the weight of the earth to hold him inside so he couldn't drain her power.

'And she'll never stop stealin' folks, and hidin' them away. Mark my words.'

'But why?' said Leander.

'Why does the cat chase rats?' Pellar asked.

'Hunger?' said Felix.

'Sport?' said Leander.

'Instinct?' said Charlotte.

Pellar nodded. 'The cat can't tell you why. He only knows that he *must*. Can't help the way he's made. Same with Augustina. She must.'

'She uses us, too,' said Charlotte. 'To make money, she needs us. It's her greed that keeps her going, too.'

'Perchance.' The man dusted biscuit crumbs from his lap, then leaned forward. 'But it's more than that. She wanted money. I gave her money. She wanted company. We travelled side by side. I bought her all the finery she asked for. When she had this odd fancy to conjure spirits for a livin', didn't I make it happen? I provided everything she wanted. Still, even when I asked her to stop takin' children, she stole the boy. Couldn't help herself.'

How many souls had she taken altogether? How many are trapped elsewhere, like Pellar? Felix wondered, a sharp pain radiating through his chest at the thought.

Felix had seen Pinchbeck steal four other children, apart from Charlotte and Leander. Did this mean some of them might be trapped somewhere, and not dead as he'd always believed?

'Evil is her nature,' Pellar continued. 'She's festerin' on the inside. There's no reasonin' with her. She won't stop unless we stop her.'

'You'll help us, then?' said Charlotte.

'Aye.' He got shakily to his feet. 'Quickly. Show me where she is.'

The man began walking towards the churchyard gates, faster this time, despite his uneven gait and hunched posture. The children scrambled to follow him. Felix's heart was in his throat – after years in limbo, it seemed everything was happening at once. He wanted to clamp his hands over his ears to shut out the world and think for a moment. Pinchbeck had stolen and discarded even more children than Felix had ever suspected. It was so cruel and ruthless. But she had kept Felix all these years. He was special to her. Wasn't he?

'Which way? Hurry, before she wakes.'

They led him along the winding lane towards Pinchbeck's carriage. Leander raced a little way ahead, then jogged back impatiently, but Pellar moved at his own unchanging pace.

'What do you need?' asked Charlotte. 'Herbs? Candles?'

'Bare hands shall do it,' said Pellar, expression grim.

'How will you undo the magic?' said Leander. 'Is it a spell, or—?'

'Nay,' said Pellar. 'I'm goin' to kill her.'

'You can't!' said Felix. Bad enough to betray Pinchbeck this far. Now they were sending an executioner for her! And Pinchbeck had always threatened that if harm should befall her . . . 'We're all under her spell. If you kill her, all of us will die.'

'There's no choice. The spell can't be broken. Dyin' is better than the purgatory I've been in!'

Charlotte and Leander shared the same open-mouthed expression of horror.

'What year is it?' the old man said.

'Seventy-six, sir,' said Leander.

'Eight years I've been trapped in there. Eight years of torture. And look at you.' He pointed at Felix. 'Not an inch taller nor a day older than when I met you. Eight years she's stolen from you.'

A new feeling was stirring in Felix's chest. A feeling he didn't have a name for. Pellar was right. Pinchbeck had done a terrible thing to all of them. It was as though Felix had been blind to her wickedness all this time, so wrapped up in his search for his brother, so grateful for food and companionship that he didn't see her for what she was.

'Listen, bairns. I'm dreadful sorry for the wrong you've been done. You didn't deserve this fate.' He wiped a sleeve across his forehead. 'If I could go back and stop her, I would. But it's too late. And I can't stand by and let her do this to another child. Not while there's breath left in my body.'

Felix persisted. 'But sir, you'll die, too.'

'A sacrifice I'm willing to make. I'm ready to meet my maker. At least I shall have the pleasure of standin' side by side with Augusta to see her judgement handed down by the Almighty.'

Leander stood in front of Pellar, hands on hips. 'You can't do this to us! You talk of saving children, well, what about us?' he said. 'We're children, too.'

'If I don't kill Augusta, more children will meet your tragic fate. Is that what you want, boy?' Pellar waved the ring box in Leander's face. 'She told me being inside a Cabinet was like sleepin'. More lies. Years I've been stuck in that place – no light, no feelin', nothin' but the sound of my own nightmares. This was my punishment for not helpin' her. She deserves to die.'

'But *we* don't!' Charlotte joined Leander.

'I'm sorry, but you were dead the moment you met her.' He shoved his way through the children. 'I'll spare you my sufferin'. Believe me, little ones: a swift death is better

172

than being for ever in a box. I have to stop her, whatever the cost.'

'Is there no other way?' said Felix. 'You were a wise man, I remember. You must have some inkling of how to undo her magic.'

'An inklin'. Aye. There might be another way, but there's no time to waste sparin' thoughts on that. Every hour she walks the earth is a danger.' Pellar paused and looked Felix up and down, and Felix saw a flash of the old, kind Pellar in his expression. 'Still a wee boy, after all these years. A pity, lad. A real shame. Let us put an end to this. Take me to her.'

'Run!' Felix dashed past the old man and up the lane, trusting the others would follow. He could tell the man would not be persuaded, so now they had to get Pinchbeck far away before Pellar reached her.

'Do as you will, children!' Pellar shouted after them. 'We'll meet again once I've found my gun.'

173

15

The Tower: Downfall, Upheaval, Disaster

CHARLOTTE

The three children raced through narrow streets, over the bridge and out to the edge of town. Charlotte kept glancing over her shoulder, expecting to see that ghoulish man at her back, but there was nobody there. Her worn shoes slipped on patches of ice and she struggled to keep up with the boys in their sturdy boots.

They were at the carriage in minutes, the horses unsettled by their hurried arrival. Charlotte peeped inside to check Pinchbeck was still asleep.

'She hasn't stirred.'

Felix coaxed the horses back on to the road.

'Hurry,' said Charlotte as they clambered on to the driving seat. 'If Pellar gets to Pinchbeck, we're all dead.'

Maybe they were dead anyway. Charlotte couldn't imagine

what excuse they could give for moving the carriage away from Coven.

'The horses are tired.' Felix's expression was bleak.

'They won't let us down,' said Charlotte, and tried to believe it. 'Any distance will help. Pellar's a captive, like us. He must be bound by the same rules. The further he is from Pinchbeck, the weaker he'll be.'

Charlotte urged the horses on and the coach rattled forward. Charlotte was sure she'd never heard it creak so loudly, nor the horses' hooves echo with such force over the stones, but Pinchbeck slumbered on.

At least the noise meant their voices wouldn't carry.

'Do you think it's true, then?' said Leander. 'There is no way to break her spell?'

'He didn't say that. He said that there was no time to waste thinking on it. Which might mean there *is* a way, no matter how unlikely. We must believe that,' said Charlotte. 'Or there's no hope.'

She glanced at Felix who was strangely quiet. He was staring ahead, seemingly lost in his own thoughts.

Just hours ago, Charlotte's greatest fear was that Pinchbeck would smash her Cabinet and she'd die, but Pellar's words had sparked fresh terror. Maybe the half-crazed old man was right – death was nothing compared to the horror of wakeful eternity in a box. Her mind drifted back to her uncle. What she'd give for the comfort of Litchfield House, for kind voices and soft sheets and stories by the fire.

'You all right?' asked Leander.

'I was thinking of home.'

'You'll go back one day.'

She couldn't allow herself to entertain such dreams. She offered him the best smile she could manage, but shook her head.

'I'll help you,' he said. 'Promise.'

'Thank you, Leander,' said Charlotte. 'I wish I'd been kinder to you when you first arrived. I was . . . I was scared – I'm still scared – but it's not your fault. You were tricked just like us. And you were really brave back there in the graveyard. I'm glad that you're here. We're going to need all your courage now.'

She gazed out over the empty hillside rather than let Leander see how close to tears she was. She wouldn't cry. She was more courageous than that. The horses thundered on.

After they had driven for two hours, Leander needed to relieve himself and they pulled up beside the hedgerow. The first hint of dawn gave the sky a pinkish hue. Charlotte stretched her limbs, wriggled her fingers and marched about to warm herself. Leander was barely back from the brambles when a low groan came from the carriage.

It rocked with the shifting weight inside – Pinchbeck must still be clumsy from the tincture. Charlotte hopped up on to the driving seat, instinctively seeking higher ground, and Leander followed suit. Felix stood, stroking Marigold's mane, perhaps to soothe himself more than the horse.

Pinchbeck would know immediately that the carriage

had moved. She'd be suspicious. *Be calm. Act like you've done nothing wrong.* Charlotte tried to calm herself.

Pinchbeck gave a wordless yell when she stepped on to the track.

'What game is this?' she cried. 'Where are we?'

Charlotte wanted to invent a clever excuse, but nothing came. Her mind kept returning to the demented ghost pursuing them, ready to hunt Pinchbeck down and condemn them all to hell. Pinchbeck hobbled over to them. She looked to have aged ten years overnight – Pellar's release must be weakening her faster still.

It didn't make her any less terrifying. Physical strength wasn't needed to command them into their Cabinets, or smash Charlotte's delicate lantern.

'You,' said Pinchbeck, pointing a finger at the spot between Charlotte's eyes. 'You did something to my drink. Tell me, or live to regret it!'

'Perhaps ... perhaps it was a little too strong?' she stammered.

'Liar.' Pinchbeck's voice was steady and controlled which was much more worrying than when she shouted. 'There's no room in heaven for liars, Charlotte.'

Her eyes were narrow and bright as she moved closer, close enough that Charlotte could see a few wiry grey hairs sprouting from a mole beside her nose which wasn't there before. The image of a tail swishing behind her in the darkness came into Charlotte's head from nowhere, but vanished almost as soon as it arrived.

'Well. Why are we not in Coven as I commanded?'

None of the children answered. Charlotte could almost feel Leander's heart pounding behind her. She hoped he'd have the sense to keep his mouth shut for once.

'Not only do you disobey me, you're too cowardly to explain yourselves.' Pinchbeck's mouth stretched into a chilling smile as she focused her gaze on Charlotte. 'You've always been trouble. Rude. Defiant. And now there's no reason for me to tolerate it any longer. I've a special punishment for you.'

'Wait!' shouted Leander. Felix stepped in front of Pinchbeck, arms outstretched.

'Don't think you're off the hook, boys. You're all going to learn what happens when you disobey me.' Her stare was still fixed on Charlotte.

'Don't hurt them,' Charlotte begged.

'*Abeo!*' Pinchbeck cried.

A crushing pain flooded Charlotte from inside out as her body faded away from her mind. There was a click and a shiver as the lantern was locked shut. She could not escape.

What would become of her now?

FELIX

Felix was wracked with an agony he had not felt since Isaak first disappeared. His conscience clawed at him. And, locked in with his violin but unable to touch it, he couldn't soothe his mind with melody.

What had become of Charlotte and Leander? Had

Pinchbeck broken their Cabinets? Felix was still alive so the violin case must be intact. For now. He pushed with his mind, trying to emerge, but he couldn't. His Cabinet was closed. He was at Pinchbeck's mercy.

What had he done? He had promised to serve Pinchbeck faithfully in exchange for her help to find Isaak, and now Felix had broken their agreement. If Pinchbeck was to discover the full extent of his mutiny, would he ever get the chance to search for his little brother again?

But he had to help Charlotte. *I sacrificed my brother for her, and may have lost them both.*

Worst of all, Felix could do nothing but wait.

LEANDER

The locket was closed. Leander was sealed inside his Cabinet.

Although this was not the first time Pinchbeck had closed the locket, it was the worst. Previously, when she had closed their Cabinets on the way into a seance, Leander had always felt calm, knowing it was not for long. This time was different. Pinchbeck was angry.

What if she destroyed their Cabinets? Decided it was easier to get rid of them all?

He tried to force his way out, but nothing happened. Not even the pain he felt when he first tried to resist being pulled inside – nothing at all.

Leander felt so desperately alone. More alone than he'd been when he slept by himself in the library because now he had come close – so close! – to finding himself part of a family again. It hadn't been long, but he had come to think of Felix and Charlotte as true friends. And now … had he lost them for ever?

Leander had been so naive to trust Pinchbeck. *Whatever happens*, he told himself, *if I get out of this locket, I will do whatever it takes to free us all.*

16
Wheel of Fortune: A Sudden Twist of Fate

LEANDER

'*Exsisto!*'

A sharp gust of air swept over Leander as the locket was unlatched. Relief was quickly followed by fear, as bitter as chicory, wondering what might await him. But he didn't resist – there was no pain as he stepped, blinking, into the world. Felix emerged from his violin case half a breath behind him.

Leander waited for Charlotte to appear, but she wasn't there. The spot in the carriage where her lantern normally rested was occupied instead by a large jar half filled with broken glass. Felix gave the tiniest shake of his head – a warning not to say anything – and Leander bit his tongue to keep from crying out.

Pinchbeck stood smiling before them, uncomfortably close in the cramped carriage. Her hand rested on the shelf next to the jar, making sure the boys noticed it. She had changed into a green gown and the peacock hat from their first meeting. He noticed that her hair was darker and her skin seemed fresher than before.

Because she has one less Cabinet draining her, thought Leander. *Because Charlotte is gone.*

Charlotte had been right. Pinchbeck didn't want her any more. The monster had used Charlotte for a purpose and then discarded her like she was nothing. Leander clenched his jaw, fighting to look calm when he wanted to scream.

'Good morning, boys. Please see to the horses.' She sat by the hamper from Lord Litchfield's estate, unwrapped a fruit pie and took a dainty bite. 'Behave nicely and you can have some of this fine food.'

The boys climbed out of the carriage in silence. They were in a town, with a short row of houses some hundred feet behind them and the edge of a market just in sight in the opposite direction. The horses were grazing on a patch of rough grass at the side of the road.

'Charlotte's gone!' The words burst out of Leander as soon as they were a few paces away. It was all he could do to whisper. 'Pinchbeck *killed* her.' Vomit burned in his throat and his eyes stung.

Felix pulled Leander by the sleeve until they were on the opposite side of the carriage to Pinchbeck, out of her line of sight. 'That wasn't Charlotte's Cabinet in the jar.' He sounded calm, but was as white as a sheet. 'The glass was the wrong colour. Blueish. And thick.'

'What is it, then?'

'The lemonade bottle from the hamper, if I had to guess. Pinchbeck wants us to think it's Charlotte's lantern so we won't look for her.' Felix rubbed the flank of the chestnut horse and gently led her back to the carriage.

Leander rubbed his fists against his eyes, trying to wipe away the image of Charlotte's lantern smashed into a thousand pieces. He imagined her staring into his eyes and pleading for help as she gradually turned to dust and blew away on the wind. 'Are you certain?'

'She's trying to scare us into line.' Felix began hitching up the first horse. Leander tried his best to help, tightening straps where Felix pointed.

'Then Charlotte might still be here?'

'Not in the carriage,' said Felix. 'Or she'd have appeared when Pinchbeck said "*abeo*", hidden or not. The command works on all Cabinets within earshot.'

Not dead then, but not here, either.

'Which means Pellar was telling the truth. Pinchbeck must keep all her old Cabinets hidden somewhere.'

Leander's heart leaped. If Charlotte was alive, there was hope. 'How can we find her?'

'Shh,' Felix reminded him. He shaded his eyes and squinted up at the sun. 'We may have a chance still.'

A lady with a basket walked by.

'Excuse me, miss, what day is it?' said Felix.

'Friday the first,' she replied without stopping.

'Thank you,' said Felix, then waited until the woman was

out of earshot before continuing. 'It's the same day. Pinchbeck shut us away at dawn and it isn't even noon yet. She had to hide Charlotte's Cabinet, travel here, let the horses graze.'

'So Charlotte must be near,' said Leander, picking up Felix's meaning. 'We can't leave this town without her.'

Pinchbeck wasn't foolish enough to stay near the scene of her crime for long. If the horses hadn't needed to eat, they'd most likely have been gone already.

'How do you take off a horseshoe?' asked Leander, an idea forming. He peeped round the side of the carriage to see if Pinchbeck was paying attention, but she hadn't left the carriage.

'If it's already loose, I can do it,' said Felix. 'Is she losing one?'

'No. But if she did . . .'

'. . . Pinchbeck might stay until the farrier can see her. Worth a try.'

There was a modest collection of tools in the carriage, but neither boy wanted to risk Pinchbeck's wrath by going back inside.

'Scout about in the dirt,' suggested Felix. 'Find me a flat stone with sharp corners. A bit of slate will do.'

They searched the muddy undergrowth at the side of the lane, picking up handfuls of twigs so they could claim to be gathering firewood if Pinchbeck saw them. Once Felix found something that would work, they returned to the horses. It would have to be Marigold, they both agreed, for she was the more flighty of the two, and so more likely to refuse to pull.

'Talk to her, keep her soothed,' Felix instructed Leander.

He took one hoof between his hands and held her leg tight between his knees. Leander heard him whisper, 'Forgive me, Marigold.'

Marigold stirred and twitched her ears. Leander murmured nonsense words to keep her calm. *If Pinchbeck catches us . . .* Felix wedged the stone in as best he could, positioning it where it would make her foot sore as she walked on the hard road. He straightened up and gave her a little rub by way of apology.

'Are you done?' Pinchbeck called. Leander heard the carriage door swing open.

'Almost,' said Felix, and Leander looked away and gripped the leather bridle iron-tight to disguise his shaking hands. 'The horses are tired; they need to rest.'

'They'll rest when we get to the city. News of my seance and ghost photography will be spreading by now. I'm sure the papers will want to speak to me.' The corner of Pinchbeck's mouth curled up into the slightest hint of a smile, almost daring them to ask about Charlotte. Leander couldn't trust himself to speak. After a centuries-long moment, Pinchbeck said, 'Hop up here, then!' and climbed on to the driving seat. Felix and Leander did as they were told.

Marigold did not let them down. Almost immediately, she began to limp slightly, lifting her left hoof a little higher off the ground. She slowed, despite Pinchbeck's urging, and when the dirt track became cobble, just past the market, refused to pull.

Marigold shifted her weight from hoof to hoof, raised

her head and shook it in warning when Pinchbeck tried to check her sore foot. Pansy was unsettled, too, sensing her companion was hurt.

Pinchbeck unhitched Marigold and led her on to the grass, though the ground was so hard with frost it was unlikely to offer much relief.

'Felix, run back into town,' Pinchbeck ordered, still holding on to the horse. 'Get directions to the farrier. Tell him to come out here as soon as possible.'

'Can I go with him?' asked Leander.

Pinchbeck narrowed her eyes.

'I want to see how they make the horseshoes,' Leander said with a smile and a shrug.

'Leave your locket here,' said Pinchbeck, holding out her hand.

Leander reluctantly took off the locket and gave it to her.

'Remember, dear boys, I have your Cabinets. If there's a moment of disobedience ...'

She didn't finish her sentence. She didn't need to for the threat to be understood.

The boys set off running.

'We won't have long to search for Charlotte, but it's something,' said Felix.

'Do you think we're looking for another grave?'

'No. Pinchbeck couldn't dig up a grave in daylight.'

'What then?' Leander shoved his hands into his pockets for warmth.

They crossed the road, past a public house called The

Four Ashes and a tailor's shop. 'Pellar said there are ways of keeping magic contained. Pinchbeck must be using charms and symbols,' said Felix.

'Like what?'

'The spellbooks talk of crosses, prayers, rosaries?'

'Those are everywhere! Every house ...' Leander felt like he'd swallowed a brick. It was impossible. They had no clues, no idea how many hiding places Pinchbeck had, no guarantee Charlotte would be in one of them. Was their best plan really just to wander around in the cold, looking for crosses?

He'd barely befriended Charlotte and now she was lost. He felt panicky and guilty – it hurt. This was what he got for trying to make friends and belong. He should have stayed in the library, alone. He didn't need other people – all they brought was pain.

He thought of his mother and wished his locket was round his neck, not hanging within reach of that wicked woman.

The two boys reached the farrier's workshop. A little girl scrubbing the front step with a donkey stone told them he was with a customer, but she'd pass on their message. They gave Pinchbeck's name and described where the carriage was waiting, and the girl wrote it on a slate in a spidery hand.

'Pinchbeck, you say?' A well-dressed man paused on his way out of the workshop. 'What Christian name?'

'Augustina, sir,' said Felix.

'Would she be Augustina Pinchbeck, the spiritualist?'

'Why?' said Leander. Felix jabbed his elbow into Leander's ribs. 'I mean, if it's not impolite to ask, sir, do you know her?'

The man frowned, then shook his head. 'I've heard the name, that's all.' He swept out of the door and away.

The farrier emerged, wiping his hands on his apron. 'Tell your mistress that I'll be there before sunset. I have to tend to another matter, and then I'll come.'

FELIX

Leander wanted to search for Charlotte right away. He was practically quaking with impatience, but Felix insisted it was better to return to the carriage first.

'Play at being good. After last night, Pinchbeck will be on the lookout for misbehaviour,' he said to Leander as they headed back.

With luck, Pinchbeck would decide to find lodgings and he and Leander could search through the night for Charlotte. But there was a chance that Pinchbeck might press on anyway. And who knew when they might pass through this town again? They needed another excuse to leave Pinchbeck before the farrier arrived.

'When we get back, I'll suggest we go busking in the marketplace. Pinchbeck won't turn down money.' Felix spoke with more confidence than he felt. She might let Felix go, but make Leander stay with her, and the boy might get himself in trouble without Felix to watch over him. He felt responsible for keeping Leander safe.

'Yes!' Leander bobbed on his toes, bouncing with nervous energy.

Felix's fingers itched for the pressure of the violin strings, the smooth and steady sway of the bow to loosen the tightness in his muscles. And perhaps, the faintest whisper of hope stirred in his chest, perhaps Charlotte would hear his music and know they were coming.

As they walked, Felix took out his holey stone and raised it to his eye, checking the surrounding area. *One never knows. I could be lucky.*

'What's that?' asked Leander.

'A holey stone. Hagstone.'

'But what is it?'

'It's a rock with a hole worn through the middle by flowing water. People say if you look through one, you'll find all the hidden and magical things human eyes don't notice.' He let Leander hold it and turn it over in his hands. 'Pinchbeck gave it to me, years ago, to . . .' He didn't want to talk about it, but he and Leander needed to trust each other. 'To help me find my little brother, Isaak.'

'Did you find him?'

'No.' He sighed. 'I still hope.'

'What do you think happened to him?' said Leander.

'I don't know.' Felix knew there was a good chance that Isaak was dead. He had been too small to look after himself, and it seemed impossible that he wouldn't come back to Felix if he could. He had no one else in the world, and nowhere else to go.

'It was nice of Pinchbeck to give you this magic stone, wasn't it?' said Leander, holding it up to his eye. 'What with all the horrible things she's done.'

Felix nodded. It was nice of Pinchbeck – uncharacteristically nice, considering how she often treated others. But Felix was different – he had always gone with Pinchbeck willingly, and wanted her seances to succeed. He didn't think of himself as stolen so much as employed.

It was increasingly uncomfortable to reflect on his agreement with Pinchbeck, when her recent actions had been so very wicked. In the past, it had been easier to overlook her cruel side and focus on everything she had given him. But more and more, Felix was torn between his loyalty to Pinchbeck and his love for Charlotte ... and now his growing fondness for Leander.

'Nothing looks different.' Leander handed the stone back to Felix.

'No,' said Felix, putting it away in his pocket. 'It never does.'

They rounded the corner leading to the lane with the carriage on and immediately something felt wrong.

Movement at the carriage up ahead; a disturbance.

Felix grabbed Leander's sleeve, urging him to stay quiet. Felix recognized trouble when he saw it.

Hold your nerve, watch and wait. The others are counting on you, he thought.

No one was looking in their direction, so the boys approached cautiously. Three men stood by the carriage, including the gentleman they had met at the farrier's shop.

Two of them held Pinchbeck between them. She was not struggling, but her face was full of poison.

Felix and Leander hopped into a ditch and crawled as near as they dared, trying to make out what was being said.

'The constable is acting on my instruction,' the gentleman from the shop said, his back to the children.

'And *you* are?' Pinchbeck's voice dripped with disdain.

'The magistrate of this parish.'

Felix took a deep breath. What would it mean for their quest if Pinchbeck was arrested?

'I understand you were recently the guest of Lord Litchfield,' the gentleman continued.

Leander made a sound: half gasp, half whimper. The gentleman looked over his shoulder. In panic, Felix almost fled to his Cabinet, then stopped himself, worried that Leander wouldn't have the sense to disappear, too. And he didn't want to leave the other boy exposed and alone. They stayed low, bellies to the ground, for twenty eternal seconds until the man began talking again.

'I've heard some troubling reports.' The gentleman turned his attention back to Pinchbeck and the boys raised their heads far enough to see over the ratty grass.

'Yes,' said Pinchbeck, her voice honey-smooth. 'People are often troubled by my work. Alas, I am cursed with a gift and must use it to help people. His Lordship was pleased with the results.'

Despite sleeping in her carriage, Pinchbeck looked respectable with her neat hair and fancy hat. She held herself with poise and spoke like a lady, and made it clear she expected to be treated as one.

'I'm here with regard to his niece,' said the magistrate.

Leander pressed a little closer to Felix's side.

'A tragedy. She appeared to me as a spirit. It was my sad duty to tell Lord Litchfield of her demise.'

'We have reason to believe you have the girl in your possession. Kidnap is a most grievous offence, Miss Pinchbeck.'

'*Madame* Pinchbeck,' she corrected him haughtily.

Joy washed over Felix like a high vibrato. Lord Litchfield must have found Charlotte's note and it convinced him to alert the magistrates! Leander must have been thinking the same thing and the boys shared a hopeful smile.

Pinchbeck laughed. 'You must have misunderstood. Lord Litchfield's niece died five years ago.'

'Just doing my duty, ma'am. I'm sure you understand.'

Felix clutched Leander's sleeve, half afraid the boy would leap up and blurt out the whole story. But, if Pinchbeck saw them, she'd command them into their Cabinets before they said a word. She'd manage to explain it away if the men saw anything strange – she was a medium after all. Disappearing children would only strengthen her claims that she was communing with spirits.

He felt Leander shaking, and then realized that he was shaking, too. Excitement and desperation tore at Felix's insides. He dug his fingers into the dirt to anchor himself as his mind whirred with possibilities. If Pinchbeck was taken by the constable, they would be able to search for

Charlotte without her interference. And, once they'd found her, Charlotte could send word to Lord Litchfield and then perhaps he'd come and help them. They wouldn't be able to travel all the way back to Litchfield House, of course – they'd be insubstantial if they strayed so far from Pinchbeck – but they could send a telegram.

He watched as Pinchbeck stood, erect and haughty, with the air of someone confident in her innocence. One of the men had let go of her arm and she slipped her hand into her dress pocket. Her eyes were alert and, though she looked calm, she was obviously worried. She looked round and the boys lowered their heads.

Above them, there came the familiar *bang-rattle* of the carriage door slamming shut. A deep voice spoke. 'No one here, Your Honour. No room to hide a child.'

'I must object,' said Pinchbeck. 'This is hardly the way to treat a lady.'

Please don't let them give up.

Another figure emerged from the carriage. His voice was higher pitched, barely a man. 'Found this, sir.'

Felix dared to peek. The boy passed something shiny to the magistrate.

'Well, look at this,' said the gentleman.

It was the silver sugar bowl from Litchfield House that Leander had brought with him in hopes of selling to Pinchbeck. This could be the luck they were waiting for.

The magistrate continued. 'I may not be able to prove you are a kidnapper, *Madame* Pinchbeck, but there's no doubt you are a thief. Constable, detain her. Send word to Lord Litchfield. Court will convene Monday morning. Keep a close watch on this villain.'

LEANDER

The boys agreed a plan in the quietest of whispers as Pinchbeck was marched off by the constable.

'We need to know where they're taking her,' said Felix. 'So we aren't stranded too far away. I'll follow at a safe distance.'

'I'll get the Cabinets,' said Leander. 'Then come after you.'

Felix shook his head. 'I'll come back for you. Don't get yourself lost.'

As Felix sneaked away, Leander stayed in the ditch and watched the constable's men search the carriage, praying they wouldn't move or break the Cabinets. They took a money bag and the pinboard of jewellery, mumbling that they were certainly stolen, then left, agreeing to leave the carriage behind until the farrier came for the injured horse.

The instant they were out of sight, Leander dived in. What luck! With Pinchbeck out of their way, they would find Charlotte. They had to. He dug out his old sack and stuffed it with anything that looked useful. He found his locket – thankfully hidden by the drapes and unnoticed by the men – and put it on. Felix's violin case had been pulled out, but left behind. The instrument was so old and tatty they probably assumed it was worthless. Leander fastened the case to protect the violin. Though he hated to shut Felix's Cabinet, he could not carry it otherwise.

The carriage was in complete disarray from the search. Glass jars had been smashed, allowing powders and potions to form a foul-smelling sludge on the floor. He took the shovel, a penknife, a small lamp and a tinderbox. He decided to leave the spellbooks and the book of fairy tales behind. They were heavy, and he was sure they had no more help to offer. The tarot cards might be useful to Felix, but they were scattered about on the floor and there wasn't time to collect them all. Maybe it didn't matter. Felix had said you didn't need to pick the right cards, but that *'the cards decide what they want to tell you'*. He grabbed them by the fistful and threw in as many as he could.

Crumpled on the floor, muddy from a boot print, lay Charlotte's yellow ribbon. Leander shuddered as he thought of her scared and alone somewhere.

He hesitated to leave the food hamper, but it was too big to carry and the men could be back at any moment; he settled for stuffing his pockets with handfuls of dried fruit. The bag tore as he slung it over his shoulder so he snatched up a blanket and heaped the things on top, gathered the corners together and heaved the whole uncomfortable bundle up on to his back.

How far away would Pinchbeck be taken? Felix said he would come back for him, but he could at least start walking in the same direction as the constable's men. He couldn't risk becoming insubstantial.

Onward. No time to waste. Pinchbeck was captured, at least until court on Monday, and they had the freedom to search for their friend. Luck was finally smiling on them.

CHARLOTTE

It was dark. Charlotte was used to that. The walls of her lantern were glass but, once inside, she could see nothing. Darkness did not scare her. What scared her was the absence of sound.

Even in her Cabinet, there was always something to hear: distant voices, muffled hoofbeats, birds singing.

Wherever she was now, it was silent.

By trying to escape her fate, it seemed she had only hastened it, like the classical myths she had once studied in her uncle's library. Another foolish mortal. Except, of course, she wasn't mortal, as far as she could tell, and if she was imprisoned it would be eternal.

Was this what Pellar had spoken of? Had Pinchbeck hidden her away in some secret place like buried treasure, forgotten for all the ages?

Was this what she had to look forward to – no light, no sound, no feeling – for ever?

Without physical form, Charlotte couldn't even weep.

17

Justice:
Law, Truth, Clarity

LEANDER

A breathless Felix raced towards Leander before he reached the end of the road.

'This way ...' He pointed back the way he'd come. 'They took her to the constable's house. I saw them search her pockets ... Her book – her commonplace book – they took it. Which means we can get it.'

The book which Pinchbeck had guarded so jealously, kept about her person day and night, made all her notes in. 'If she was going to write down where Charlotte is—'

'Exactly!' Felix was pink-cheeked and hopeful. 'Let's go.'

After handing Felix his violin case and tightening the grip on his bundle, Leander trotted behind him through narrow, winding streets lined with neat brick terraces and tiny stone cottages.

'This is wonderful,' said Leander. 'If we find Charlotte, we can get word to Lord Litchfield somehow, can't we? Do you think he can help us?'

'I hope so,' said Felix. 'This way, to the right.'

'I hope Pinchbeck goes to prison for ever!'

'I only hope she doesn't get sent far away. If they took her to the city by carriage, we'd never catch up before we turned insubstantial. Mind the puddle.'

That was a sobering thought. Even with Pinchbeck locked away, they weren't completely safe. But at least it gave them breathing room. Time to find Charlotte. Time to plot a way to get free. Fat drops of water began to splash down from the sky and drip from the uneven roofs and guttering. By the time they reached their destination, it was a proper shower.

The constable's house was squat and shadowy like a brown toad. It was set back from the road, a little distance from its neighbours and behind it sloping grass led up to the woods. They tiptoed to the back of the house, passing a small, windowless outhouse half sunk into the ground.

'Pinchbeck is locked in the root cellar,' Felix whispered, pointing at the outhouse. 'They must use it as a prison cell.'

Leander shivered at the thought of her just beyond the stone walls, waiting in the darkness. Their footsteps were as quiet as their breath.

'See there?' Felix pointed to a small window. The wooden frame was warped and swollen with damp – easy enough to pull open. Leander had broken into harder places. 'They searched her in that room and put everything she was carrying into a bag before they locked her up.'

Leander was taller than Felix and, with a boost, he was able to drag himself through the window. The floor indoors was higher, and it was only a small drop down to it, so it was easier to land quietly.

He found himself in a room that was something between an untidy parlour and an office. A tired old chair stood before a rickety desk strewn with papers, and hanging on the wall above was a needlepoint reading *Cleanliness is next to Godliness*. It was covered in dust.

'In the corner,' whispered Felix, his eyes just visible as he peeped over the window frame. 'Look under the desk.'

A familiar mix of thrill and shame brewed inside Leander as he crossed the floor. More than a few times, cold and hunger had pushed him into doing something criminal, and he'd become good at it. He tested the floorboards gingerly before transferring his weight.

Yes, there was a bag there, sitting alongside a pile of rusted chains and a coil of rope. Pinchbeck's coin purse was inside, a few crumpled handkerchiefs, a brass ring and—

He held the book up.

'Yes, that's it. Hurry.'

Pocketing the book, Leander replaced the bag and returned to the window. Felix gasped. His hands grabbed the frame as he tried to pull himself through.

'What's wrong?' Leander glanced round and saw what Felix was staring at. Something small and brown had fallen out of the bag and was rolling towards the door.

'Isaak—?' whimpered Felix.

Isaak? Cogs and gears turned frantically in Leander's head and then he remembered that Isaak was the name of Felix's brother. Did the object belong to him? If so, that meant it was . . .

A Cabinet.

Pinchbeck stole Felix's brother.

'I'll get it,' Leander said. Felix was still trying to scramble through the window. Leander spun on his heels to chase after the thing, but the door swung open in his path. A woman stepped through, and screamed.

'Go!' shouted Leander. Felix darted away from the window and Leander took a running jump, flinging himself through behind him. The woman swiped at his ankles, barely missing.

'Get back here!' she shouted after them. He ran with all his might, fingers locked tightly round the precious book. Ahead of him Felix rushed on, his violin case slung over his shoulder and the blanket bundle bumping against his legs.

Once they were deep in the woods, the boys huddled below the lowest branches of a large evergreen, wet and cold and shaken by their near miss. Leander brought out the commonplace book from his coat. He handed it to Felix.

Felix was staring at a spot in the dirt and took the book without breaking his gaze. He was trembling hard, and Leander had a hot-stone feeling in his stomach that it wasn't because of the weather.

'Felix?' He touched the boy's shoulder gently. 'Felix?'

No answer. It was scary to see Felix this way. Felix, the calm, clever, sensible one.

'The little round box that fell out of the bag . . . was it your brother's?' Leander guessed.

Felix glanced at Leander and then back to the dirt. The violin case was still on his back and his fingers gripped the strap so tightly his knuckles were white. He moved his head a fraction of an inch, which Leander took as a nod.

Felix coughed. 'He kept his best marbles in it.'

Leander's mouth went dry and he forced himself to swallow. 'Did Pinchbeck catch your brother, too?'

Silence.

'Do you think Isaak has been here all along?' asked Leander. The words tasted sour and stale. *'Augustina collects spirits,'* Pellar had said. How many prisoners did Pinchbeck have? How many children had she tricked into giving up their souls?

Felix didn't, or couldn't, reply. A realization, stronger than the wintry wind, swept over Leander. He *did* need other people. He didn't want to be without Felix and Charlotte. Their friendship, though as new and delicate as a spring snowdrop, was the best thing he'd had since his mother died. Now Charlotte was lost, and Felix was giving up, and without them he couldn't hope to defeat Pinchbeck.

'I'll get it for you, I will. As soon as it's dark, I'll go back and find it. Do you hear me?'

Felix gave another nod, stronger this time.

I can do this. If Felix can't take care of me, I'll take care of him. This idea was strangely comforting. *That's what a family does.*

'We'll find your brother, I promise.'

201

Plunk. A raindrop landed on the cover of the commonplace book.

'But first we need to find Charlotte,' he urged. 'And this book might be our answer. I can't read it like you can.'

Felix nodded.

The rain kept coming. The tree was wide and thick, but somehow droplets managed to trickle through the branches. Leander unwrapped the bundle he'd taken from the carriage, and did his best to tuck the blanket into the boughs to make a shelter. A handful of tarot cards, caught up in the folds of the blanket, fell down on to the muddy ground and mingled with the carpet of twigs and moss. Leander and Felix huddled together in the dim light as Felix opened the book.

It was small and roughly bound. The pages were as fragile as the oldest of the spellbooks, and dirty edges showed they were well thumbed. Some were torn and carefully mended with silk thread. They smelled of spent gunpowder and yeast. Felix turned the pages reverently, as though Pinchbeck's magic might spill out.

Words and drawings covered the pages leaving not a half-inch wasted. Tiny, complicated pictures. Sketches of animals and the stars, and endless charts of numbers. But mostly words, written with a thick pen in a small, tight hand, making it nearly impossible to distinguish where one word ended and the next began.

'What's it say?' said Leander, peering over Felix's shoulder.

'Not all the words are English.' He flipped a page. 'This

is English, here, but nothing about captured spirits. It's a recipe, I think. And this –' he flicked to the next page – 'is Latin.'

'Can you read it?' Leander squinted at the page, hoping to see a word or two he recognized from church.

'No. Charlotte can read some Latin if – *when* – we find her. I only know the words they write on gravestones.'

'What's this?' Leander pointed to words in a different shade of ink, encircled by a snake.

'I don't recognize those letters.'

'Keep going.'

They continued through the book, Felix reading out the parts he could understand. There were more recipes, strange prayers and, at the back, a list of addresses. All homes at which Pinchbeck had performed seances, complete with notes on each of the family members.

'That's how she's so convincing,' Felix explained. 'She collects information before she visits. Makes it seem like the dead are telling her the family secrets.'

There were lots of rats. Detailed pen-and-ink drawings with labels, including an entire page drawing of a rat skeleton. More rat-banishment poems like the one they had found in the carriage. All manner of quotes and verses mentioning rats and their superstitions. And, on the edges of many pages, scribbled pictures of rats so realistic Leander expected to see a whisker twitch.

'What's this?' Leander jabbed his finger at an onion-shaped drawing filled with rows and rows of thin, winding lines. It reminded him of the long-dead hedge maze in the grounds of Litchfield House.

'A labyrinth.'

'What?'

'If a ghost or a witch comes across one— Oh!' A tarot card fell on to the open book. The Moon. Leander glanced up – it must have been caught between the blanket and the tree branches. Felix seemed cheered by this omen. 'The Moon. Secrets. Mysteries. We're close.'

He turned to the next page. 'A witch ball. Lists of herbs and stones. She could be using any of this to hide Charlotte. She's been building magical barriers to hold Cabinets, so she can go on without being weighed down by the charms.'

Above them, rivulets of icy water were making their way through the dense branches. The blanket Leander had propped up was sagging as it absorbed the rain, and drops began to bleed through.

'A man covered in mud?' Leander pointed at a strange image in the corner of the page.

'A clay statue. People used to say you could catch a soul in one.'

'Can you?'

'Well, Pinchbeck can't. She needs something that can open, like our Cabinets. But clay ... this soil is full of clay. I wonder ...'

The next page was nothing but lines and lines of Latin. Any of this might tell them how to rescue Charlotte, and yet without her they couldn't read it. Leander picked up a stone and threw it in frustration; it clattered down through dead tree branches.

Then there was a map, roughly drawn and smudged in places, but definitely a map. Leander could make out roads and little boxes for buildings, a snaking stream and a heavy, blocky line two-thirds of the way up the page. There was a break in the line, a finger's width across, and beside it a spot where the nib had poked a black hole through the paper.

'The Four Ashes,' said Felix, pointing to a label. 'We passed that earlier. Here's the church and there's the bridge we crossed to get to Pinchbeck's cell.' A drop of water fell on to the page, rolling down the paper like an inky tear. The boys shuffled right back against the tree trunk.

Above the hole in the paper was a symbol drawn in red-brown ink. Triangles and a curly line.

'I recognize that ... It was on Pellar's grave!' said Leander. His heart gave a single hard thud, like it wanted to escape from his ribs and race towards the town gates. 'Is it ... ?' He could barely find the words. 'Is it a sign? Is her hiding place ...'

'It has to be,' said Felix. 'Charlotte's in the town wall!'

As though the heavens agreed, there came a monstrous clap of thunder. The blanket finally gave way under the weight of the water. The boys were instantly soaked and the precious book was washed practically clean as torrents of rainwater left cloudy puddles in place of Pinchbeck's writing.

Felix shoved the book into his pocket. They stood and ran, leaving everything else behind them.

We're coming, Charlotte, Leander thought. *We're coming!*

205

18

High Priestess: Mystery, Intuition, Impatience

LEANDER

They stuck to the trees as far as they could. Leander tripped and stumbled; running through the woods was exhausting but, after he was almost caught at the constable's house, they needed to avoid being out in the open.

Eel-like roots made the ground uneven, and dry, thorny shrubs tore at every inch of bare skin. A low branch snagged at Leander's neck and yanked him backwards. Losing his footing in the slippery mud, Leander came down hard on his buttocks in an inch-deep puddle. Felix, a few paces ahead, turned back and helped him to his feet, and they continued.

It felt like they were racing against nature itself, tearing through the prickly undergrowth. The storm swelled above them, drenched clothes sticking to their skin, sucking out the last warmth from their tired muscles.

At the edge of the woods the pair dashed from the cover of the trees into the nearest lane. The walls on Pinchbeck's map were at the furthest corner of the town. Felix led the way, snaking down alleys and through rain gutters, slipping on cracked flagstones, on and on and . . .

There!

The walls were crumbled and broken but wide and thick. Felix quickly began hunting for any openings or cracks, while Leander rounded the gatepost to check the other side.

'Felix!' Leander had to shout to be heard over the storm.

'Do you see something?'

'I feel strange!'

Ever since they'd left the trees, Leander's body was getting heavier and heavier. Here by the wall he felt dizzy. The air around seemed to be straining against him, thicker somehow, the ground distant beneath his feet.

'I feel it, too. We're too far from Pinchbeck. If Charlotte isn't here, we're in trouble. We may not be able to go any further before we lose all substance.'

The thought was as chilling as the winter rain. Leander rapped his fist against the mossy wall. He was still solid, for now.

The evening was gloomy and it was becoming harder to see. A blanket of black cloud hung overhead and the street lamps were not yet lit. *The lamp. I took a lamp from the carriage, but we left it in the woods!*

Except . . .

Except a big, flat stone had clean lines where the moss had been pulled away.

'Felix,' called Leander again. There was a mark on the rock, a reddish brown loop. Was it—? He tugged at the moss, which came away in clumps like rotten cloth. The symbol was there. The same triangles from Pinchbeck's book and Pellar's gravestone. He had found it!

Felix rushed to his side, violin case dipping into the mud as it hung over his shoulder. They worked together to prise the rock from its place, fingers raw. There was a small hollow behind it, then a rough layer of damp clay, still slick and shiny.

They worked swiftly, hardly caring for the rain and icy wind and the thunder crashing overhead. Charlotte was here. She had to be here. If she wasn't . . .

Felix pulled at the clay with his fingers and Leander used a sharp stone. Behind the clay was a gap about six inches deep, then a solid metal wall. Small objects littered the space – bundles of dried leaves, oddly shaped rocks and ancient yellowed feathers. A pattern painted on the rock in smudged charcoal resembled the labyrinth in Pinchbeck's commonplace book.

'Charms. Charlotte must be in there,' said Felix.

'Or *something* must,' said Leander.

They hesitated and looked at each other, both thinking the same thing. Pinchbeck could have any number of hiding places. What if the spirit wasn't Charlotte? They might unleash another vengeful ghost; another Pellar.

'If someone else is in here, they'll be in their own Cabinet,' reasoned Felix. 'We know what Charlotte's lantern looks like. If we find anything else, we won't open it. Not yet. Agreed?'

'Yes,' said Leander. A fresh gust of wind blew stinging raindrops into his eyes.

On further inspection, the metal wall was the door to a stout metal box. A safe. It had obviously once been painted black, but the paint was chipped and peeling, with rust beneath. A small circle of metal covered a deep keyhole, with fresh scratches around it. On the circle was an engraving, rough and rusty, but unmistakably a rat.

'It might not be locked.' Leander wiggled his finger into the keyhole and pulled hard. Rust marks stained his skin, but the door did not budge. He felt round the edge of the box, hoping to pull the whole thing out, but it fitted so tightly in the space that not a wisp of smoke could have crept between metal and stone.

'It's as though the wall was built around it.' Leander leaned back on his haunches, and Felix dived in to try, his face as blank as the stone, his trembling arms giving away his desperation.

The wall was as tall as Leander, with huge old rough-hewn rocks overlapping each other and forming a barrier two feet thick. Even if they had all the time in the world, they stood no chance of removing enough stones to dig the box out, especially as weak as they were.

'It's no good. We need the key,' said Felix.

Leander felt a warm trickle on his rain-numbed cheek; a tear. At least the rain would hide it from Felix. Another dead end. They had searched the carriage and lived in it – there were no keys among Pinchbeck's ghoulish collection. And the constable had emptied Pinchbeck's pockets when she was arrested, so the key couldn't be on her person.

'It could be anywhere,' said Leander. He sat down in the mud, not caring about the frigid water on his skin. A little voice in his mind told him to lie down, give up, let the winter night take him.

'Think,' said Felix. 'We opened every drawer and box in the carriage. There must be somewhere we haven't checked. Where would Pinchbeck hide a key that no one would ever look?'

'Don't know,' said Leander. His eyes wandered back to the locked box and its engraving –

He had it.

'Rats!' he shouted. 'The rat skeleton jar! No one would open—'

But Felix was already running.

Leander scrambled to his feet, pausing to shove the flat stone back over the opening in case somebody else noticed it. He caught up with Felix, breathless, but not tired, a new energy surging through him at the sight of Felix's determination. The storm cheered them on, as loud and grand as an orchestra.

They had to be right. The rat skeleton was in the biggest jar. There was plenty of room for a key in the cloudy liquid, and both the lock and the map had the picture of a rat . . .

We'll find the key, and rescue Charlotte, and she'll read the Latin words in the commonplace book and somehow, somehow it will give us the secret to our freedom.

The heaviness in his limbs was fading – because he was closer to Pinchbeck, or because he was buoyed by hope?

As they skirted the woodlands near the constable's house, they saw the black bulk of the carriage beside it. The men had moved it while the boys were on their quest. No sign of the horses, who must have been taken to shelter. They edged nearer, watchful for any sign of the constable's men.

Path clear, they scurried over to the carriage, hugging the shadows like cockroaches. Although the rain had made wet rags of their clothing and sliced at their reddened skin, it was also the blessing that kept other people indoors.

The carriage was even messier than before. All of the drawers had been opened and tipped out. Two shelves had been knocked askew and their contents lay in a higgledy-piggledy heap. Things were missing here and there. The men had collected evidence of Pinchbeck's thieving ways – or lined their own pockets.

The rat jar had been on one of the now-broken shelves. The boys dropped to their knees to dig through the remains, relying on their sense of touch as much as their eyes. A hot, sharp pain stabbed through Leander's hand. He pulled it back to find there was blood on his knuckle, almost black in the darkness.

'Careful,' he whispered to Felix. 'Broken glass.'

He licked away the blood, found a cleanish rag and wrapped it round his hand to protect it from the dirt.

Suddenly Felix held something aloft. The skeleton jar! Leander bit his lip to stop himself weeping with relief as Felix twisted the stopper free. He poured out the sour, murky liquid on to the pile of rubbish, cringing as the bones poked out and touched his fingers. He straightened the jar and they heard the clink of metal on glass.

Voices came from outside.

No! They were so close. This couldn't be happening. Rainwater and terror on Leander's skin turned to ice as the voices grew louder.

Felix swung the violin case off his back and shoved it under the bench, wedging it open. He flung the key inside and vanished after it.

Leander tried to disappear as well. He willed his flesh to fade, slowed his breathing, imagined nothingness.

It didn't work.

A thick, hairy hand opened the carriage door.

Now. Go. Vanish, please! Nothing. Leander put his hand to his throat, but the locket wasn't there. The woods. The branch that had caught at his neck and then snapped him free. He had lost it.

The constable grabbed him by both shoulders and yanked him out of the carriage.

'Aha! You're the little toerag our Martha's been fancying a ghost. I've gotcha, lad.'

*

Charlotte pushed as hard as she could, but it was no use. Escape was impossible when the lantern was latched shut. She listened for the slightest sound – some tiny hint of where she might be or what was happening. Earlier she'd heard a rasping noise, but it had stopped.

This is what Pellar had felt, sealed up in a leaky coffin in some long-forgotten grave.

How she longed for Felix's music, or Leander's idiotic questions, or, best of all, the scratch of her uncle's ink pen as he worked in his study.

Comfort. She needed comfort. Stretching her mind back into the past, she sought out a warm memory to soothe herself.

The smell came first. Wood polish and paper, solid and warm, mingled with the springtime scent of cut grass and loamy earth. In her imagination, she danced down the corridor and her lilac dress – a new one her uncle had brought from London – swished and swirled about her. She opened the library door. Her uncle put down his paper and smiled.

'Your Majesty,' he said with a little bow. 'Oh, Charlotte, it's you! I thought you were the fairy queen, all dressed in bluebell petals!'

Charlotte giggled and spun in a circle. How old was she? Seven, eight? Only a few months under his sweet care. 'What news today?'

'Only dull and dreary things in the papers,' he continued. 'Though I wanted to show you this.' A new book, the papery edges dusted in gold.

'What is it?'

'A little book of stories for a good girl who has been learning her letters.'

She squealed. 'Thank you! Can we read it now?'

'I was hoping we would.'

The big brown armchair was their favourite spot for reading together. Charlotte tried to recall the cool leather under her fingers, and the way the light from the windows pooled in warm patches at their feet.

But it couldn't block out the miserable nothingness of this tomb.

What were the chances of Leander turning up with that very book in his sack? And the story of the Rat King . . . she couldn't shake the notion it was important. The part at the end, where he used too much magic and got stuck in his rodent form . . .

There was more to the memory.

'This book has a secret,' said her uncle. He opened the cover and gently bent back the block of pages, causing the edges to fan out. The gold seemed to disappear, and a picture emerged, the tiniest fraction of the image painted across the edge of every page. A hidden illustration, visible only when the paper was spread just so. He closed the book, and the picture disappeared.

What was the picture? Charlotte couldn't bring it to mind;

it slipped away like a dream upon waking. The answer was frustratingly close, just beyond her grasp.

What did it matter anyway? She was helpless. Stuck. Alone.

And the boys – what had become of the boys? Had they just left her to her fate? Or were they imprisoned, too?

19

The Devil:
Despair, Obsession,
Wickedness

LEANDER

Leander struggled and twisted as the constable dragged him into the house by his ear. In the little office room, rough hands pinched and poked and shoved as his pockets were searched; the constable's face was a picture of disgust as he pulled out a handful of sodden crumbs and sticky fruit.

Who was he? Where did he live? Who were his parents? Why was he in the carriage? What did he steal? Why did he break into the house?

Question after question was fired at him and throughout it all Leander played dumb. It was slightly warmer inside the house, but this room had no fireplace. Now he wasn't racing about, his sodden clothes were icy and heavy and his teeth began to chatter. He still said nothing.

'He's obviously backward,' said the woman, watching from

the corner. The same woman who had chased him out of the house earlier. She had a plump face with a prominent nose and her belly was swollen with child.

'Better an idiot than a ghost, eh, Martha?' the constable teased. The woman scowled and folded her arms across her apron. The man shook Leander. 'I shall keep you out of trouble until I can get you before the magistrate. We don't like thieves around these parts.'

'Where will you put him?' asked Martha.

'Out with the woman. It's probably her rotten son.'

'Am not!' said Leander with a snarl.

'It does talk, then,' said the constable.

'He'll freeze out there,' said the woman.

'Be a good lesson.' The constable reached for a key hanging on a rusty hook by the window frame.

'I don't want to think of him in the cold, Sam. He's just a child, whatever she has him mixed up in.'

'He's a *thief*, Martha. You want him in the house with you?'

Martha sighed and opened a dusty chest by the wall. She pulled out a threadbare blanket and draped it over Leander's shoulders.

The constable sighed. 'Women,' he said, but he let Leander keep the blanket.

He bundled Leander out of the doorway and hauled him towards the root cellar. The thought of being trapped in a tiny room with Madame Pinchbeck terrified and disgusted Leander. He made a last attempt to wrestle himself free and sprint for the woods, but the constable's fingers were as strong as iron manacles, and Leander was exhausted from terror and from running and running. All he could hope was that Felix was on his way to find Charlotte and would then return for him.

They'll come for me before the night is out, he told himself, and tried hard to believe it.

The constable banged on the door with the side of his fist. 'Some company for Her Ladyship.'

He unlocked the door and slid aside the bolts top and bottom. Leander glimpsed Pinchbeck's wizened features as a shaft of light fell upon her from the constable's lamp. She sat on a wooden stool with her cloak wrapped round her, a cup of water and a bowl of soup at her feet. The ceiling was so low, the feather in her hat brushed against it.

'Let me out at once. Don't you see I'm a lady of stature?'

'We gave thee a candle. More than most folk get.'

The constable shoved Leander down three stone steps and the door slammed behind him.

Leander squashed himself into the corner furthest from Pinchbeck, but the cellar was so small he could have easily reached out and touched her. He pulled the thin blanket tightly round his shoulders, trying to stretch it over as much of his body as possible. A drop of water fell from his hair and dripped off the end of his nose.

'Good evening, Leander,' said the familiar voice. 'I was wondering when you'd come.'

*

Leander was captured, Charlotte missing, Pinchbeck arrested.

For the first time in forever, Felix was alone.

He emerged from the violin case and secured it over his shoulder. The key clasped tightly in his hand, he peered through the carriage window to see if his path was clear. From a safe distance he saw Leander shoved through the door into the constable's house and, a few short minutes later, stuffed into the same dark cell as Pinchbeck. Poor wretch.

Why didn't Leander go into his locket? The one good thing Pinchbeck had given them was a perfect hiding place, the ability to vanish into their Cabinets. Why didn't he use it?

His mind wandered to Isaak's wooden box rolling across the constable's office. Pinchbeck had cheated him – all these years she'd let him search for his brother, and she'd had him all along. Sorrow and disbelief and anger clanged together in his head: a cacophony of misery. A fire had been lit inside him, and the last scraps of loyalty to Pinchbeck were burned away.

All this time, a small part of him had hoped he could free Charlotte and Leander, and somehow stay with Pinchbeck. But not any more. All those years, every time he thought she was helping him, showing him kindness, caring for him, it had been nothing but lies. She was controlling him. She had the thing he wanted most in the whole world, and she'd kept it from him. Any bond he once felt for her was severed for ever.

But there was no time to brood. If Felix wanted to free himself and the others, he had to act.

Maybe Charlotte would know what to do next. At least he had the key. Beyond that, he couldn't guess what would happen.

CHARLOTTE

Charlotte spilled out of the lantern. She took a deep, gasping breath, air rushing into her lungs. Disorientated, she flailed around for something solid to lean against and the hard, rough stone wall pressed back against her. She was real again.

Being solid was sweeter than honey on a summer's morning.

And there was Felix behind her, holding the lantern. She flung herself against him, her arms tight round his thin, wet body, and she breathed in his scent of rosin and rainwater.

'Is Pinchbeck here?' She glanced around, body tense, waiting for the monster to lumber out of the darkness.

'No. You're safe,' said Felix.

She hugged him again. 'How long was I—'

'A day. Just a day.'

Only one day? It seemed much longer. She had spent full days in the lantern before, but this time she was exhausted. The fear of being trapped for ever had shaken her to the bones.

But there was no time to wallow in self-pity; she must pull herself together. 'Where's Leander? Did Pinchbeck hurt him?'

'No,' said Felix. There was anguish in his eyes. 'The constable caught him.'

'Constable? I don't understand.'

'It's . . . I don't know where to start and we don't have much time. We need to work fast.'

'I'm so weak. Was it really only one day?'

'We're a long way from Pinchbeck. Almost as far as we can go. You'll feel stronger when we get closer. And look.'

Charlotte crouched beside him and peered into the darkened hole. There was a rusted iron safe, wide open, and ragged bundles of decaying herbs. Felix kneeled in the mud and reached his entire arm into the hole.

'She had this surrounded with charms and sealed up with clay. This is how she stops the Cabinets from using up her energy.'

'Where is Pinchbeck?'

'In a cell. A cellar really. Your uncle must have found the note because the magistrate was looking for you. She's . . . Oh.'

With a final tug, Felix pulled out a coarse drawstring bag. He carried it to where a gas street lamp cast a circle of milky light and Charlotte followed, clutching Felix's shoulder as he loosened the strings. She already knew what he would find.

Cabinets. A whole bag of them. Twelve or fifteen at first glance, an assortment of ordinary objects only they would have recognized as magical. A silk purse. A snuffbox. A medicine bottle. And something else, which made her heart tighten. The bottom of the bag was filled with shards of glass and pottery. *Broken Cabinets.*

How many people had Pinchbeck condemned to death this way? She pictured the woman gleefully tossing these treasures into a sack and stuffing it into the box, not noticing or caring whether the fragile pieces shattered against the hard metal.

Charlotte covered her eyes with her apron, as though it could shield her from the unfolding horror. 'Open them.'

'Not yet,' said Felix. 'We don't know who they are, or what state they'll be in. They could be dangerous.'

Charlotte knew he was right. They should take the sack, and look after it until it was safe to open the Cabinets. But first they had to rescue Leander. They needed to get back to him as fast as possible. She was relieved to be out of her Cabinet, but nothing would feel right until the three of them were back together. 'Why did—'

The crunch of boots on gravel interrupted her. Felix clutched the bag to his chest as they turned to see who was approaching. Night was falling and, beyond the town gates, the world was in darkness. They could barely make out the shape of a man on the road, but his feet made an uneven stomp-scrape as he limped along. Charlotte and Felix stood side by side as the figure emerged into the lamplight.

Edmund Pellar.

He trudged towards them, looking as wild and weird as he had in the graveyard, coated with a fresh layer of mud and grime. He wheezed as though the effort of travelling such a distance had taken every bit of his strength.

'Where is she?' he hissed.

'Not here,' Charlotte snapped. How did he find them? If she had strayed so far from Pinchbeck, she would never have found her way back. She hadn't counted on his fortitude. 'How did you— How are you still solid?'

'I'm gettin' closer, I can tell. Gettin' stronger with each step. That's how I knew I was headin' in the right direction.' He paused to hack and splutter into a grubby handkerchief. His eye caught the open hole in the wall. 'Found one of her little cubbyholes, have you? I shouldn't trouble yerselves. It'll all be over soon.'

'You shan't find her.' Felix spoke with venom, but inched nearer to Charlotte's side.

'Come this far, en't I?'

'Help us,' Charlotte pleaded. 'You and us, together . . .'

Pellar laughed.

Charlotte and Felix could outrun this twisted, broken man, and he'd have no chance of keeping up. But that wouldn't stop him. He had tracked Pinchbeck here, despite his cough and his limp, despite being weakened by time and distance. Pellar could be their ally, but his burning need for revenge would destroy them all.

'There's no use protectin' her. Tell me where she is and we can get this over with. It's for yer own good.'

Felix inched backwards. 'She's locked away where you can't reach her.'

Pellar stooped until his eyes were level with theirs. He twitched as if he was trying to smile, but had forgotten how.

'Holed herself up, eh? No matter. Fire will clear a building of rats. If Augustina lacks the courage to face me, I shall burn her out. Like vermin.'

Felix lunged at Pellar. He snatched something from the man's chest with a mighty tug and Pellar staggered forward, almost butting heads with Charlotte. Felix was off and away, still clutching the bag of Cabinets to his chest. She ran after him, gripping her lantern.

Pellar gave a cry of pain, which quickly faded into a long, maniacal laugh. He didn't chase them, but shouted, 'Keep it, lad! I'll still find her. I can smell her.'

Charlotte and Felix dashed away, fighting the weakness in their limbs. They threw themselves down the first alleyway and zigzagged from street to street, over cobbles and dirt, until they were long out of sight of Pellar.

Felix came to a sudden halt. 'Leander,' he said between pants. 'What about him?'

Felix was clearly drained from his day's adventures, pale, winded and shivering. He struggled to regain his breath.

'Leander is *with* Pinchbeck. They're locked together in the same cell. We have to reach them before Pellar does.'

More than anything else, Felix's panic scared Charlotte. He was right: if Leander and Pinchbeck were trapped together, and Pellar followed through with his threat, they'd both be burned alive.

Felix bent double and put his hands on his knees. 'Leander figured out where the key was to free you. We were getting it out of the carriage when the constable's men caught him.'

Emotions swept over Charlotte and she leaned against a wall lest they wash her away. Leander had been arrested trying to save her. He had tried to help her even though she'd been so cruel to him. How she wished she could go back to that first night and speak some words of kindness to him.

'Why didn't he go into his locket?' she asked.

'I think . . .' Felix pressed his hand to his brow.

'What? What's wrong?'

'He might have lost it.'

Charlotte didn't know what would happen if a Cabinet was lost. Leander's locket contained a piece of his soul. If it was gone . . .

Felix uncurled his fingers. 'This is what I took from Pellar.' He was holding a hagstone on a piece of broken string. 'I think he was using it to track Pinchbeck.'

'That should slow him down.'

Felix pulled out his own hagstone and held them both in his open palm. 'I've never seen anything through mine.' He lifted Pellar's stone to his eye and gasped.

'What is it?'

'Look!' He thrust it into her hand. 'Look at me.'

The houses and fences were unchanged, but Felix looked different. There was an odd shimmer around him, a milky, misty sheen in the air like the spray from a waterfall. Charlotte moved the stone away and the shimmer was gone.

She picked up his other stone, and looked through that. Nothing.

She compared them side by side. Pellar's was smoother. The rock was thinner around the hole. Felix's stone was crude and chunky. The hole was rough on the inside.

'This is the one Pinchbeck gave you, isn't it?'

'Yes.'

'She lied, Felix. Water didn't make this hole. It's not a real hagstone at all.'

Felix took it in his hand and squeezed. 'Of course she lied. It's always been lies!' He threw the stone and it clattered on to a rooftop somewhere out of sight.

Charlotte felt her friend's pain, hard and sharp and brutal. But there was no time to mope – she needed to keep Felix focused. Keep him fighting.

'We have to help Leander,' she said gently.

'If we rescue Leander, Pinchbeck will be free as well.'

'And, if Pellar reaches them first, he'll kill them both. Kill us all.' The words tasted like curdled milk. Free Pinchbeck when she was so close to being punished? She deserved to suffer. There must be another way. 'If we find Leander's locket, we could lower it in through a window, and he could disappear into it.'

'There are no windows. And we don't have time to search for the locket.'

'What about using Pellar's hagstone to find it?'

'It could be anywhere. We've been all over the town, through the woods,' said Felix, rubbing his knuckles over his forehead. 'And it's tiny, and Pellar . . . Oh, wait! I forgot! We found Pinchbeck's book!'

Felix fumbled the remains of the commonplace book out of his pocket and pushed it into Charlotte's hands.

'Leander and I used it to find you. Some of it's in Latin and we couldn't read it, but maybe there's something here?'

It was damp. Soggy pages were stuck together, crumbling into wet lumps as she tried to prise them open.

'It's ruined,' said Charlotte. 'I can't read a thing.' The pages were stained with smears of black ink, years of Pinchbeck's secrets destroyed.

Felix took a deep breath. 'That's that, then.' He was being so brave that Charlotte loved him more than ever. 'We have to get them both out of the cell before Pellar finds them. We can't leave Leander – he's one of us now. He's family.' He set off walking.

Charlotte nodded as she trotted after him. 'If Leander can't disappear into his locket, we'll have to get the cell door open somehow. Even if that means Pinchbeck escapes, too,' she said. The thought of freeing Pinchbeck was like a sharp stone stuck in her throat. Their choices were probable death at the hands of Pinchbeck, or certain death at the hands of Pellar.

'We can at least hide our Cabinets,' suggested Felix. 'Far enough away so we can't be forced inside, no matter how many orders she shouts.'

'Or we could make a magical barrier between us and our Cabinets – like the one in the hiding place?'

It would be guesswork at best, and, even if they could make one, Charlotte didn't know if it would work, but they were

227

out of options. The thought of being back where they started, despite all their efforts, was just too much.

'You must stay hidden,' said Felix, turning to face her. 'Pinchbeck mustn't know I found you. She mustn't see you at all.'

'What if someone else let them out, then we could both stay hidden?' Charlotte suggested. She could already feel her limbs growing stronger as they moved nearer to Pinchbeck.

'Who in their right mind would release her?'

20

The Hanged Man, Reversed:
Imprisoned, Trapped,
Helpless

 LEANDER

This must be what death feels like.

The suffocating scent of Pinchbeck's floral perfume mixed with the wet-dog stench of the old blanket and the earthy scent of the bare floor. Leander tried to imagine himself as a smaller boy playing at hide-and-seek in the coal-hole. The scent of baking bread and the warmth in his mother's voice as she pretended not to see him. Her laughter as she wiped the smudges from his cheek with her apron.

'I appreciate the company,' said Pinchbeck. 'Though I'd have preferred you to let me out. Where's Felix?'

Leander shrugged. Felix and Charlotte would come for him. They wouldn't leave him here to rot with Pinchbeck – would they? He felt sick. No one ever wanted Leander. Why would they put themselves in danger to save him?

'I suppose you can't pick the lock, then?' she asked.

'No.'

'Useless. I thought I was hiring myself a skilled thief. I might have thought twice if I'd known how stupid you were.'

'Hiring me? You stole me.'

'How did you get caught?'

'I went back to the carriage.' Leander drew his feet in and made himself as small as possible.

'Why didn't you vanish into your Cabinet until they were gone? You're no use to me in here.'

He wouldn't explain himself to Pinchbeck. Without her deviousness, Leander would still be in the relative safety of the library with only the wrath of Mrs Smart to worry about. Pinchbeck had stolen his life, and Charlotte's life, and Felix's life, even Pellar's.

And she had promised he could speak to his mother. All lies. He knew that now.

'You're a monster.' The words spilled out before he could stop them.

There was a silence, then Pinchbeck laughed. 'Silly boy. After I've been so kind to you.'

Her beautiful dress was dusty and creased, her skin sagging, like the ruins of a cathedral, dignified but decaying. The light flickered, and for half a second it seemed as if Pinchbeck flickered, too – Leander was sure he saw sharp yellowish teeth protruding from her bottom jaw. He blinked, and the image was gone.

Leander said, 'What have you done with Charlotte?'

'It was for your own good. Her or you. You'd thank me if you knew what was good for you.'

'Never.'

'Mind your manners, boy. I've already dispatched one rude child – I'll not think twice about doing it again.'

'You'll be hanged for kidnap and murder first.'

'You'd better hope not.' She fixed him with an iron gaze, eyes almost black in the candlelight. 'My death will be the end of you, too.'

'I know that broken glass in the jar isn't Charlotte's lantern,' he said. 'Is she dead? Tell me.'

'Charlotte is safe,' said Pinchbeck. 'Somewhere the cruel world can't hurt her. Somewhere she won't have to worry about hunger, or pain, or the ravages of old age. She's one of the lucky ones, Leander.'

'If you don't want her any more, why not just let her go?'

'But I *do* want her, little one. I want all of you. All you poor, forgotten, unwanted things. Didn't I take you in when no one else would? Haven't I fed and clothed you? All the suffering I've saved you. This world's no place for orphans, son. Orphans like you waste away in the workhouse or die down the mines. But that will never happen to you. Because of me.'

'I'd take my chances,' said Leander. 'Besides, Charlotte was loved by her uncle and you took her anyway.'

'Pah!' Pinchbeck spat. 'Charlotte was better off with me than that old fool. He should have respected my talents. Charlotte's fate rested in his hands, not mine.'

231

She shifted her position, sighing with the effort. Her hair was whiter than it had been that morning, and Leander hoped that meant Felix had managed to free Charlotte, that it was the weight of too many spirits draining Pinchbeck's power. He wondered if Pinchbeck would sense when Charlotte was rescued, or if she'd blame the cold, cramped cell for her stiff, weary bones.

'Don't be frightened, Leander. Felix will save us. My faithful, loyal Felix won't let me down.' She leaned her head back against the wall and closed her eyes.

Leander didn't even know what to pray for. If the others opened the cell to save him, Pinchbeck would be free, too. But otherwise prison awaited Leander when he was hauled before the court as a thief. He couldn't imagine what might happen if he and Pinchbeck were taken to different towns.

Would it hurt as they were pulled apart?

Leander blinked, fighting his drowsiness and fear. He tucked his legs beneath him, trying not to think about how rats would love a grim, dusty cellar like this, trying not to think about them running over his feet in the darkness . . .

Pinchbeck had started to doze in her corner and he watched her through sleep-sticky eyes. He was disgusted to breathe the same air as her. Yes, she was definitely getting older, but other things seemed different, too. Had her fingernails always been so long and sharp? There was a mole on her face he hadn't noticed before, with three long grey hairs sprouting from it, like the witch in the storybook.

The candle stub in the room was burning low – soon

the light would be gone and he'd be plunged into darkness with that monstrous woman The flickering light cast long, ghoulish shadows on to the walls. Tiredness tugged at his eyelids, but Leander's mind was restless and he couldn't give himself over to sleep. Pinchbeck's head drooped and the candlelight transformed her shadow into something inhuman – the brim of her hat became a long, pointed nose, the feathers two little ears, until a giant black rat towered over them.

Leander gasped and the noise snapped Pinchbeck awake.

She straightened herself up and her shadow changed back into a woman. The illusion was broken. Just a trick of the light and his tired, anxious imagination?

'What are you looking at, boy?' she snarled. 'Behave.'

Leander couldn't explain, though, why the mole on her face was gone.

FELIX

Felix led Charlotte to the cell. The walls were made from huge, heavy stones sunk into a large mound of earth. The door was tight-fitting and solid, and thick iron bolts were the proof it stored something more dangerous than vegetables.

The shape reminded Felix of a kiln and he imagined it filling with searing heat.

They kept a wary distance and watched the constable's house. Two men said polite farewells at the doorway and headed off into the night, talking of the beer waiting for them after a long and strange day. Presently, the constable himself came to the door.

'No more, my dear,' Felix overheard him say. 'There's no one getting out of the lock-up, and I shan't be long at the inn.'

A woman replied from within, but Felix couldn't make out her words.

'Settle before the hearth where it's warm. Don't be standing in a draught in your condition.'

The door closed and he left in the same direction as his men.

Felix whispered to Charlotte, 'That woman almost caught Leander when he stole the commonplace book. The man said she thought Leander was a ghost.'

'She's probably heard what Pinchbeck does for a living. It'd make any sensible woman uneasy.'

An idea was beginning to take shape for Felix. 'If the constable's wife believes Pinchbeck can conjure ghosts, then let's be ghosts. We'll haunt her house, and she'll open the cellar to be free of the witch!'

'How will it work?'

'She's having a baby. There's none more superstitious than an expectant mother.' He felt a hot pang of guilt at his own suggestion.

'Oh, Felix. That's wicked.' Charlotte was an oil painting in the shadows: all sharp lines and dark smudges. 'Let's do it!'

They'd scare the woman into opening the cell door, then scramble for the woods before they were seen. Success was far from certain, but it was the best idea they had. After all, hauntings were what they were good at, what Pinchbeck had trained them for all these years.

To the carriage yet again. Though it had been home for years, Felix was beginning to hate the thing; it was tainted by suffering and loss.

'Oh!' Charlotte exclaimed.

He saw the devastation with fresh eyes through her reaction. However much Pinchbeck deserved it – *And she does*, Felix reminded himself. *She kept Isaak prisoner all along* – it was strange to see her precious collection destroyed. It would pain her to lose her treasures.

Good. It didn't hurt her to cast Charlotte aside, or to keep my brother from me, or—

'Do you think my uncle will come?' Charlotte's voice broke through his thoughts. She had found a candle stub to light.

'The magistrate said he'd send word when they arrested her. They found a sugar bowl from your uncle's house, but there was no sign of you. Will that be enough?'

'If he doesn't come, no one can help us. Once Pinchbeck and Leander are free ...'

She didn't need to finish the sentence. *We'll be back where we started – worse than where we started because she'll know we betrayed her. We can't stop her.*

They gathered their tools. Strands of thread as fine as spider-silk. Fairy bells. Long, thin sticks meant for tapping and tipping.

'I miss home,' Charlotte said with a resigned sadness to

235

her voice, like the change from a major to a minor key. Felix looked up, meaning to comfort her.

She leaned back on her heels and wiped a strand of hair from her eyes. Felix laughed. 'You're glowing!'

'I'm flushed—' she began. He took her hand and held it up to show her the eerie yellow sheen on her fingers.

He sifted cautiously through the debris for the container. 'The phosphorescent powder, look. There's still some left.'

The jar of yellow-grey powder gave off a mysterious light as it moved from the shadows to the candle beam. The glass was cracked and powder seeped out, colouring his fingers like an artist's pigment.

'Perfect.'

'Are you ready?' said Felix.

'No – wait – one more thing. The book of fairy tales – is it still here?' she asked, starting to search.

She found it under a blanket, undamaged. Holding it close to the candlelight, she opened the covers and twisted the papery middle to the side. A picture came into view.

'What is it?' Felix asked.

Flowers. A bundle of roses and forget-me-nots.

'Oh,' said Charlotte, crestfallen. 'I was sure there'd be a clue, but it's just a pretty painting.'

'Marsh and Blight,' said Felix, already searching for the heavy tome. 'That's got golden pages, too . . .'

They lifted it up, fanned out the pages.

Nothing. Charlotte bit her lip. 'Try the other side. From the back.'

Flipping the book over, Felix spread out the pages again. There was something there.

It was old, faded, but beautiful and detailed. In the dim light, Felix could make out what looked like a row of boxes and bottles and jars. Beside every container was a drawing of a man, each one smaller than the last, as if he was shrinking. By the end of the row, the man had become a rat.

'This is the answer,' said Charlotte. 'This is important. I know it is.'

'But what does it mean?'

As Felix looked closer, he saw that the detailed border was decorated with flowers and vines and stars, and there, near the centre, was a violin. Beside it a lantern. 'Our Cabinets,' he whispered to Charlotte.

'But how . . .'

The candle flickered and went out.

'Come on,' said Felix. 'Let's get Leander before Pellar finds them.'

Back outside, they surveyed the house. It was small – two rooms and a pantry downstairs. The office, with the small window Leander had climbed through earlier, and a kitchen. Peering through the keyhole, Felix saw the woman resting in the easy chair, knitting a tiny sock in the lamplight. A cheery rag rug lay between the coal-black hearth and a sturdy wooden table. Copper pans, shiny and bright, caught the light from where they hung on the wall.

It was a real home, cosy and safe – for now.

A small lean-to pantry led off the kitchen. It had a tiny

window – it'd be difficult to squeeze through, but easy to disappear if their Cabinets waited outside. Another way to escape if things went wrong. They placed their Cabinets against the kitchen wall, propped open so they could enter and exit at will.

Charlotte's apron pockets were stuffed with supplies. In the woods behind them, nocturnal creatures stirred, and every snapping twig or rustle of wind reminded them Pellar was approaching.

It was time.

'Now,' said Felix.

He kneeled down and laced his fingers to boost Charlotte through the same window Leander had entered earlier. She crossed the room quickly and silently. Felix watched and listened for any sound of movement from the kitchen. He felt nervous and excited as he always did before a performance, though this one had far bigger stakes than a normal seance. Pinchbeck might even be proud of them for conjuring up a haunting by themselves.

On the opposite wall Charlotte daubed crude letters with a pot of grease, blowing the powder against it to leave smudgy, glowing words. *Let them go. No harm will come*, warned her uneven writing. It was rough but would do the job if the woman could read.

Felix waited until Charlotte had finished and tucked herself into a corner before picking up his violin and playing a high, sharp note.

*

238

The music of Felix's violin felt like fresh water on a hot day to Leander. It began with a single drawn-out note, followed by a series of mismatched tones. Pinchbeck, who had been snoring softly, immediately twitched awake.

'My boy,' she purred. 'I knew he would come.'

The gentle melody began to swell. A frantic hope filled Leander's body and lifted him to his feet, head almost touching the ceiling.

The music was a message. Felix was letting him know he was near. Help was coming.

Pinchbeck evidently thought the same. 'Felix has never let me down. He knows what side his bread is buttered. We shall be on our way in no time.'

21

Two of Wands:
Inspiration, Planning,
Progress

Charlotte heard Felix play a few more discordant notes and she waited impatiently for the woman to come and discover her message. Sounds of movement came from the kitchen, but the door didn't open.

Charlotte sprinted over to the little desk and knocked over the chair, then darted back behind the door.

That did it.

The woman bustled in, wearing an expression of mild alarm and carrying a candle. Muttering and tutting, she stooped to pick up the chair, then gasped when she saw the ghostly message. Charlotte dashed into the kitchen. She did not stop to check if the woman had spotted her. Hopefully, if she had, Charlotte was nothing more than a swish of fabric.

She heard a sharp thud. Felix had thrown a hard rubber ball through the window to distract the woman. Charlotte pulled out a strip of what Pinchbeck called ectoplasm – spirit residue. Really it was fine white gauze, which Charlotte had frayed and dipped into the glowing powder. She draped it over the door frame between the rooms like cobwebs.

She ran for the pantry, but the door was locked, so she flung herself beneath the table. Her heart was racing. She was a little excited, despite her worry and guilt at their unkind plan. She crouched, ready to jump out and touch the woman if she needed more convincing.

An ominous grating noise seemed to come from the bricks themselves as Felix scraped a piece of slate over the outside walls. Charlotte heard creaking floorboards – the woman was pacing anxiously, but stayed where she was.

Three sharp knocks sounded. Their agreed signal. Charlotte took a great breath and, in unison, she and Felix screamed with all their might.

A clatter. Rapid footsteps. A *thunk* and a rattle.

The ectoplasm caught the light beautifully as the woman opened the door, candle in hand. Charlotte felt a flash of shameful pride in her handiwork. The ghostly threads brushed the woman's cheek, startling her. She flailed wildly, and the flame of her candle touched the glowing gauze.

Whoosh!

The material burned faster than anything Charlotte had ever seen. The powder became fire in a bright white flash, then crumbled to ash in half an instant. Howling with terror, the woman dropped the candle and it caught on her skirt.

The flame lapped hungrily as though the powder had

241

whetted its appetite. Charlotte scrambled out from her hiding place. The woman half fainted as Charlotte tried to bat out the flames which inched upward, threatening to consume her. Their eyes met in shared alarm.

The woman swooned to the ground, eyes rolled back. Charlotte threw herself on top of her, doing her best to smother the flames with her apron.

It could only have been moments. The flames had made an eight-inch path up the woman's clothing and her underskirts were charred, but the fire was out. Tendrils of white, sulphur-smelling smoke hung in the air. Shaking, Charlotte rose to her feet, only to be knocked over again by Felix barrelling past her into the kitchen.

'Charlotte! Your apron!'

She looked down, numb with shock, and dumbly observed the corner of her apron burning.

I'm on fire.

It registered slowly, as though she was reading it in a book and not watching it happen. Felix returned in a heartbeat and threw a jug of milk over her, dousing the flames.

He dropped the jug and was on his knees, scrabbling beneath the table, stretching to reach something in the dusty corner. Charlotte stared at the poor woman senseless on the floor.

'Come on,' Felix said, halfway out of the window already.

She hurried after him, sliding on the wet floor. The jar of powder had tipped over in her apron pocket and was spilling down her dress.

Scooping up their Cabinets, they ran for the trees.

Charlotte wailed. 'Oh, Felix. We hurt her!'

Felix squeezed her hand but said nothing. His eyes were trained on the house, watching for any sign their plan had worked.

'She was almost burned alive!'

'So were you.'

The scorch marks on Charlotte's apron stopped an inch or two from where the phosphorescent powder was sitting in her pocket. If the flames had reached the powder, she would have gone up like the ectoplasm, no chance of rescue. If Felix hadn't acted so quickly . . .

She heaved and threw up what little was in her stomach.

'We're fools,' said Felix. 'We should have searched for the keys while the woman was in her faint.'

Another wave of nausea hit Charlotte at the memory of the woman's motionless body. 'But she has to be the one to open the door, or Pinchbeck will see us.'

'And if she doesn't wake?'

Charlotte had the sensation of a sudden fall. Surely they hadn't—

'I don't think she's dead,' Felix added hastily. 'But what if she doesn't come round before her husband gets home?'

'We left our message. Maybe he'll release them.'

'Leander's punishment will be worse if the constable thinks he and Pinchbeck have been bewitching people. He'll gather the men. We'll wait a moment, then we have to go back.'

The next few minutes felt like torture to Charlotte, and she could see her anguish reflected in Felix's face. Foolish! Why hadn't they thought of the consequences if they failed?

And then ... 'She's there!' Felix exclaimed.

The woman was emerging from the back door of the house.

'She's alive,' whispered Charlotte, a tingle of relief spreading across her back.

The woman held a small lamp over her head and glanced around. She took half a step, then stopped to check again, like a rabbit that has had an encounter with a fox. A glint of light reflected on something in her hand. A key.

The haunting had worked after all. The woman was going to release Pinchbeck and Leander. They had done it! Leander was saved from Pellar, at least. A moment of small victory.

But what next? Leander was still in Pinchbeck's clutches and they had to stay close to the hideous woman because they had failed to break her spell.

A sob rose in Charlotte's throat, so big it threatened to swallow her. All of this and they were not one step nearer to freedom.

FELIX

'Come on,' Felix urged Charlotte. 'We should move now, hide our Cabinets while the woman lets them out and then hurry back to get Leander away from Pinchbeck.'

He grabbed Charlotte's hand and pulled her away from the

house. Together they stumbled to the next street and Felix spotted a half-collapsed outhouse.

'Here!' he hissed and ran towards it.

Hastily, they put the lantern and the violin case inside, along with the sack they'd found in the hiding place. They jammed the door closed with bits of broken brick.

'Should we gather up some feathers and herbs from the carriage?' Felix suggested. 'Try to make a magical barrier?'

'No time,' said Charlotte. 'We'll just have to hope that the walls and distance will stop her from ordering us back inside. We need to catch up with them, find a way to let Leander know we haven't abandoned him.'

They turned and ran back towards the constable's house again.

Now that their own Cabinets had been stored away, Felix's mind turned to the little wooden box in his pocket. A little box that radiated with heat and hope. Isaak's box.

He hadn't told Charlotte that he'd taken it from the constable's house, or what was inside. The news was too good to share; if he spoke the words aloud, it might cease to be real, a dream that dissolves in daylight.

Charlotte knew what Isaak meant to Felix. She'd encourage him to open it.

But he must wait. He had waited years; he could wait a few hours more until Leander was safe. If he released his brother – for surely, certainly, this must be his Cabinet – Isaak would be confused and frightened. If he panicked or shouted, or was too weak to keep up, it could put them all in more danger. Felix had to keep himself under control for a little while longer.

He allowed himself the tiniest peek through the holey stone to confirm it. Yes, the same misty haze he had seen around Charlotte. Definitely a Cabinet. There were scratches in the wood, marks that hadn't been part of the decoration. Symbols crudely carved into the lid, similar to the symbol painted over Pinchbeck's hidey-hole and carved into Pellar's headstone. A tiny silver chain, as thin as embroidery cotton, was wrapped twice round the box.

Charms. Pinchbeck had put extra charms on Isaak's Cabinet. That must be why he never appeared when Pinchbeck said '*abeo*' and summoned the others from their Cabinets, even though he was close by.

Such cunning. This was no accident or misunderstanding. Pinchbeck knew all along that this Cabinet held Felix's brother. She had gone to great lengths to keep it hidden from him, and to prevent accidental summoning. She'd let Felix search and suffer all those years. For what purpose? To control him? To keep him loyal to her?

The last eight years had been a lie.

He tightened his fists and gathered his resolve. There was time for anger later. He had Isaak's Cabinet now. That was the important thing.

When they were safe – could they ever be safe again? – he'd open it and savour the reunion. It had been so long, he could barely recall Isaak's face. He cupped the wooden box in his hand, enjoying the weight of it.

The wood was a little swollen from damp, old and fragile. He would need to open it with great care. He wouldn't rush and risk breaking it. Isaak had been here all along. At least he would have heard Felix's music. At least he knew his brother was near.

LEANDER

Though the walls of the cell were thick, Leander had heard all manner of strange things: scratching, banging and a most unholy scream. And then the door opened.

After the total darkness of the cell, even the oil lamp was unbearably bright. Leander squinted out at the woman who had offered him a blanket earlier – Martha. She was dirty and dishevelled, and her face glistened with tears. What had happened to her?

'Out with you!' cried Martha. 'Begone!'

Pinchbeck was up and out before she'd finished speaking. She was impressively light on her feet for an old woman who'd been in a cold stone box all evening. Leander scrabbled to his feet and followed. He shrugged off the blanket and held it out to the woman who glared at him, nostrils flared and lips a thin line.

'Thank you for your kindness, miss.' He tried to hand her the blanket again, but she put her hands behind her back and the blanket fell to the ground. Leander bent to pick it up.

'Boy!' Pinchbeck glided on and Leander trotted obediently after her. He looked for Felix, but could see little beyond the lantern's dome of light. 'The carriage, no time to waste. Felix will catch up. He can't get far without me, and he knows it.'

'It's—' Leander hesitated to tell her. 'They made a mess of your carriage. And the horses have been taken.'

'We must find some. Any horse will do. Use your head, boy. Where's the nearest stables?'

There were stables at the inn, and the farrier's place.

'Hurry, boy! The devils will be after us.'

He didn't want to help Pinchbeck, but he didn't want to be caught by the constable again, either. All he could do was stay out of trouble, and trust that the others would find a way to help. Leander pointed a trembling finger. Maybe he could lead Pinchbeck to a stable a little further away. It was his small act of rebellion.

'Get moving, then. Quick and quiet.' Pinchbeck was breathing heavily with the effort of the brisk walk.

Leander kept his eyes to the ground for fear his face would reveal his secrets. And then, from the edge of his vision, a flash of movement.

His heart soared. It was the others. They hadn't left him! Pinchbeck marched on unaware. Leander fell behind, out of her view. They passed a gnarled tree, its great roots pushing up the paving slabs. And there, crouched in its shadow, were Charlotte and Felix. What a sight! Head to toe in water and filth, ash-stained and ragged, Charlotte looked more like a homeless waif than the Lady of the Manor.

Leander had to control himself, not draw any attention to

them. He continued to trudge behind Pinchbeck who was muttering about inconvenience and injustice.

Felix and Charlotte kept pace alongside them, flitting from bush to alley, sticking to the shadows. Charlotte put her finger to her lips. As if he needed to be told!

He was so focused on thoughts of escape and the others that he almost missed the stable entirely.

'Here, miss.' He tugged on Pinchbeck's sleeve. In a wide gap between two houses lay a dirt track, which led to a modest stable behind. Pinchbeck smiled the same syrupy smile she had first given him over a cup of bark tea.

'Good boy.' She cupped his cheek affectionately with her gloved hand. 'Keep watch out here. Whistle if someone comes. We shall make London after all.'

She still trusts me. Even after his outburst in the cell, it seemed Pinchbeck believed Leander would obey. 'Yes, Madame.'

She headed down the path and paused at the stable door. 'And, once we're in London, we'll have a special seance, just for you to speak to your mother, shall we?'

Leander did his best to smile.

22

Nine of Swords:
Worry, Fear, Nightmares

CHARLOTTE

The moment the stable door slammed behind Pinchbeck, Charlotte and Felix flew towards Leander. Charlotte flung her arms round his neck and held him tight.

'Your locket, where is it?' she asked in a hushed, urgent voice.

'We've hidden our Cabinets,' said Felix. 'Five minutes' walk away. We think it'll be too far for her to order us inside.'

'I think I lost my locket in the woods. I—' Leander's eyes were wide and wet.

'We'll find it,' said Felix. 'As soon as Pinchbeck is behind bars again, we'll hunt until we find it. Don't worry. The good news is that, without it, you can't be ordered back inside, either.'

'Listen, we have very little time.' Charlotte gave Leander no opportunity to reply. 'Our only hope is to have Pinchbeck recaptured alone, and pray my uncle comes to our aid. But Pellar intends to burn her alive.' She pulled him down the track so Pinchbeck wouldn't hear. 'We've seen him. He's near. Felix will keep Pinchbeck here. I'll get the constable.'

Leander tried to speak. She put her hand on his lips.

'It's up to you to find Pellar and stop him. Whatever happens, you can't let him reach Pinchbeck. If he kills her, we all perish.' She took her hand away.

He nodded, puffed out his chest. Brave. 'Stop Pellar. How?'

'Trick him. Trap him. Anything.'

'Take this.' Felix pressed the holey stone into Leander's palm. 'This one works – it's Pellar's. It might help you find him.'

'How will I know it's safe to come back?' Leander's bottom lip was trembling, but he stood firm and resolute.

'We'll find you. Towards the town gates, that's where we lost him,' Felix said.

'Wait—' Leander called as they turned to leave. 'What happens when they catch Pinchbeck? We still don't know how to free ourselves from her magic.'

A long pause. 'If she's locked away, we can stay somewhere nearby with our Cabinets . . . It might be the best we can do,' said Felix.

'The book – the Rat King,' said Charlotte. There was a truth in those pages, she knew it. The secret picture on the spellbook showed a man shrinking down into a rat, just like the Rat King in the story. Was it possible? 'If we can make Pinchbeck transform . . .'

251

'It's just a story,' said Leander.

'They're all just stories – none of this is possible. Cabinets and ghosts and her, whatever she is. Stories come from somewhere, don't they? If there's a speck of truth ...' said Charlotte.

Suddenly Leander grabbed her wrist. 'I saw something ... in the cell. It looked—'

A noise from the stable. 'There's no time,' said Felix. 'I'll try to keep her here.' He ran up the path and into the lair of the beast.

Charlotte gave Leander's hand a little squeeze for courage. 'You can do it, Leander. Go.'

She rushed off towards the inn, and heard Leander's footsteps going in the opposite direction as he heroically set off. He was so brave. If anyone could stop Pellar, Leander could. Her heart was rock-heavy for the two boys, each on their way to face their own terrible danger.

This won't be the last time I see them. It won't. Just keep running.

Frozen feet hit the stony road over and over again.

Felix touched his brother's Cabinet one more time before slipping into the stable. A burning oil lamp hung from a rusty bracket. Pinchbeck was as bold as ever: an escaped criminal stealing a horse, with the gall to light the lamps as she went.

There was only one horse here. Would she try to rig it up to the carriage anyway, or did she plan to escape on horseback?

252

'I told you to stay out,' said Pinchbeck, her back to the door. 'Since you're here, get to untangling the rope.' She turned and, seeing Felix, said, 'Oh, it's you, dear boy! Fine work tonight. I knew I could rely on you.'

Felix crouched by the pile of soggy, fraying rope and made a show of working loose the knots. 'Yes. They'll be hunting for you soon enough. Wise to stay low, not risk the open road.' He meant to slow Pinchbeck down, but it was sound advice. There would be few travellers in the harsh weather. They'd stand out more on the road than if they bedded down and kept quiet.

Did he *want* her to escape?

No! Of course not. Pinchbeck had betrayed him, lied to him for years, and there was nothing to stop her finishing off Felix and the others for good. Any loyalty he still felt was his foolish heart playing tricks. Echoes of their years together, nothing more.

'Where's Leander?' asked Pinchbeck.

'Playing lookout. He said you told him to.'

'Hmmm . . .' Her tone made Felix uneasy.

'I'm better with horses.'

'You don't know where mine are?'

'I don't,' said Felix with genuine regret. Pansy and Marigold were good girls. He hoped someone could find them a home. They had a few healthy years in them yet.

Pinchbeck had the horse loose and was leaning on the wall. 'I'm weary.'

'You must be tired from sitting in that cell.' Felix did his

253

best to keep his voice light and steady. 'I had to wait till the constable's wife was alone.'

'It's more than tired, boy.'

A few seconds passed in uncomfortable silence. Pinchbeck tapped her finger on a wooden beam. *Tap. Tap. Tap.*

'Faster, boy. You're dawdling.'

'The rats have been at this. It's nearly gnawed through. Is there another?' He was conscious of every move under Pinchbeck's gaze, like an actor who had forgotten his lines.

Pinchbeck didn't answer. When Felix looked up, she was staring at him intently.

'Where's your violin?'

Felix's stomach rolled. They had taken a gamble by hiding their Cabinets. If the distance didn't work, Pinchbeck could force them back inside and they'd be helpless.

'Where's your violin, Felix?'

'I left it with the carriage.' He feigned a renewed interest in the rope and pretended not to notice her gaze boring into him.

'With the carriage?'

'Yes,' he said, then, quickly changing the subject, 'I could cut off the rotten part of the rope probably.'

Not far away, Charlotte would be bursting into the inn and shouting for the constable. Somewhere Leander was leading Pellar on a merry dance round the town. Felix believed in them. They believed in him. He must act more convincingly than ever before.

'It isn't like you to be parted from it. That was foolish.'

'Yes, I suppose. I was fretting over you.'

'One might think you're hiding it on purpose. Keeping it away from me.' There was quiet danger in her voice, and the depth of silence that followed made Felix wish for the return of the storm.

'Why would I do that?' Felix even managed a smile as he stood up and dusted his hands on his trousers. He must be carefree, but not overly so. Worried about their escape, but not afraid of Pinchbeck. For comfort, he touched the wooden box in his pocket, making the smallest movement he could. He kept eye contact with Pinchbeck as he did so.

Her brow furrowed. Had she noticed? She had the alert stillness of an animal ready to pounce and Felix prepared himself to flee should she lunge.

Instead, Pinchbeck did something unexpected.

She started to cry. A fat, lazy tear trickled down her cheek.

'You wouldn't give up on me, would you?' Her expression, so cold a moment before, was despondent and sad.

'N-no,' said Felix, wrong-footed by this sudden change.

'All our years together. Did I not take good care of you? We've had some happy times, have we not?'

It was like a punch to the stomach. There had been good times. The home Pinchbeck took him from was no home at all. She was capable of dreadful things, but most days had been pleasant. The work had even been fun sometimes. Back when it had just been the two of them, they had invented so many of her seance tricks. One thing they had in common was that they both enjoyed an audience. He was a street child – he would never have had the chance to play his violin in all those fancy homes without Pinchbeck.

'Of course,' said Felix, forcing a tiny laugh, pretending not to notice her tear.

'Didn't we have some grand adventures?'

Pinchbeck had realized something was wrong. Perhaps she didn't know exactly what, but things were not going her way. He knew this was her way of reaching out to him, of begging him for help. She leaned heavily on the wooden wall, countenance grey and tired.

'We can still be great, you and I, when we take our act to London. This nastiness with the constable is nothing.'

It would be easy to go with her. If he told the truth, it'd all be over. She'd be so pleased, she might even let him have Isaak back—

'The others have never been anything but a bother,' Pinchbeck continued. 'But we have a special bond, don't we, Felix? We can go on together. Just the two of us as it used to be.'

Stop. Her words pulled Felix from any thoughts of betraying his friends. How easily she discarded Charlotte and Leander, how quickly she expected to be able to manipulate Felix. Whatever loyalty he had felt for Pinchbeck was gone. He'd spent as many years with Charlotte as he had with Isaak. Was she not his sister, too? He wouldn't let this woman – this villain! – take another family from him.

It was hard to keep a gentle expression when he was

in turmoil. Pinchbeck was waiting for a promise. Felix pretended not to notice anything was wrong.

'Is there anything I can use to cut this rope?' The horse was fretting as though it understood what was unfolding. Felix hunted for any tools lying around, deliberately turning his back on Pinchbeck to show a lack of concern. 'Ah, here—'

He reached for a hoof knife hanging above him. Pinchbeck's arm whipped out with the speed of an adder's tongue. She had Felix by the shirt and yanked him closer.

They were nose to nose. Felix's toes slipped on the straw-covered ground as she pushed him against the wall.

'What have you done, boy?'

Even in her weakened state, Pinchbeck was more than a match for a thin, ten-year-old boy who hadn't eaten or slept in for ever. If Felix hadn't been stolen, he'd be a man of eighteen, as strong and sturdy as his father.

'What have you done?'

'What do you mean, Madame?'

'Why am I so weak? Why are you acting so strangely? You've turned on me, haven't you?'

'I've always been loyal.'

Pinchbeck continued to glare.

'You've been a mother to me.' The words were rat droppings in his mouth. Felix's body was aflame with panic and the desperate prayer of the condemned man. 'You're helping me find my brother.'

Pinchbeck eased Felix back on to his feet and smiled. 'Of

257

course, you've always been faithful, my boy, that's why I've had you longest of all.' The smile grew wider. 'Show me what's in your pocket.'

Felix dared not move. Where was Charlotte with the constable? Someone had to come. *Please.*

Pinchbeck reached into Felix's coat pocket and drew out Isaak's box.

'I . . .' Felix fought to drag air into his lungs. There was no hope of regaining her trust.

'Now we both know where we stand. Where is the other little wretch? Gone for the constable, no doubt? Remember, child, there's no happy ending for you without me. Your fate is sealed to mine. Be a good boy and call them off.'

She lifted Isaak's Cabinet above her head and held it to the lamp.

'You know what happens if I burn this.'

23
The Star:
A Glimmer of Hope

LEANDER

It felt to Leander as if he'd been running for ever. This time he was running alone, into unthinkable danger. The darkness was suffocating.

Charlotte and Felix were safe, but for how long? And Leander was searching for Pellar – a terrifying creature who would sacrifice the children to get his revenge.

It was surely madness, but Leander no longer felt afraid. He'd used up all the fear he had. Fear was gone; strength was gone; hope was gone. Yet somehow his legs kept moving. It was frustratingly slow, a bad dream in which he ran and ran but never gained any ground.

It was late now and the little town slumbered around him.

How can they sleep when the world is ending? Leander thought. How were they not woken by the deafening roar of the blood rushing through his body?

After he had put some distance between him and the stable, he slowed his feet to listen to the night. Noises spilled out from homes – a child crying for his mother, low voices over a late supper. The streets themselves remained quiet. Leander looked through the holey stone, though he wasn't sure what he was supposed to see. Then a vague shimmer from far away led him through the streets. A clue from the stone or just his imagination?

He paused as he heard a sound round the next corner. Footsteps? *Yes.* A slow but solid gait, heavier on one side than the other. Leander tried to remember the way Pellar had moved in the graveyard. Could it be? A rough, gravelly cough answered his question.

Gathering all his courage, Leander stepped out within arm's reach of Edmund Pellar. The man looked as peculiar and disturbing as before, though he stood a little straighter now, as if the long walk had somehow refreshed him. On his back he carried a thin cloth bag, the strap slung over his shoulder and across his chest. It had to contain his gun.

Leander expected Pellar to speak, but he did not. Instead, he continued walking at the same pace with no change of expression, as if Leander was no more than a creature scurrying across his path. Leander held firm. Pellar marched past, knocking him aside with his shoulder.

'Mister Pellar!' Leander called after him. The man grunted. Leander walked alongside him, skipping sideways to stay in his line of sight. 'Mister Pellar, I'm the one—'

'I know who you are. That woman has sent you out

into the cold to mislead me. She is a coward, afraid to face me herself.'

'She doesn't know you're coming.' Leander touched Pellar's arm, and he roughly shrugged him off.

'All the better, then.'

'Wait!' Leander stepped directly in front of Pellar, causing the man to trip. 'Please, please wait, sir. We're so close to having her captured.'

'The other boy said she was locked up already. You are all lyin',' Pellar growled.

'She *was* locked up! She was caught by the constable. I was too! They got me free, but that meant she was released as well and now she's stealing a horse, but Charlotte can—' The story spilled out like tangled yarn and he hung from the man's coat as Pellar kept walking. 'She'll be locked up again soon and then she'll be easy for you to find. Only please give us a little time to free ourselves so we don't perish with her.'

'I've done enough waitin', child.' He swung round a corner, heading towards the middle of the town, closer to Pinchbeck and Felix.

'You're going the wrong way,' Leander tried. Pellar gave a hollow half-laugh.

'You shan't fool me.'

'Sir,' Leander pleaded, 'if you have any kindness left in your heart—'

Pellar stopped and shook his head.

'You shouldn't have been pulled into Pinchbeck's

wickedness,' he said to Leander. 'It wasn't fair nor right. But it has to end this way.'

Leander was burning despite the chill of the night. He couldn't, wouldn't believe Pellar. There *must* be another answer.

Pellar held Leander's shoulders firmly, but there was no menace in the gesture. 'I won't let her take another child. I can't have that on my conscience. I'll give her one last chance to repent and give it all up. But make no mistake: I will shoot her when she refuses.'

'I won't let you.' said Leander.

CHARLOTTE

The inn wasn't far. If only Charlotte could run faster. Pinchbeck would be in a hurry to get away.

Ouch! A loose cobble made her stumble and wrench her ankle. She found her balance, testing her foot. It hurt but it held her weight. She gritted her teeth against the pain and pushed on.

She'd burst in and shout for the constable. Say someone was trying to steal a horse. That was the best plan. No time to waste explaining the whole story. She feared they wouldn't listen, her looking so wild in her burnt and stained clothing and her odd luminous smudges.

As she drew closer to the inn, her heart leaped. A carriage was pulling up in front of the inn. A carriage bearing the Litchfield crest.

Uncle!

Charlotte's legs were suddenly string beneath her weight and her head was full of stars. Salvation was within reach.

She hobbled the last few yards, shouting with all her might and waving her arms above her head. Soft light spilling from the inn caught the powder on her dress and turned her into a glowing apparition. The driver was dismounting and jumped aside as she swept past. She yanked the carriage door open with such force she almost fell over.

'Uncle!'

'Hey, you!' yelled the driver behind her.

'Uncle? Are you there?' In the gloom, she could barely make out two shapes. An elderly man, thin and hunched, stared back, wide-eyed and alarmed. Behind him a sour-faced woman wore a matching expression.

The heavy hand of the driver clamped down on Charlotte's shoulder and began to pull her away.

'It's me! It's Charlotte!' she pleaded, shrugging off the man's grip with new-found strength. She put her foot on the step. The woman shrieked and cowered away. 'Please, Uncle. You have to recognize me.'

Her uncle continued to stare and a second man joined the driver, pulling Charlotte backwards. She was not strong enough to resist two of them. They dragged her away, her fingers losing their grip on the door and her shoes slipping on the uneven ground.

'Wait!'

The old man's voice was loud and deep enough to echo

round the square, despite his frail appearance. The men stopped pulling, big hands still tight on her shoulders. Charlotte held her breath. Her uncle struggled to his feet and laboriously climbed down from his carriage, followed by the woman, who hung back, holding the door like a shield.

He shuffled towards her, leaning heavily on a silver-topped cane.

'Charlotte? My Charlotte?'

'Careful, Your Lordship,' said the woman. 'The streets are full of beggars and thieves.'

Lord Litchfield ignored her. 'Could it really be you?'

For a short eternity, the whole world was still. Then they surged towards each other and Charlotte fell against his chest. His arms folded round her. The years had not been kind; he was thin and small. But his smell – the scent of him, his clothes and hair – and she was a child again, listening to a story on his lap by the fire. Her cheek brushed against the soft silk of his cravat – mourning black.

'Honeybee. Are my eyes playing tricks?' He moved back to examine her at arm's length, some of her mud and powder left behind on his travelling coat. He did not notice. 'I found the letter, but I hardly dared believe . . . Safe.'

Charlotte desperately wanted to wallow in this moment for ever, but everything hung in the balance. This was not her happy ending – not yet.

'I'm not safe. Others are in danger, too. Pinchbeck—'

'That infernal woman. I knew it! Where is she?'

'In a stable, stealing a horse to flee. The constable is—'
She pointed at the inn, too overcome to finish her sentence.

'Mrs Smart, instruct the constable to follow us immediately.'
The woman scowled but hurried to the inn.

'Charlotte.' He squeezed her arms as though checking she
was real. 'Take me there.' He signalled for the driver to return
to his post and, with obvious effort, clambered up after him.
Charlotte followed.

She pointed out the way to go. Wind blustered round
them, whipping up her hair and clothes. Her teeth chattered
and her stomach churned. It felt as if the whole world was
somehow ending. But her uncle was there. *If I die today, at
least we were together one last time.*

Lord Litchfield kept a firm grip on her hand. The hurried
footfalls of the constable's men joined the rumbling of the
carriage. The noise was too loud for her to explain or try
to talk. Instead, she thought of the boys and silently prayed
Pinchbeck was still in the stable. She and Felix should have
agreed on a sign that he could leave if Pinchbeck moved
on. And Leander – had he reached Pellar? Had he come to
any harm? She shouldn't have sent him alone. Of the three
of them, he was the newest, and the most naive. What
had she done?

What choice did I have?

The horses' hooves beat out a message. *Dan-ger-com-
ing-dan-ger-com-ing-dan-ger—*

It was too loud. So much noise . . . No chance of catching
Pinchbeck unawares . . .

'Stop!' she shouted, and the carriage pulled to a halt. She was down as soon as the wheels stopped turning. The driver leaped from his seat and a moment later the constable and three other men thundered up behind them.

Suddenly she saw a breathless Leander come rushing from the opposite direction, followed by the determined stride of Edmund Pellar.

24
Judgement:
A Final Reckoning, Absolution

Fear clawed at Felix's belly, so strong he could hardly draw breath. The wind howled round the little stable as they faced each other, Pinchbeck still clutching Isaak's Cabinet.

'Leander is outside, keeping watch.' His voice cracked. 'Please don't burn it.'

'Call him, then.'

Felix hesitated. She waved the tiny wooden box dangerously close to the top of the lamp flame. If it burned, would Isaak burn, too?

'Wait, I—'

'If Leander is waiting outside, you'll have no problem calling him in.' Still holding the box out towards the flame, she edged her way along the wall and unhooked the curved hoof knife.

I should have grabbed it! Now she had his brother and a weapon.

Was it too late to beg? To give it all up for his brother?

The horse gave a small whinny and her ears twitched. There were sounds from the street. It might be Charlotte, or else the stable owner had heard them.

'I'll get him,' said Felix.

'Quickly.'

He darted to the wide stable door and pushed. Movement out on the road; people were gathering at the end of the path.

'She's here!' a man shouted from the road.

Felix looked back at Pinchbeck in terror, knowing the ruse was over.

'You've betrayed me,' she said. 'I knew it.'

Should he run, or try to grab Isaak's Cabinet?

He hesitated a moment too long. Pinchbeck lunged at him, the wooden box still clutched between gnarled fingers. Wheezing with the effort, she yanked Felix by the collar and held the curved blade of the hoof knife against his neck, then shuffled forward into the open doorway.

'Stay back!' she shouted to the people outside. 'Or I'll kill the boy!'

LEANDER

Leander had failed. Pellar was unstoppable.

Noises up ahead. He rounded the last corner to the lane and was met by a commotion.

A carriage stood abandoned in the road near the stable. Not Pinchbeck's. Leander saw Charlotte on the path leading towards the closed stable, a smartly dressed old man next to her with his hand on her shoulder.

Lord Litchfield. Just as Leander remembered him.

Their plan had worked. Five or six men were running up the path towards the stable. Among them he recognized the constable.

Is Pinchbeck still inside? And Felix?

'Round the back!' Lord Litchfield said with the air of a man used to giving orders. Two men, one in livery, bounded round the side of the stable. The doors of nearby houses were opening, some by inches, others swung wide as people came to see what was happening.

Pellar was only thirty yards from the stable path, and closing. Leander had raced as fast as his tired legs could go, but the man had kept pace, his long stride uneven but relentless.

Charlotte turned towards the sound of the man's footsteps and Leander watched her face as she first saw him and then Pellar, her expression changing from joy to horror in an instant.

But Leander wasn't giving up now. If he couldn't stop Pellar walking, he'd at least stop him from shooting. He charged and lunged for the gun bag on the man's back. He grabbed it and yanked hard enough to make Pellar stumble backwards, but the strap across his chest was too strong to give. Pellar snatched at the air to stop his fall and Leander tried again to pull the weapon free.

Man and boy fell together, limbs tangled. The butt of the

gun hit the ground next to Leander's head and the jolt caused it to fire into the air, leaving a smouldering hole through the bag.

Crack-BOOM!

The bang of the gun echoed in Leander's skull and brought a strange stillness to the air. Everyone froze.

Pinchbeck was a silhouette in the lamplit doorway. Under her arm was a squirming shape.

Felix! Pinchbeck had a knife to his throat.

As Leander was distracted, Pellar flung him aside and got to his feet.

The constable pointed at Leander. 'That boy was locked up with her! Grab him!' A tall man darted across the road and twisted Leander's arm up his back until he was doubled over, unable to do anything but watch.

'Repent, Augustina!' shouted Pellar, his hoarse voice somehow carrying over the commotion.

Pinchbeck turned, her expression moving from surprise to horror to an unconvincing attempt at a smile.

'Edmund,' she said. 'My love—'

'Witch,' interrupted Pellar. 'Betrayer.' Patiently, with twisted, unsteady hands, he set about reloading his gun.

Leander looked on in horror. *Why is no one stopping him?* But all eyes were fixed on Pinchbeck.

'Don't let him—' Leander tried to pull away from his captor, who gave his arm another wrench. Pain shot through it like a spike of hot ice.

'Where have you been, husband?' said Pinchbeck, her grip on Felix tightening.

270

'I shall give you one chance to renounce your evil.'

'Help me, my love.' Pinchbeck sounded so pathetic Leander almost felt sorry for her, but the knife in her hand belied her words. 'We can be together again. I've missed you.'

The constable's men edged forward, surrounding Pinchbeck and the stable at a wary distance.

'Stay back!' Pinchbeck shouted. 'Don't make me kill him.' Felix squirmed like bait on a hook and Pinchbeck grunted with the strain. Something fell from her hand and rolled across the paving slabs in a steady circle. Felix stretched out his hand towards it, though it was too far away for him to reach.

'He's got a gun! You have to stop him!' Leander struggled, but the man holding him cuffed him across the ear and ignored his pleas.

'Give yourself up, woman.' Lord Litchfield spoke fearlessly to Pinchbeck. He began to walk towards her with slow, measured paces. Leander's heart was in his throat to see it. 'You've no chance of escape. Let the boy go, and you might avoid the gallows yet.'

Such bravery. The lord was smaller, older, weaker. He had no weapon, yet still he inched towards her. The constable's men waited, prepared to pounce the moment Felix was safe.

'Come on, son,' Litchfield said in softer tones to Felix, arms outstretched. 'Pull yourself free of her.'

Felix tried, his fingers digging into Pinchbeck's arm, heels scrabbling in the dust ... Pinchbeck pulled him tighter. Her hair was completely white now. Red face, teeth clenched – Leander could see it hurt her to hold on, but hold on she did.

271

In the stable, the horse was stamping and fretting, at risk of bolting. Pinchbeck ignored it.

'I can't,' said Felix.

'You can do it, Felix!' shouted Leander.

'Leander!' Felix yelled back. 'Isaak's box!'

The object Pinchbeck dropped. It was Isaak's Cabinet! In all the chaos and with so many people milling about, it could get trampled underfoot.

Leander lifted his heel and stomped as hard as he could, scraping his boot down his captor's shin. The man cried out and loosened his grip enough that Leander could twist to face him. He bit the man's forearm as hard as he could.

'You little—!' the man yelled but Leander was already away. He pushed through the constable's men and ran between Lord Litchfield and Pinchbeck. He grabbed Isaak's Cabinet.

Pinchbeck snarled in frustration.

'I've got it, Felix!' Leander shouted. He raced towards Charlotte, well away from Pinchbeck's reach. 'I've got Isaak. I've got him.'

CHARLOTTE

Charlotte could hardly breathe. Felix, underfed and frozen, had not the strength to fight, though Pinchbeck was older and weaker than ever with four spirits weighing on her. She was cornered, but still fighting, hissing at the gathering crowd. How much longer could she hold out?

'I've got Isaak's Cabinet,' panted Leander as he ran towards her. He was ice-white and looked about ready to drop.

Isaak's Cabinet. A flash of clarity. 'We need to get the Cabinets!'

Charlotte sprinted back towards the yard where they had hidden their Cabinets, pain shooting through her sore ankle with every step. Leander followed at her heels. Left at the corner, through the alley, hop over the gutter, round the wall.

If she opened the violin case, then Felix could disappear. Pinchbeck might be able to force them into their Cabinets, but there's no way she could lock them before being caught by the men in the stables. So they'd be able to just come straight back out.

'Here.' She pointed out the hiding place to Leander.

Leander kicked away the broken bricks and yanked open the outhouse door. He slung the violin case strap over his head and Charlotte picked up her lantern, then noticed the bag they'd found in the wall.

If each one contained another captured spirit, and too many spirits made Pinchbeck weak, then maybe ...

Elation and hope propelled Charlotte along faster than ever. Everything was beginning to make sense. The book. The rats that were everywhere Pinchbeck went. The strange comment to Charlotte about how she should have been a man instead ... as if she could have *chosen*. What if she had? What if she hadn't always been in that body?

'The bag—' Charlotte started. There wasn't enough time

to explain and she was breathless from the effort. 'More Cabinets. More Cabinets make her weaker.'

'Yes!' Leander shouted. 'We can open them all. Then she'll be too weak to fight off the men.'

'There was a secret picture.' She stumbled and had to grab on to a wall to take the weight off her ankle. 'Ouch.'

'Here, I've got you.' Leander came to her side and put his arm round her waist. 'Lean on me.' She placed her arm over his shoulder and he helped her walk.

'There was a picture in the spellbook. A secret one. It showed a man turning into a rat. There were pictures. Of our Cabinets.' She winced in pain. 'Your story – the Rat King. I think it's her.'

'In the fairy tale ... the Rat King used up all his magic and was stuck as a rat for ever,' finished Leander.

It was impossible. Surely it was impossible. And yet ...

'Run ahead,' said Charlotte. 'I'm too slow. I'll catch you up. Run and open the Cabinets.'

'I don't want to leave you,' said Leander.

'Go! Felix needs us!'

LEANDER

'Felix!' Leander appeared round the corner of the street, waving the violin case in the air. He stood by the wheel of Lord Litchfield's carriage and set down the bag of Cabinets very gently, afraid of damaging them. With trembling fingers, he unlatched the violin case before quickly starting to open the sack of Cabinets.

Felix's eyes closed in relief and he melted away from Pinchbeck's grip, vanishing to nothing. A murmur of confusion and fear rippled over the onlookers.

'*Exsisto!*' Pinchbeck roared. Felix had no choice but to emerge, taking solid form again beside Leander.

This led to much shouting and the horse, thoroughly spooked, reared up on its back legs and bolted. The constable's men threw themselves back into the bushes to avoid being trampled as it clattered off through the crowd.

Pinchbeck grabbed a pitchfork. The men recovered and advanced on her once again, but she swung and jabbed, forcing them back.

But now something else was happening. Pinchbeck's command hadn't only summoned Felix. Gradually, one by one, other shapes began to take form around Leander and Felix.

Charlotte's plan was working!

Slowly, the spirits solidified, some taking longer than others to find their substance. Each was different – some poured out like treacle and others crackled into being. How long had these pour souls been trapped? A tall, wiry boy with red hair and a crooked nose. A lad with deep brown skin in a red embroidered suit. Two children with white-blond curls and matching frock coats. Shock and wonder painted their faces.

'*Abeo!*' shouted Pinchbeck.

Felix disappeared. The other spirits also vanished, forced back inside their Cabinets. But not Leander – his Cabinet was still lost. There was no time to spare. He jumped back into action.

'The sack,' Leander urged Felix. 'Help me open the Cabinets.'

Reaching into the bag, he pulled out a glass jar and strained to remove the stopper. He bit the old cork and pulled it free with his teeth. Next a silk purse. His fingers fumbled at the muddled knot in the string. With their Cabinets open, the spirits inside were free to emerge.

And then Felix appeared again.

'Here,' said Leander, passing him Isaak's box. Felix desperately pulled at it, trying to open the warped lid.

At last Charlotte arrived. Leander was overcome with relief and hope that the three of them were finally back together. Charlotte hobbled over to them and immediately began to help, pulling out a square tin and prising off the lid.

'Devils!' screamed Pinchbeck, her voice already hoarse and limp. She was hunched over now, her eyes completely black, the white of her hair seeming to spread over her flesh.

It was true. She *was* the Rat King, and her magic was about to run out.

Pellar laughed a dark, hearty, vengeful laugh, still holding the gun. Could he see it, too?

'*Abeo!*' croaked Pinchbeck, but with no real power now. The spirits once again became vapour, swallowed into their Cabinets, but it was futile. With their Cabinets open, they reappeared at once, unwilling to be contained a moment longer. Leander lifted out the last Cabinet – a leather spectacle case – and snapped it open.

Pinchbeck howled. Leander looked up in time to see her

staggering backwards into the stable, pitchfork trembling in her twisted fingers, shoulders stooped, all fight draining away. More than that, she was changing, every part of her body twisting and stretching and shrinking, fur spreading, eyes growing darker. She was no longer human, halfway between woman and rodent. The weight of all those captured souls was draining the last of her magic and she was transforming. Surely Pinchbeck would release them now, if such a thing was possible. Surely she would save herself from becoming a rat.

Only Felix wasn't looking at the transformation of Pinchbeck. Instead, he was staring at the shimmering, transparent form of a small boy who had emerged from the battered wooden box Felix had at last managed to prise open. Felix sank to his knees and put his arms out to the boy, who ran to him, becoming more solid with each step.

'Isaak!' Felix cried.

'You shan't take me alive,' Pinchbeck croaked, snatching the oil lamp and casting it to the floor. In an instant, the straw and wood were engulfed in flames.

The constable leaped back from the fire and the stable door swung shut. A final image of Pinchbeck was seared in Leander's brain: her skirts encircled by tongues of flame, as though hell itself had opened up to claim her.

She's dying!

Charlotte clung to Leander's shoulder. Pinchbeck would be consumed by the fire. They had won, and they were going to die anyway.

25

Death:
Endings, Transition,
Metamorphosis

LEANDER

Shoving, shouting, crying. Was it over? Was this where he would die?

In an act of foolish heroism, some men tried to get into the stable, to save Pinchbeck or to catch her – Leander wasn't sure which.

'Get her!' the men were shouting. 'Take her alive!'

The newly rescued spirits of ten or twelve children cowered and wept, wandering between the frightened and baffled locals.

Lord Litchfield fought his way through the people to his niece. Leander was bundled out of the way by people carrying water in buckets and jugs in a useless attempt to douse the flames. The fire was already reaching its long fingers up the walls and threatening the roof. Pinchbeck could not possibly survive.

Charlotte sat on the step of her uncle's carriage, crying in long-overdue sobs, and Lord Litchfield lifted Felix's chin to check he hadn't been cut by the knife.

Leander was the only person who remembered Edmund Pellar.

He watched in dumb silence as Pellar walked calmly towards the stable and bent to scoop something up, which he then dropped into a small sack. He tied it with a knot and tucked it into the pocket of his greatcoat.

And then Pellar strode away.

Leander chased him down, catching up with him in the next road.

'No need to follow me, child. You did it.'

'The fire – it will kill her. We'll all die!'

'It shan't kill her because she isn't there.'

Leander opened his mouth to argue. Pellar took out the sack from his pocket. Inside Leander could make out the bulging, wriggling shape of a rat. 'She's safe with me.'

'That's Pinchbeck? The rat?'

'Aye. The rat.' Pellar's eyes sparkled, and the whisper of a smile played on his lips as he put the sack back.

'How? Why?' The shadow in the cell, the hairs on her cheek . . .

'You left her no choice. The spirits were out, her magic exposed. Perchance she could have held out a little longer, but capture was inevitable. What then? The gallows? Not Augustina Pinchbeck. Better to go on her own terms.'

'But if she could turn into a rat why didn't she do it before? When she needed to escape the cell?'

'Think, boy. The only way for her form to change was for her to give up all her precious captives. Everythin' she'd worked for. Do you think she'd do that if there was any other choice?'

'Is that really her? Are you sure?' Leander had seen her changing with his own eyes, but he could hardly believe it. And she had been so much bigger, and the fire had spread so quickly.

'I'd show you, but the other lad took the thing—'

'This?' Leander drew the hagstone from his pocket and peered through it. Sure enough, there was an odd misty-purple glow around Pellar's pocket where the rat was. 'Oh.'

Pellar nodded, and held out his hand for the stone. Leander gave it back.

'So what now? Are we free?'

Pellar threw back his head in laughter. 'Free, child? Can't you tell? Can't you feel it with every ounce of your being?'

And Leander could. Underneath the cold and the ache and the exhaustion, there was a pleasing hollowness in his chest, as though he was breathing a little deeper. 'Is it truly over?'

'For you, it is over. For Pinchbeck –' he reached into his greatcoat and pulled out the writhing sack again – 'maybe not.'

'Are you going to kill her?'

'Oh no. I shall show her the same mercy she showed us. A lifetime in a cage should be a good start.'

'Why didn't you tell us what to do?' asked Leander. 'That

280

we only had to release the other spirits to weaken her power so much that she'd have no choice but to set us all free?'

'I had no inklin' there were so many, nor that Augustina would be so desperate. You were clever, and you were lucky. I should know. I was in the business of luck. Here.' He shoved the rat bag back into his pocket and unpinned something from his waistcoat. He pressed it into Leander's palm. 'For luck, with my gratitude.'

It was Leander's locket, chain intact.

'Where did you—'

'No more questions, child. Some things in this world should remain mysteries. Now go! Go to your friends! Taste your freedom! Rejoice in it!'

Then he walked away into the night.

Leander rubbed his fingers over the cool, reassuring shape of his mother's locket.

'Leander?' came Charlotte's voice from far away. 'Leander!'

And Leander started running for what he hoped would be the last time.

26

King of Cups:
Generosity, Kindness,
a Father Figure

FELIX

The fire raged as though the earth itself was determined to burn away any memory of Pinchbeck and her crimes. Charlotte's uncle tried to usher them to the warmth and safety of the inn, but the children refused to go until the wood was consumed and the stable no more than a skeleton of glowing charcoal.

Pinchbeck was reduced to the vile rodent that she was. Leander explained Pellar's intention to keep her caged and tormented. A just end? Not quite as much as she deserved. All those years she had dragged Felix up and down the country, letting him believe he was searching for his brother. And she'd had him captive all along. There were a million things he needed to say to Isaak, but the only words Felix could find were, 'I love you.'

Eleven other spirits had been released. Eleven stolen lives.

Eleven shattered families, not counting the three broken Cabinets they carefully pieced together from the shards at the bottom of the sack. Felix recognized some of them as the poor children Pinchbeck had stolen during their time together. Others, it seemed, were far older.

Felix didn't even know how to feel. Elated. Angry. Betrayed. Overjoyed. Even a little sad – he knew Pinchbeck deserved her fate, but he had cared for her, and the fire hadn't been quite strong enough to burn away every trace of those memories.

The other spirit children were disorientated. Some were older than Charlotte, others little more than toddlers. Why would Pinchbeck steal such small children? What possible use could they be? Some cried while others laughed and leaped into the air, delighting in their physical form again. As the hours passed, they gradually became aware that they were free and could no longer disappear into their Cabinets. A joyful notion, but one that raised more questions. Most of the children were far from home. All had been imprisoned for many, many years – most even longer than Felix. Their families were likely dead or scattered to the wind. Some of the children didn't know their own last names. Three spoke no English. Reunion with their loved ones was impossible.

The owner of the inn was not happy when asked to provide lodgings for fourteen children. It was a tiny place, not accustomed to more than the occasional traveller. A good deal of money exchanged hands to allow them to sleep higgledy-piggledy on the floor of the inn's two guest rooms. They couldn't very well wander the streets all night, Charlotte's uncle said, and nothing useful could be done until morning.

Leander and Isaak supped on hot gruel, side by side. Felix sat with them, but found it hard to eat. All he wanted to do was stare at them.

'What are you thinking?' said Leander. 'You're miles away.'

'I was thinking how lucky I am to have my brothers back.'

'Brothers?' said Leander with a smile.

'Brothers,' said Felix. 'I'm glad you came along and messed everything up.'

'Me too,' said Leander.

Isaak reached across the table to squeeze Felix's hand. He hadn't spoken since the fire, but Felix wasn't worried. They were together now. Safe. Isaak was probably bubbling with the same confusing mix of emotions as Felix. He would speak when he was ready.

One by one the spirit children – *Just children now*, Felix supposed – were taken up to the two tiny bedrooms upstairs to sleep. Felix went outside with his violin to try to make sense of what had happened.

He lifted the bow and let his tale spill out through the still night air. He played quick, high notes like tiny, pattering paws, and long, slow, lamenting wails. Felix closed his eyes and let the music tell the story of the Rat King, and three stolen children running through the night, and a long, long journey home.

'I heard you,' came Isaak's voice when the last note hung in the air. 'I always knew you were looking for me.'

'I had a promise to keep,' said Felix.

CHARLOTTE

Though she was exhausted, Charlotte's mind was too busy to sleep.

The other children had settled at last. Felix and Isaak slept curled together like cats, while Leander burrowed beneath soft blankets. The housekeeper, Mrs Smart, had been instructed to take care of the little ones, but the woman was as gentle as limestone and soon became impatient with their fretting. Charlotte soothed them into a big shared bed, and a little before dawn they were finally all asleep. Among them was a small, fair-featured little girl Charlotte had never expected to see again. Rosa. The last of Pinchbeck's victims, at least until Leander came along. Charlotte pulled a blanket up over Rosa's sleeping frame. It was a miracle, as though she had risen from the dead.

Charlotte wandered into the hallway and sat down on the bare wooden stairs, still covered in the mess of her adventure. She rested her head against the panelling and picked at the loose threads on her dress.

'May I join you?'

Charlotte jumped up.

'Sit down,' said her uncle. 'Rest.'

She sat on the stair and he creaked and groaned his way down beside her.

'You were lost in thought,' he said.

'I was trying to make sense of everything. I can't believe we're together finally. And yet nothing will be the same as before.'

'No. I am grateful nevertheless.'

They sat a while, content. Dry mud on the hem of her dress was beginning to flake off. It was calming to think of mundane things like cloth and mud. Far easier than thinking of flames and magic and a dozen children without homes.

'I'm so sorry,' said her uncle at last.

'You had no way to find me.'

'More than that, Charlotte. It was my fault you were taken.'

'I traded her my lantern. That's how she caught me.' Charlotte didn't know how to explain. It all sounded so impossible. 'We argued, do you remember? I wanted to go to the parties and you said ...'

'You were too young.' The old man nodded.

'You'd been so busy with work. I thought you were going to send me away.' She sniffed. 'I wanted an adventure. It sounds so stupid now. I only thought we might be gone a few days. I wanted you to miss me, I suppose.'

'It wasn't your fault.' Litchfield sighed. 'She stole you for a reason, Charlotte. To hurt me. Revenge for my misdeeds.' He dabbed at his eye with the corner of his handkerchief.

'No,' said Charlotte. 'It wasn't like that.'

She put her small hand into his bony one, skin as soft and thin as chiffon. He had wasted away without her.

'Do you remember the work I did? My writing?'

'You wrote about mediums, and how they were frauds. I remember some of them coming to the house, even though you would never let me watch. Pinchbeck was one of them.'

'The fashion for seances disgusted me. It started as a harmless game, I'm sure, but it went too far. These mediums who claim to talk to the dead, they're all charlatans. The worst part is how they prey on grieving families. Using their pain for profit. It's unforgivable.'

Charlotte felt heavy with guilt. Unforgivable. For so long, she had pushed aside her doubts about their work – she had no choice but to take part – but, now that it was over, years of regret and shame waited to overwhelm her.

'I wrote about the tricks they used to fool others, thinking knowledge would stop people being so easily taken in.' He sighed. 'Augustina Pinchbeck sent me a letter, and said she was a true medium. Offered to prove it and I allowed her into our home.'

'I know, we were introduced. That's why I stopped to talk to her that day in the woods – I wouldn't have spoken to a stranger. But that's not your fault. She wanted to get her hands on a rich girl. If not me, she would've taken the next girl she found.'

Her uncle shook his head. 'No, I think it was more than that. I did a bad thing.'

'Oh?' said Charlotte.

'When I invited her to perform, I intended to expose her as a fake. I expected to catch her with trick candles and fake limbs and all the usual paraphernalia. But there was nothing.'

'She did use those things,' said Charlotte. 'She must have deliberately left them behind when she met you.'

'I was baffled. Couldn't guess how she did it. There was a haunted violin played by a ghost in the dark. I held it in my own hands and couldn't solve the mystery.'

'Felix.' Felix performing his music in her own parlour before she ever knew him, her own dear uncle cradling his violin . . .

'She gloated. She had bested me. I *knew* it was a trick, but I couldn't prove it.' He closed his eyes, shook his head at the memory. 'So I lied.'

'Lied?'

'I couldn't say she was the real thing. It would undo all the good I'd done with my articles. I had witnesses, and I needed them to verify my report.' He cleared his throat and lowered his voice. 'I hid a few props of my own among her things. When we raised the lights, everyone believed she had put them there to trick us.'

'She must have been angry.' Pinchbeck would never tolerate being humiliated in such a way.

'Furious. She swore I'd live to regret it. And then she left. I published my articles, and heard no more about her.'

Charlotte let his words sink into her mind like rocks into deep water.

'Is that when she took me?'

'A month later. I had no reason to think it was connected. You'd disappeared on your morning walk. I feared you had fallen in the woods, or toppled into the lake.'

288

So it hadn't been a chance meeting. Pinchbeck had planned her kidnap.

'Why did you invite her back?'

'Years of sitting alone and wondering. Wealth buys a certain privilege. There were searches – your name was spread as far as I could manage. Weeks became months and I knew you must be dead. Still, it consumed me. I saw no one, rarely left my study.'

Charlotte rested her head on his shoulder. Her absence had tortured him, as Isaak's disappearance had torn at Felix. All the lost children asleep upstairs had left someone behind, suffering the same way.

'Then in the paper – barely a week or two ago – a photographer claiming that not only could she contact the dead, she could capture their image. Augustina Pinchbeck, the one medium I couldn't disprove—'

'She might have the answers after all.'

'Yes.'

'I was there, Uncle. I was in your parlour that day.'

'I thought I'd never see you again, yet there you were, as I remembered you. And later I found a letter.'

'My note.'

'Too strange to be real, but it was your handwriting, and the honeybee you drew ... I sent word through old friends to stop Pinchbeck at any cost. The rest you know.'

She threw her arms round his neck, tears flowing down her cheeks as he embraced her.

'How can this be, Charlotte?'

'I can't explain it. And I don't know what will happen now.' She wiped her face with one sleeve, the fabric rough against her weather-chafed cheeks. 'I suppose . . . perhaps we will begin to grow old, now the magic is done.'

At least she hoped so. They deserved to grow up and grow old like everyone else. Pinchbeck's spell was broken; the Cabinets were just ordinary objects again. Surely their bodies would be allowed to age at last. She had been the same for so many years, it would feel strange to see her body change and grow.

'I will see you are cared for always. No more harm shall befall you. I promise.'

'Felix and Leander, too? I won't be parted from them. I wouldn't be alive without them.'

'And the boys, too. As long as I live. All of them.'

LEANDER

Leander woke slowly from sweet dreams, stretching out his sore limbs. He could tell it was daylight before he opened his eyes and he remembered: *It's over.* He savoured the glorious sensation, enjoying the warmth of the soft blankets against his skin. He had slept for a long time and some of the others were already up. Felix was gone. A small boy slept curled up at the end of the bed, and a lanky youth was snoring on the rug.

Leander rolled over and started. Mrs Smart was standing over him.

'I knew it was you, toad.' Her voice was hushed but bitter.

'Mrs Smart—'

'Laid there like the cat who got the cream. I don't know how you did it—'

'What are you talking about?' He sat up and scratched his head. Mrs Smart was less scary here, in this warm, light place. After all the dangers he had survived.

'The master's taking them all back to the big house, to find them a trade or a home to go to.'

A home.

'But not you, swine.' Mrs Smart stood, hands on hips, bending over to glower at him. 'There's no place in that house for you. Wait till the master hears of your thieving ways.'

'Wait until he hears of yours,' Leander hissed. Mrs Smart sneered.

'The boy criminal turns up with the master's missing girl? Somehow you're responsible for whatever villainy happened to her.'

'How could I be? I was seven years old when she went missing!'

'And she hasn't aged a day in years. For all I know, you're the same breed of devil. These little children will have a home, but you, you'll rot in the workhouse as you deserve. I'll see to it.'

Would they believe this horrible woman? Mrs Smart had often used the master as a threat, reminding Leander how much he hated thieves, how cruel he'd be if he found Leander sleeping in the library. But Charlotte spoke of a loving uncle who cherished her. If he was willing to find homes for all those children, surely he'd forgive Leander his misbehaviour.

'Charlotte will tell him the truth.' Leander folded his arms and stared right back at her.

'Does Lady Charlotte know what you are? A dirty thief? A beggar? She's a high-born lady. She'll have no time for you now she's back to her station.' Mrs Smart smiled like a weasel. 'Or we can come to an arrangement, you and me.'

'She knows who I am,' said Leander with more courage than he felt. A tiny doubt crept into his mind. Charlotte had grown to care for him, but that was when she had nothing and no one else. She had her home back now. Would she really still want him around? Being alone after everything he had gone through seemed too much to bear.

'Get out, witch.' Charlotte was standing in the doorway.

Mrs Smart snapped her mouth shut, surprised, then pursed her lips.

'Leander, come and have breakfast. We have a long journey ahead.'

Relieved, Leander scrambled out of bed and pushed past the scowling woman. Charlotte stared at Mrs Smart with the same fierceness he'd seen that first day in the woods. She guided Leander out into the corridor and down the stairs. Music from Felix's violin drifted in from the street.

'She shouldn't be here, but Uncle's health wasn't good enough to travel alone.' Charlotte pushed open a door to where seven or eight children were eating bowls of porridge under the bemused gaze of the innkeeper's wife.

'She won't bother you again. I won't allow it.'

27

The World: Completion, Success, Accomplishment

LEANDER

Coaches were ordered; hampers were filled. People ran to and fro, packing and preparing for the journey ahead. They were squeezed into three carriages. Leander, Charlotte, Felix and Isaak rode in the front one with Lord Litchfield.

'I want to thank you, boys.' Lord Litchfield sat beside Charlotte, looking brighter and healthier than Leander had seen him before. 'Charlotte has told me everything. I'm not sure I understand it yet, but I know that you are good and brave. You will have a home at Litchfield House for the rest of your lives. I will treat you as my own sons. I give you my word, as a gentleman, that you will be taken care of.'

'Lord Litchfield, thank you,' said Leander, blinking hard to stop hot, happy tears from spilling down his cheeks.

'Call me Uncle,' said the old man. He rested his head back and closed his eyes with a small, contented smile.

An uncle. Brothers and a sister. A family.

The procession of carriages clattered up to Litchfield House. This time Leander entered the big house by the front door.

There was a great deal of excitement. The few servants left after the master's long years alone rushed about, trying to cope with a suddenly busy household and the reopening of many forgotten rooms. The children did their best to help, but a few spoke no English, and none could properly make a bed.

Lady Charlotte, as the servants called her, was given her old rooms. They were exactly as she had left them, but covered in a thick layer of dust. Mrs Smart, as it turned out, was a poor housekeeper. She had not returned with them.

The rooms were cleaned swiftly and the stale smell was driven out with vast bunches of hothouse flowers which her uncle – *our uncle* – had sent up to cheer her.

The spirit children were slotted into the house wherever they would fit. A makeshift nursery was cobbled together. There was talk of finding positions for the bigger children and schools for the babies, but Lord Litchfield said it would take time before they were ready for the wide world. They were bewildered and uneasy, wild and playful, and drove the maids to distraction. The cook, on the other hand, was delighted to have so many eager mouths to feed, and, whenever one of the children went missing, they were sure to be found in her kitchen being spoiled with bread and cake.

Lord Litchfield was as good as his word – Leander was shown to a room with a huge bed and a fireplace all for him. It was the grandest thing he had ever seen. He placed his mother's locket underneath his pillow for safekeeping. Felix and Isaak would share a room, refusing to be separated again even for a night.

The big house seemed so different now that Leander didn't have to sneak around. He walked the length of every corridor and opened every door. He returned to the library. It seemed smaller than he remembered. At the front of the house he found Charlotte sitting on the steps, staring out at the moss-covered fountain.

'It'll be beautiful again by the springtime,' she said. 'We'll have everything cleaned and repaired. Everything back as it should be.'

A gust of wind whipped round the building, shaking bare branches and sending dry leaves skittering in circles. Something brushed against Leander's ankle, the wind holding it against him. He picked it up. It was one of Pinchbeck's tarot cards. *How did that get here?*

'Four of Wands,' said Leander.

'What does it mean?'

And, for the first time, Leander knew exactly what the cards were trying to say.

'It means home.'

Author note

The Victorian era is my favourite period in history to research, because the Victorians left so much behind for us to study – buildings, newspapers, advertisements, and most exciting of all, photographs.

Having a portrait painted is slow and expensive, so throughout much of history, only rich people could afford a picture of themselves. The faces of everyday people are missing from our galleries and records. But fast, cheap photography gave us thousands of photos of ordinary people. We can see people who lived nearly 200 years ago, exactly as they looked on the day the photo was taken.

The oldest existing photographs were created around 1826, though they look grainy and rough. Improvements happened quickly and by the 1840s huge numbers of people were having their photos taken. In these early days, it took several minutes to capture a picture. People had to stay completely still or the picture would be blurry. It's quite hard to hold a natural-looking smile for three minutes at a time, which is one of the reasons why Victorian photos look formal and stuffy. The other reason is fashion – people thought a serious expression looked dignified.

Victorian photographs were made by coating sheets of glass or metal (called 'plates') with a special chemical called silver nitrate, which reacts to light. The silver nitrate changed colour depending on how much light reached it, capturing the image. Then the plate was bathed in different liquids to stop the picture darkening or fading.

By 1876 when this story takes place, cameras had improved and photos could be printed onto card instead of delicate sheets of silver and glass. This made them even more popular as they could easily be copied, sent through the post, or sold as souvenirs.

Just as cameras became more advanced, photographers were learning and experimenting with trick photography. A clever photographer could layer images together to make it seem like a woman was sitting inside a wine glass, or a man was holding his own severed head.

Some photographers decided to make 'ghosts' appear on their pictures. Some, like Pinchbeck in *The Vanishing Trick*, used double-exposure – exposing the same 'plate' to light twice, effectively making two photos on top of each other. Any objects (like furniture) which were in both pictures would look solid, whilst anything only in one picture would look see-through and ghostly.

If you'd like to know more about Victorian photography, or to see some of the photos which inspired *The Vanishing Trick*, go to my website www.jennispangler.com and click 'more information'.

The Victorians were fascinated by ghosts, so 'spirit

photography' became very popular. In both England and America, mediums held seances and claimed to speak to the dead. It may seem surprising to us that so many Victorians believed in ghosts and seances, but lots of sensible and educated people did. Even Queen Victoria attended some seances.

The 1800s were a time of huge change in the UK, with advances in science and invention changing the way people lived. At the beginning of the century, cunning folk made their money by selling a mixture of herbal remedies and magic. You might have consulted someone like Edmund Pellar to cure a tummy ache, lift a curse, or find a thief. By the end of the century the cunning folk had died out because modern medicine and the police force were beginning to take shape, and people were letting go of their old beliefs in magic and superstition. But interest in mediums and seances was still gaining popularity. Perhaps people weren't ready to give up on magic entirely.

Perhaps we still aren't.

Acknowledgements

This story would never have made it to the page if it wasn't for the support of some wonderful people.

My wonderful husband, Styl. When I announced I wanted to write a book, he made my dream a priority and made sure I had time and space to work. He is the best partner I could ask for, and I am so lucky. My beautiful children, Daphne and Jasper, who are an endless source of enthusiasm and imagination. I love you all so much.

My amazing parents, John and Dawn, who made a lot of sacrifices for my education, and who really believed it when they said I could do anything I put my mind to. They deserve thanks for so much more than this book, but it will do for a start.

My grandparents, Charles and Mabel, who love books almost as much as they love each other.

My amazing friends – Emma Norry, who has read so many versions of this book and pushed me not to give up on it. Lindsay Galvin, who thought that maybe Pinchbeck would be better as a woman (she was right!). Laura Oldham, who is always on board whenever I say, 'I've had an idea . . .' And Stuart White, who created the #writementor community which has helped more than I can say.

I'm so grateful to Lauren Gardner, my brilliant agent, for taking a chance and being a huge cheerleader for my work. To Jane Griffiths, my editor, and the whole team at S&S for all your hard work and support. And a massive thanks to Chris Mould for his gorgeous illustrations, which are better than I ever dreamed.